The Library
of
Indiana Classics

There is something jaunty in a tam-o'-shanter, particularly a red one
Page 79

The House of a Thousand Candles

By

Meredith Nicholson

With Illustrations by
Howard Chandler Christy

Indiana University Press
Bloomington

First Midland Book Edition 1986

The Library of Indiana classics is available in a special clothbound
library-quality edition and in a paperback edition.

©
All rights reserved

Manufactured in the United States of America

Library of Congress Cataloging-in-Publication Data

Nicholson, Meredith, 1866–1947.
The house of a thousand candles.

(The Library of Indiana classics)
I. Title.   II. Series.
PS 3527.I35H68   1986   813'.52   85-45892
ISBN 0-253-32852-7
ISBN 0-253-20381-3 (pbk.)

To Margaret My Sister

CONTENTS

THE HOUSE OF A
THOUSAND CANDLES

THE HOUSE
OF A THOUSAND CANDLES

CHAPTER I

THE WILL OF JOHN MARSHALL GLENARM

Pickering's letter bringing news of my grandfather's
death found me at Naples early in October. John
Marshall Glenarm had died in June. He had left a
will which gave me his property conditionally, Pickering wrote, and it was necessary for me to return immediately to qualify as legatee. It was the merest luck
that the letter came to my hands at all, for it had been
sent to Constantinople, in care of the consul-general
instead of my banker there. It was not Pickering's
fault that the consul was a friend of mine who kept

1

track of my wanderings and was able to hurry the
executor's letter after me to Italy, where I had gone to
meet an English financier who had, I was advised, un-
limited money to spend on African railways. I am an
engineer, a graduate of an American institution famil-
iarly known as "Tech," and as my funds were running
low, I naturally turned to my profession for employment.

But this letter changed my plans, and the following
day I cabled Pickering of my departure and was outward bound on a steamer for New York. Fourteen
days later I sat in Pickering's office in the Alexis Building and listened intently while he read, with much
ponderous emphasis, the provisions of my grandfather's
will. When he concluded, I laughed. Pickering was a
serious man, and I was glad to see that my levity pained
him. I had, for that matter, always been a source of
annoyance to him, and his look of distrust and rebuke
did not trouble me in the least.

I reached across the table for the paper, and he gave
the sealed and beribboned copy of John Marshall Glenarm's will into my hands. I read it through for myself,
feeling conscious meanwhile that Pickering's cool gaze
was bent inquiringly upon me. These are the para-
graphs that interested me most:

I give and bequeath unto my said grandson, John Glenarm, sometime a resident of the City and State of New

York, and later a vagabond of parts unknown, a certain property known as Glenarm House, with the land thereunto pertaining and hereinafter more particularly described, and all personal property of whatsoever kind thereunto belonging and attached thereto,—the said realty lying in the County of Wabana in the State of Indiana,—upon this condition, faithfully and honestly performed:

That said John Glenarm shall remain for the period of one year an occupant of said Glenarm House and my lands attached thereto, demeaning himself meanwhile in an orderly and temperate manner. Should he fail at any time during said year to comply with this provision, said property shall revert to my general estate and become, without reservation, and without necessity for any process of law, the property, absolutely, of Marian Devereux, of the County and State of New York.

"Well," he demanded, striking his hands upon the arms of his chair, "what do you think of it?"

For the life of me I could not help laughing again. There was, in the first place, a delicious irony in the fact that I should learn through him of my grandfather's wishes with respect to myself. Pickering and I had grown up in the same town in Vermont; we had attended the same preparatory school, but there had been from boyhood a certain antagonism between us. He had always succeeded where I had failed, which is to say, I must admit, that he had succeeded pretty frequently. When I refused to settle down to my profession, but chose to see something of the world first,

Pickering gave himself seriously to the law, and there was, I knew from the beginning, no manner of chance that he would fail.

I am not more or less than human, and I remembered with joy that once I had thrashed him soundly at the prep school for bullying a smaller boy; but our score from school-days was not without tallies on his side. He was easily the better scholar—I grant him that; and he was shrewd and plausible. You never quite knew the extent of his powers and resources, and he had, I always maintained, the most amazing good luck,—as witness the fact that John Marshall Glenarm had taken a friendly interest in him. It was wholly like my grandfather, who was a man of many whims, to give his affairs into Pickering's keeping; and I could not complain, for I had missed my own chance with him. It was, I knew readily enough, part of my punishment for having succeeded so signally in incurring my grandfather's displeasure that he had made it necessary for me to treat with Arthur Pickering in this matter of the will; and Pickering was enjoying the situation to the full. He sank back in his chair with an air of complacency that had always been insufferable in him. I was quite willing to be patronized by a man of years and experience; but Pickering was my own age, and his experience of life seemed to me preposterously inadequate. To find him settled in New York, where he had been established through my grandfather's generosity, and the executor of my grandfather's estate, was hard to bear.

But there was something not wholly honest in my mirth, for my conduct during the three preceding years had been reprehensible. I had used my grandfather shabbily. My parents died when I was a child, and he had cared for me as far back as my memory ran. He had suffered me to spend without restraint the fortune left by my father; he had expected much of me, and I had grievously disappointed him. It was his hope that I should devote myself to architecture, a profession for which he had the greatest admiration, whereas I had insisted on engineering.

I am not writing an apology for my life, and I shall not attempt to extenuate my conduct in going abroad at the end of my course at Tech and, when I made Laurance Donovan's acquaintance, in setting off with him on a career of adventure. I do not regret, though possibly it would be more to my credit if I did, the months spent leisurely following the Danube east of the Iron Gate—Laurance Donovan always with me, while we urged the villagers and inn-loafers to all manner of sedition, acquitting ourselves so well that, when we came out into the Black Sea for further pleasure,

Russia did us the honor to keep a spy at our heels. I should like, for my own satisfaction, at least, to set down an account of certain affairs in which we were concerned at Belgrad, but without Larry's consent I am not at liberty to do so. Nor shall I take time here to describe our travels in Africa, though our study of the Atlas Mountain dwarfs won us honorable mention by the British Ethnological Society.

These were my yesterdays; but to-day I sat in Arthur Pickering's office in the towering Alexis Building, conscious of the muffled roar of Broadway, discussing the terms of my Grandfather Glenarm's will with a man whom I disliked as heartily as it is safe for one man to dislike another. Pickering had asked me a question, and I was suddenly aware that his eyes were fixed upon me and that he awaited my answer.

"What do I think of it?" I repeated. "I don't know that it makes any difference what I think, but I'll tell you, if you want to know, that I call it infamous, outrageous, that a man should leave a ridiculous will of that sort behind him. All the old money-bags who pile up fortunes magnify the importance of their money. They imagine that every kindness, every ordinary courtesy shown them, is merely a bid for a slice of the cake. I'm disappointed in my grandfather. He was a splendid old man, though God knows he had his queer ways.

I'll bet a thousand dollars, if I have so much money in the world, that this scheme is yours, Pickering, and not his. It smacks of your ancient vindictiveness, and John Marshall Glenarm had none of that in his blood. That stipulation about my residence out there is fantastic. I don't have to be a lawyer to know that; and no doubt I could break the will; I've a good notion to try it, anyhow."

"To be sure. You can tie up the estate for half a dozen years if you like," he replied coolly. He did not look upon me as likely to become a formidable litigant. My staying qualities had been proved weak long ago, as Pickering knew well enough.

"No doubt you would like that," I answered. "But I'm not going to give you the pleasure. I abide by the terms of the will. My grandfather was a fine old gentleman. I shan't drag his name through the courts,—not even to please you, Arthur Pickering," I declared hotly.

"The sentiment is worthy of a good man, Glenarm," he rejoined.

"But this woman who is to succeed to my rights,—I don't seem to remember her."

"It is not surprising that you never heard of her."

"Then she's not a connection of the family,—no long-lost cousin whom I ought to remember?"

"No; she was a late acquaintance of your grand-father's. He met her through an old friend of his,— Miss Evans, known as Sister Theresa. Miss Devereux is Sister Theresa's niece."

I whistled. I had a dim recollection that during my grandfather's long widowerhood there were occasional reports that he was about to marry. The name of Miss Evans had been mentioned in this connection. I had heard it spoken of in my family, and not, I remembered, with much kindness. Later, I heard of her joining a Sisterhood, and opening a school somewhere in the West.

"And Miss Devereux,—is she an elderly nun, too?"

"I don't know how elderly she is, but she isn't a nun at present. Still, she's almost alone in the world, and she and Sister Theresa are very intimate."

"Pass the will again, Pickering, while I make sure I grasp these diverting ideas. Sister Theresa isn't the one I mustn't marry, is she? It's the other ecclesias-tical embroidery artist,—the one with the x in her name, suggesting the algebra of my vanishing youth."

I read aloud this paragraph:

Provided, further, that in the event of the marriage of said John Glenarm to the said Marian Devereux, or in the event of any promise or contract of marriage between said persons within five years from the date of said John

Glenarm's acceptance of the provisions of this will, the whole estate shall become the property absolutely of St. Agatha's School, at Annandale, Wabana County, Indiana, a corporation under the laws of said state.

"For a touch of comedy commend me to my grandfather! Pickering, you always were a well-meaning fellow,—I'll turn over to you all my right, interest and title in and to these angelic Sisters. Marry! I like the idea! I suppose some one will try to marry me for my money. Marriage, Pickering, is not embraced in my scheme of life!"

"I should hardly call you a marrying man," he observed.

"Perfectly right, my friend! Sister Theresa was considered a possible match for my grandfather in my youth. She and I are hardly contemporaries. And the other lady with the fascinating algebraic climax to her name,—she, too, is impossible; it seems that I can't get the money by marrying her. I'd better let her take it. She's as poor as the devil, I dare say."

"I imagine not. The Evanses are a wealthy family, in spots, and she ought to have some money of her own if her aunt doesn't coax it out of her for educational schemes."

"And where on the map are these lovely creatures to be found?"

"Sister Theresa's school adjoins your preserve; Miss Devereux has, I think, some of your own weakness for travel. Sister Theresa is her nearest relative, and she occasionally visits St. Agatha's—that's the school."

"I suppose they embroider altar-cloths together and otherwise labor valiantly to bring confusion upon Satan and his cohorts. Just the people to pull the wool over the eyes of my grandfather!"

Pickering smiled at my resentment.

"You'd better give them a wide berth; they might catch you in their net. Sister Theresa is said to have quite a winning way. She certainly plucked your grandfather."

"Nuns in spectacles, the gentle educators of youth and that sort of thing, with a good-natured old man for their prey. None of them for me!"

"I rather thought so," remarked Pickering,—and he pulled his watch from his pocket and turned the stem with his heavy fingers. He was short, thick-set and sleek, with a square jaw, hair already thin and a close-clipped mustache. Age, I reflected, was not improving him.

I had no intention of allowing him to see that I was irritated. I drew out my cigarette case and passed it across the table.

"After you! They're made quite specially for me in Madrid."

"You forget that I never use tobacco in any form."

"You always did miss a good deal of the joy of living," I observed, throwing my smoking match into his waste-paper basket, to his obvious annoyance. "Well, I'm the bad boy of the story-books; but I'm really sorry my inheritance has a string tied to it. I'm about out of money. I suppose you wouldn't advance me a few thousands on my expectations—"

"Not a cent," he declared, with quite unnecessary vigor; and I laughed again, remembering that in my old appraisement of him, generosity had not been represented in large figures. "It's not in keeping with your grandfather's wishes that I should do so. You must have spent a good bit of money in your tiger-hunting exploits," he added.

"I have spent all I had," I replied amiably. "Thank God I'm not a clam! I've seen the world and paid for it. I don't want anything from you. You undoubtedly share my grandfather's idea of me that I'm a wild man who can't sit still or lead an orderly, decent life; but I'm going to give you a terrible disappointment. What's the size of the estate?"

Pickering eyed me—uneasily, I thought—and began

playing with a pencil. I never liked Pickering's hands; they were thick and white and better kept than I like to see a man's hands.

"I fear it's going to be disappointing. In his trust-company boxes here I have been able to find only about ten thousand dollars' worth of securities. Possibly— quite possibly—we were all deceived in the amount of his fortune. Sister Theresa wheedled large sums out of him, and he spent, as you will see, a small fortune on the house at Annandale without finishing it. It wasn't a cheap proposition, and in its unfinished condition it is practically valueless. You must know that Mr. Glenarm gave away a great deal of money in his lifetime. More-over, he established your father. You know what he left,—it was not a small fortune as those things are reckoned."

I was restless under this recital. My father's estate had been of respectable size, and I had dissipated the whole of it. My conscience pricked me as I recalled an item of forty thousand dollars that I had spent—some-what grandly—on an expedition that I led, with con-siderable satisfaction to myself, at least, through the Sudan. But Pickering's words amazed me.

"Let me understand you," I said, bending toward him. "My grandfather was supposed to be rich, and yet you tell me you find little property. Sister Theresa

got money from him to help build a school. How much
was that?"

"Fifty thousand dollars. It was an open account.
His books show the advances, but he took no notes."

"And that claim is worth——?"

"It is good as against her individually. But she con-
tends——"

"Yes, go on!"

I had struck the right note. He was annoyed at my
persistence and his apparent discomfort pleased me.

"She refuses to pay. She says Mr. Glenarm made her
a gift of the money."

"That's possible, isn't it? He was for ever making
gifts to churches. Schools and theological seminaries
were a sort of weakness with him."

"That is quite true, but this account is among the
assets of the estate. It's my business as executor to collect it."

"We'll pass that. If you get this money, the estate is
worth sixty thousand dollars, plus the value of the land
out there at Annandale, and Glenarm House is worth——"

"There you have me!"

It was the first lightness he had shown, and it put me
on guard.

"I should like an idea of its value. Even an unfinished house is worth something."

"Land out there is worth from one hundred to one hundred and fifty dollars an acre. There's an even hundred acres. I'll be glad to have your appraisement of the house when you get there."

"Humph! You flatter my judgment, Pickering. The loose stuff there is worth how much?"

"It's all in the library. Your grandfather's weakness was architecture—"

"So I remember!" I interposed, recalling my stormy interviews with John Marshall Glenarm over my choice of a profession.

"In his last years he turned more and more to his books. He placed out there what is, I suppose, the finest collection of books relating to architecture to be found in this country. That was his chief hobby, after church affairs, as you may remember, and he rode it hard. But he derived a great deal of satisfaction from his studies."

I laughed again; it was better to laugh than to cry over the situation.

"I suppose he wanted me to sit down there, surrounded by works on architecture, with the idea that a study of the subject would be my only resource. The scheme is eminently Glenarmian! And all I get is a worthless house, a hundred acres of land, ten thousand dollars, and a doubtful claim against a Protestant nun

who hoodwinked my grandfather into setting up a
school for her. Bless your heart, man, so far as my inheritance is concerned it would have been money in my
pocket to have stayed in Africa."

"That's about the size of it."

"But the personal property is all mine,—anything
that's loose on the place. Perhaps my grandfather
planted old plate and government bonds just to pique
the curiosity of his heirs, successors and assigns. It
would be in keeping!"

I had walked to the window and looked out across
the city. As I turned suddenly I found Pickering's
eyes bent upon me with curious intentness. I had never
liked his eyes; they were too steady. When a man always meets your gaze tranquilly and readily, it is just
as well to be wary of him.

"Yes; no doubt you will find the place literally
packed with treasure," he said, and laughed. "When
you find anything you might wire me."

He smiled; the idea seemed to give him pleasure.

"Are you sure there's nothing else?" I asked. "No
substitute,—no codicil?"

"If you know of anything of the kind it's your duty
to produce it. We have exhausted the possibilities. I'll
admit that the provisions of the will are unusual; your
grandfather was a peculiar man in many respects; but

he was thoroughly sane and his faculties were all sound to the last."

"He treated me a lot better than I deserved," I said, with a heartache that I had not known often in my irresponsible life; but I could not afford to show feeling before Arthur Pickering.

I picked up the copy of the will and examined it. It was undoubtedly authentic; it bore the certificate of the clerk of Wabana County, Indiana. The witnesses were Thomas Bates and Arthur Pickering.

"Who is Bates?" I asked, pointing to the man's signature.

"One of your grandfather's discoveries. He's in charge of the house out there, and a trustworthy fellow. He's a fair cook, among other things. I don't know where Mr. Glenarm got Bates, but he had every confidence in him. The man was with him at the end."

A picture of my grandfather dying, alone with a servant, while I, his only kinsman, wandered in strange lands, was not one that I could contemplate with much satisfaction. My grandfather had been an odd little figure of a man, who always wore a long black coat and a silk hat, and carried a curious silver-headed staff, and said puzzling things at which everybody was afraid either to laugh or to cry. He refused to be thanked for favors, though he was generous and helpful and constantly performing kind deeds. His whimsical philanthropies were often described in the newspapers. He had once given a considerable sum of money to a fashionable church in Boston with the express stipulation, which he safeguarded legally, that if the congregation ever intrusted its spiritual welfare to a minister named Reginald, Harold or Claude, an amount equal to his gift, with interest, should be paid to the Massachusetts Humane Society.

The thought of him touched me now. I was glad to feel that his money had never been a lure to me; it did not matter whether his estate was great or small, I could, at least, ease my conscience by obeying the behest of the old man whose name I bore, and whose interest in the finer things of life and art had given him an undeniable distinction.

"I should like to know something of Mr. Glenarm's last days," I said abruptly.

"He wished to visit the village where he was born, and Bates, his companion and servant, went to Vermont with him. He died quite suddenly, and was buried beside his father in the old village cemetery. I saw him last early in the summer. I was away from home and did not know of his death until it was all over. Bates came to report it to me, and to sign the necessary papers in probating the will. It had to be done in the place of the decedent's residence, and we went together to Wabana, the seat of the county in which Annandale lies."

I was silent after this, looking out toward the sea that had lured me since my earliest dreams of the world that lay beyond it.

"It's a poor stake, Glenarm," remarked Pickering consolingly, and I wheeled upon him.

"I suppose you think it a poor stake! I suppose you can't see anything in that old man's life beyond his money; but I don't care a curse what my inheritance is! I never obeyed any of my grandfather's wishes in his lifetime, but now that he's dead his last wish is mandatory. I'm going out there to spend a year if I die for it. Do you get my idea?"

"Humph! You always were a stormy petrel," he sneered. "I fancy it will be safer to keep our most agreeable acquaintance on a strictly business basis. If you accept the terms of the will—"

"Of course I accept them! Do you think I am going to make a row, refuse to fulfil that old man's last wish! I gave him enough trouble in his life without disappointing him in his grave. I suppose you'd like to have me fight the will; but I'm going to disappoint you."

He said nothing, but played with his pencil. I had

never disliked him so heartily; he was so smug and comfortable. His office breathed the very spirit of prosperity. I wished to finish my business and get away.

"I suppose the region out there has a high death-rate. How's the malaria?"

"Not alarmingly prevalent, I understand. There's a summer resort over on one side of Lake Annandale. The place is really supposed to be wholesome. I don't believe your grandfather had homicide in mind in sending you there."

"No, he probably thought the rustication would make a man of me. Must I do my own victualing? I suppose I'll be allowed to eat."

"Bates can cook for you. He'll supply the necessities. I'll instruct him to obey your orders. I assume you'll not have many guests,—in fact,"—he studied the back of his hand intently,—"while that isn't stipulated, I doubt whether it was your grandfather's intention that you should surround yourself—"

"With boisterous companions!" I supplied the words in my cheerfullest tone. "No; my conduct shall be exemplary, Mr. Pickering," I added, with affable irony.

He picked up a single sheet of thin type-written paper and passed it across the table. It was a formal acquiescence in the provisions of the will. Pickering had prepared it in advance of my coming, and this assumption that I would accept the terms irritated me. Assumptions as to what I should do under given conditions had always irritated me, and accounted, in a large measure, for my proneness to surprise and disappoint people. Pickering summoned a clerk to witness my signature.

"How soon shall you take possession?" he asked. "I have to make a record of that."

"I shall start for Indiana to-morrow," I answered.

"You are prompt," he replied, deliberately folding in quarters the paper I had just signed. "I hoped you might dine with me before going out; but I fancy New York is pretty tame after the cafés and bazaars of the East."

His reference to my wanderings angered me again; for here was the point at which I was most sensitive. I was twenty seven and had spent my patrimony; I had tasted the bread of many lands, and I was doomed to spend a year qualifying myself for my grandfather's legacy by settling down on an abandoned and lonely Indiana farm that I had never seen and had no interest in whatever.

As I rose to go Pickering said:

"It will be sufficient if you drop me a line, say once a month, to let me know you are there. The post-office is Annandale."

"I suppose I might file a supply of postal cards in the village and arrange for the mailing of one every month."

"It might be done that way," he answered evenly.

"We may perhaps meet again, if I don't die of starvation or ennui. Good-by."

We shook hands stiffly and I left him, going down in an elevator filled with eager-eyed, anxious men. I, at least, had no cares of business. It made no difference to me whether the market rose or fell. Something of the spirit of adventure that had been my curse quickened in my heart as I walked through crowded Broadway past Trinity Church to a bank and drew the balance remaining on my letter of credit. I received in currency slightly less than one thousand dollars.

As I turned from the teller's window I ran into the arms of the last man in the world I expected to see.

This, let it be remembered, was in October of the year of our Lord, nineteen hundred and one.

CHAPTER II

"Don't mention my name an thou lovest me!" said Laurance Donovan, and he drew me aside, ignored my hand and otherwise threw into our meeting a casual quality that was somewhat amazing in view of the fact that we had met last at Cairo.

"*Allah il Allah!*"

It was undoubtedly Larry. I felt the heat of the desert and heard the camel-drivers cursing and our Sudanese guides plotting mischief under a window far away.

"Well!" we both exclaimed interrogatively.

He rocked gently back and forth, with his hands in his pockets, on the tile floor of the banking-house. I had seen him stand thus once on a time when we had eaten nothing in four days—it was in Abyssinia, and our guides had lost us in the worst possible place—with the same untroubled look in his eyes.

"Please don't appear surprised, or scared or anything, Jack," he said, with his delicious intonation. "I

22

saw a fellow looking for me an hour or so ago. He's
been at it for several months; hence my presence on
these shores of the brave and the free. He's probably
still looking, as he's a persistent devil. I'm here, as
we may say, quite incog. Staying at an East-side lodging-house, where I shan't i̇ ᵗᵉ you to call on me.
But I must see you."

"Dine with me to-night, at Sherry's—"

"Too big, too many people—"

"Therein lies security, if you're in trouble. I'm about
to go into exile, and I want to eat one more civilized
dinner before I go."

"Perhaps it's just as well. Where are you off for,—
not Africa again?"

"No. Just Indiana,—one of the sovereign American
states, as you ought to know."

"Indians?"

"No; warranted all dead."

"Pack-train—balloon—automobile—camels,—how do
you get there?"

"Varnished cars. It's easy. It's not the getting there;
it's the not dying of ennui after you're on the spot."

"Humph! What hour did you say for the dinner?"

"Seven o'clock. Meet me at the entrance."

"If I'm at large! Allow me to precede you through
the door, and don't follow me on the street, please!"

He walked away, his gloved hands clasped lazily behind him, lounged out upon Broadway and turned
toward the Battery. I waited until he disappeared, then
took an up-town car.

My first meeting with Laurance Donovan was in Constantinople, at a café where I was dining. He got into
a row with an Englishman and knocked him down. It
was not my affair, but I liked the ease and definiteness
with which Larry put his foe out of commission. I
learned later that it was a way he had. The Englishman meant well enough, but he could not, of course,
know the intensity of Larry's feeling about the unhappy
lot of Ireland. In the beginning of my own acquaintance with Donovan I sometimes argued with him, but I
soon learned better manners. He quite converted me to
his own notion of Irish affairs, and I was as hot an
advocate as he of head-smashing as a means of restoring
Ireland's lost prestige.

My friend, the American consul-general at Constantinople, was not without a sense of humor, and I
easily enlisted him in Larry's behalf. The Englishman
thirsted for vengeance and invoked all the powers. He
insisted, with reason, that Larry was a British subject
and that the American consul had no right to give him
asylum,—a point that was, I understand, thoroughly
well-grounded in law and fact. Larry maintained, on

the other hand, that he was not English but Irish, and that, as his country maintained no representative in Turkey, it was his privilege to find refuge wherever it was offered. Larry was always the most plausible of human beings, and with the connivance of the American consul we made an impression, and got him off.

I did not realize until later that the real joke lay in the fact that Larry was English-born, and that his devotion to Ireland was purely sentimental and quixotic. His family had, to be sure, come out of Ireland some time in the dim past, and settled in England; but when Larry reached years of knowledge, if not of discretion, he cut Oxford and insisted on taking his degree at Dublin. He even believed,—or thought he believed,— in banshees. He allied himself during his university days with the most radical and turbulent advocates of a separate national existence for Ireland, and occasionally spent a month in jail for rioting. But Larry's instincts were scholarly; he made a brilliant record at the University; then, at twenty-two, he came forth to look at the world, and liked it exceedingly well. His father was a busy man and he had other sons; he granted Larry an allowance and told him to keep away from home until he got ready to be respectable. So, from Constantinople, after a tour of Europe, we together crossed the Mediterranean in search of the fleshpots of lost kingdoms, spending three years in the pursuit. We parted at Cairo on excellent terms. He returned to England and later to his beloved Ireland, for he had blithely sung the wildest Gaelic songs in the darkest days of our adventures, and never lost his love for The Sod, as he apostrophized—and capitalized—his adopted country.

Larry had the habit of immaculateness. He emerged from his East-side lodging-house that night clothed properly, and wearing the gentlemanly air of peace and reserve that is so wholly incompatible with his disposition to breed discord and indulge in riot. When we sat down for a leisurely dinner at Sherry's we were not, I modestly maintain, a forbidding pair. We—if I may drag myself into the matter—are both a trifle under the average height, sinewy, nervous, and, just then, trained fine. Our lean, clean-shaven faces were well-browned—mine wearing a fresh coat from my days on the steamer's deck.

Larry had never been in America before, and the scene had for both of us the charm of a gay and novel spectacle. I have always maintained, in talking to Larry of nations and races, that the Americans are the handsomest and best put-up people in the world, and I believe he was persuaded of it that night as we gazed with eyes long unaccustomed to splendor upon the great company assembled in the restaurant. The lights, the music, the variety and richness of the costumes of the women, the many unmistakably foreign faces, wrought a welcome spell on senses inured to hardship in the waste and dreary places of earth.

"Now tell me the story," I said. "Have you done murder? Is the offense treasonable?"

"It was a tenants' row in Galway, and I smashed a constable. I smashed him pretty hard, I dare say, from the row they kicked up in the newspapers. I lay low for a couple of weeks, caught a boat to Queenstown, and here I am, waiting for a chance to get back to The Sod without going in irons."

"You were certainly born to be hanged, Larry. You'd better stay in America. There's more room here than anywhere else, and it's not easy to kidnap a man in America and carry him off."

"Possibly not; and yet the situation isn't wholly tranquil," he said, transfixing a bit of pompano with his fork. "Kindly note the florid gentleman at your right —at the table with four—he's next the lady in pink. It may interest you to know that he's the British consul."

"Interesting, but not important. You don't for a moment suppose—"

"That he's looking for me? Not at all. But he undoubtedly has my name on his tablets. The detective that's here following me around is pretty dull. He lost me this morning while I was talking to you in the bank. Later on I had the pleasure of trailing him for an hour or so until he finally brought up at the British consul's office. Thanks; no more of the fish. Let us banish care. I wasn't born to be hanged; and as I'm a political offender, I doubt whether I can be deported if they lay hands on me."

He watched the bubbles in his glass dreamily, holding it up in his slim well-kept fingers.

"Tell me something of your own immediate present and future," he said.

I made the story of my Grandfather Glenarm's legacy as brief as possible, for brevity was a definite law of our intercourse.

"A year, you say, with nothing to do but fold your hands and wait. It doesn't sound awfully attractive to me. I'd rather do without the money."

"But I intend to do some work. I owe it to my grandfather's memory to make good, if there's any good in me."

"The sentiment is worthy of you, Glenarm," he said mockingly. "What do you see—a ghost?"

I must have started slightly at espying suddenly Arthur Pickering not twenty feet away. A party of half a dozen or more had risen, and Pickering and a girl were detached from the others for a moment.

She was young,—quite the youngest in the group about Pickering's table. A certain girlishness of height and outline may have been emphasized by her juxtaposition to Pickering's heavy figure. She was in black, with white showing at neck and wrists,—a somber contrast to the other women of the party, who were arrayed with a degree of splendor. She had dropped her fan, and Pickering stooped to pick it up. In the second that she waited she turned carelessly toward me, and our eyes met for an instant. Very likely she was Pickering's sister, and I tried to reconstruct his family, which I had known in my youth; but I could not place her. As she walked out before him my eyes followed her,—the erect figure, free and graceful, but with a charming dignity and poise, and the gold of her fair hair glinting under her black toque.

Her eyes, as she turned them full upon me, were the saddest, loveliest eyes I had ever seen, and even in that brilliant, crowded room I felt their spell. They were fixed in my memory indelibly,—mournful, dreamy and wistful. In my absorption I forgot Larry.

"You're taking unfair advantage," he observed quietly. "Friends of yours?"

"The big chap in the lead is my friend Pick-

ering," I answered; and Larry turned his head slight‹
ly.

"Yes, I supposed you weren't looking at the women,"
he observed dryly. "I'm sorry I couldn't see the object
of your interest. Bah! these men!"

I laughed carelessly enough, but I was already sum-
moning from my memory the grave face of the girl in
black,—her mournful eyes, the glint of gold in her hair.
Pickering was certainly finding the pleasant places in
this vale of tears, and I felt my heart hot against him.
It hurts, this seeing a man you have never liked suc-
ceeding where you have failed!

"Why didn't you present me? I'd like to make the
acquaintance of a few representative Americans,—I
may need them to go bail for me."

"Pickering didn't see me, for one thing; and for
another he wouldn't go bail for you or me if he did.
He isn't built that way."

Larry smiled quizzically.

"You needn't explain further. The sight of the lady
has shaken you. She reminds me of Tennyson:

" 'The star-like sorrows of immortal eyes—'

and the rest of it ought to be a solemn warning to you,
—many 'drew swords and died,' and calamity followed
in her train. Bah! these women! I thought you were
past all that!"

She turned carelessly **toward me,** and our eyes met for an instant.

Page 29

"I don't know why a man should be past it at twenty-seven! Besides, Pickering's friends are strangers to me. But what became of that Irish colleen you used to moon over? Her distinguishing feature, as I remember her photograph, was a short upper lip. You used to force her upon me frequently when we were in Africa."

"Humph! When I got back to Dublin I found that she had married a brewer's son,—think of it!"

"Put not your faith in a short upper lip! Her face never inspired any confidence in me."

"That will do, thank you. I'll have a bit more of that mayonnaise if the waiter isn't dead. I think you said your grandfather died in June. A letter advising you of the fact reached you at Naples in October. Has it occurred to you that there was quite an interim there? What, may I ask, was the executor doing all that time? You may be sure he was taking advantage of the opportunity to look for the red, red gold. I suppose you didn't give him a sound drubbing for not keeping the cables hot with inquiries for you?"

He eyed me in that disdain for my stupidity which I have never suffered from any other man.

"Well, no; to tell the truth, I was thinking of other things during the interview."

"Your grandfather should have provided a guardian for you, lad. You oughtn't to be trusted with money. Is that bottle empty? Well, if that person with the fat neck was your friend Pickering, I'd have a care of what's coming to me. I'd be quite sure that Mr. Pickering hadn't made away with the old gentleman's boodle, or that it didn't get lost on the way from him to me."

"The time's running now, and I'm in for the year. My grandfather was a fine old gentleman, and I treated him like a dog. I'm going to do what he directs in that will no matter what the size of the reward may be."

"Certainly; that's the eminently proper thing for you to do. But,—but keep your wits about you. If a fellow with that neck can't find money where money has been known to exist, it must be buried pretty deep. Your grandfather was a trifle eccentric, I judge, but not a fool by any manner of means. The situation appeals to my imagination, Jack. I like the idea of it,— the lost treasure and the whole business. Lord, what a salad that is! Cheer up, comrade! You're as grim as an owl!"

Whereupon we fell to talking of people and places we had known in other lands.

We spent the next day together, and in the evening,

at my hotel, he criticized my effects while I packed, in his usual ironical vein.

"You're not going to take those things with you, I hope!" He indicated the rifles and several revolvers which I brought from the closet and threw upon the bed. "They make me homesick for the jungle."

He drew from its cover the heavy rifle I had used last on a leopard hunt and tested its weight.

"Precious little use you'll have for this! Better let me take it back to The Sod to use on the landlords. I say, Jack, are we never to seek our fortunes together again? We hit it off pretty well, old man, come to think of it,—I don't like to lose you."

He bent over the straps of the rifle-case with unnecessary care, but there was a quaver in his voice that was not like Larry Donovan.

"Come with me now!" I exclaimed, wheeling upon him.

"I'd rather be with you than with any other living man, Jack Glenarm, but I can't think of it. I have my own troubles; and, moreover, you've got to stick it out there alone. It's part of the game the old gentleman set up for you, as I understand it. Go ahead, collect your fortune, and then, if I haven't been hanged in the meantime, we'll join forces later. There's no chap anywhere with a pleasanter knack at spending money than your old friend L. D."

He grinned, and I smiled ruefully, knowing that we must soon part again, for Larry was one of the few men I had ever called friend, and this meeting had only quickened my old affection for him.

"I suppose," he continued, "you accept as gospel truth what that fellow tells you about the estate. I should be a little wary if I were you. Now, I've been kicking around here for a couple of weeks, dodging the detectives, and incidentally reading the newspapers. Perhaps you don't understand that this estate of John Marshall Glenarm has been talked about a good bit."

"I didn't know it," I admitted lamely. Larry had always been able to instruct me about most matters; it was wholly possible that he could speak wisely about my inheritance.

"You couldn't know, when you were coming from the Mediterranean on a steamer. But the house out there and the mysterious disappearance of the property have been duly discussed. You're evidently an object of some public interest,"—and he drew from his pocket a newspaper cutting. "Here's a sample item." He read:

"John Glenarm, the grandson of John Marshall Glenarm, the eccentric millionaire who died suddenly in Vermont last summer, arrived on the Maxinkuckee from Naples yesterday. Under the terms of his grandfather's will, Glenarm is required to reside for a year at a curious house established by John Marshall Glenarm near Lake Annandale, Indiana.

This provision was made, according to friends of the family, to test young Glenarm's staying qualities, as he has, since his graduation from the Massachusetts Institute of Technology five years ago, distributed a considerable fortune left him by his father in contemplating the wonders of the old world. It is reported—"

"That will do! Signs and wonders I have certainly beheld, and if I spent the money I submit that I got my money back."

I paid my bill and took a hansom for the ferry,—Larry with me, chaffing away drolly with his old zest. He crossed with me, and as the boat drew out into the river a silence fell upon us,—the silence that is possible only between old friends. As I looked back at the lights of the city, something beyond the sorrow at parting from a comrade touched me. A sense of foreboding, of coming danger, crept into my heart. But I was going upon the tamest possible excursion; for the first time in my life I was submitting to the direction of another, —albeit one who lay in the grave. How like my grandfather it was, to die leaving this compulsion upon me! My mood changed suddenly, and as the boat bumped at the pier I laughed.

"Bah! these men!" ejaculated Larry.

"What men?" I demanded, giving my bags to a porter.

"These men who are in love," he said. "I know the signs,—mooning, silence, sudden inexplicable laughter! I hope I'll not be in jail when you're married."

"You'll be in a long time if they hold you for that. Here's my train."

We talked of old times, and of future meetings, during the few minutes that remained.

"You can write me at my place of rustication," I said, scribbling "Annandale, Wabana County, Indiana," on a card. "Now if you need me at any time I'll come to you wherever you are. You understand that, old man. Good-by."

"Write me, care of my father—he'll have my address, though this last row of mine made him pretty hot."

I passed through the gate and down the long train to my sleeper. Turning, with my foot on the step, I waved a farewell to Larry, who stood outside watching me.

In a moment the heavy train was moving slowly out into the night upon its westward journey.

CHAPTER III

THE HOUSE OF A THOUSAND CANDLES

Annandale derives its chief importance from the fact that two railway lines intersect there. The Chicago Express paused only for a moment while the porter deposited my things beside me on the platform. Light streamed from the open door of the station; a few idlers paced the platform, staring into the windows of the cars; the village hackman languidly solicited my business. Suddenly out of the shadows came a tall, curious figure of a man clad in a long ulster. As I write, it is with a quickening of the sensation I received on the occasion of my first meeting with Bates. His lank gloomy figure rises before me now, and I hear his deep melancholy voice, as, touching his hat respectfully, he said:

"Beg pardon, sir; is this Mr. Glenarm? I am Bates from Glenarm House. Mr. Pickering wired me to meet you, sir."

"Yes; to be sure," I said.

The hackman was already gathering up my traps, and I gave him my trunk-checks.

"How far is it?" I asked, my eyes resting, a little re-gretfully, I must confess, on the rear lights of the van-ishing train.

"Two miles, sir," Bates replied. "There's no way over but the hack in winter. In summer the steamer comes right into our dock."

"My legs need stretching; I'll walk," I suggested, drawing the cool air into my lungs. It was a still, starry October night, and its freshness was grateful after the hot sleeper. Bates accepted the suggestion without comment. We walked to the end of the platform, where the hackman was already tumbling my trunks about, and after we had seen them piled upon his nondescript wagon, I followed Bates down through the broad quiet street of the village. There was more of Annandale than I had imagined, and several tall smoke-stacks loomed here and there in the thin starlight.

"Brick-yards, sir," said Bates, waving his hand at the stacks. "It's a considerable center for that kind of business."

"Bricks without straw?" I asked, as we passed a radiant saloon that blazed upon the board walk.

"Beg pardon, sir, but such places are the ruin of men,"—on which remark I based a mental note that Bates wished to impress me with his own rectitude.

He swung along beside me, answering questions with

dogged brevity. Clearly, here was a man who had reduced human intercourse to a basis of necessity. I was
to be shut up with him for a year, and he was not likely
to prove a cheerful jailer. My feet struck upon a grav-
eled highway at the end of the village street, and I
heard suddenly the lapping of water.

"It's the lake, sir. This road leads right out to the
house," Bates explained.

I was doomed to meditate pretty steadily, I imagined,
on the beauty of the landscape in these parts, and I
was rejoiced to know that it was not all cheerless prairie
or gloomy woodland. The wind freshened and blew
sharply upon us off the water.

"The fishing's quite good in season. Mr. Glenarm
used to take great pleasure in it. Bass,—yes, sir. Mr.
Glenarm held there was nothing quite equal to a black
bass."

I liked the way the fellow spoke of my grandfather.
He was evidently a loyal retainer. No doubt he could
summon from the past many pictures of my grandfather, and I determined to encourage his confidence.

Any resentment I felt on first hearing the terms of
my grandfather's will had passed. He had treated me
as well as I deserved, and the least I could do was to
accept the penalty he had laid upon me in a sane and
amiable spirit. This train of thought occupied me as

we tramped along the highway. The road now led away from the lake and through a heavy wood. Presently, on the right loomed a dark barrier, and I put out my hand and touched a wall of rough stone that rose to a height of about eight feet.

"What is this, Bates?" I asked.

"This is Glenarm land, sir. The wall was one of your grandfather's ideas. It's a quarter of a mile long and cost him a pretty penny, I warrant you. The road turns off from the lake now, but the Glenarm property is all lake front."

So there was a wall about my prison house! I grinned cheerfully to myself. When, a few moments later, my guide paused at an arched gateway in the long wall, drew from his overcoat a bunch of keys and fumbled at the lock of an iron gate, I felt the spirit of adventure quicken within me.

The gate clicked behind us and Bates found a lantern and lighted it with the ease of custom.

"I use this gate because it's nearer. The regular entrance is farther down the road. Keep close, sir, as the timber isn't much cleared."

The undergrowth was indeed heavy, and I followed the lantern of my guide with difficulty. In the darkness the place seemed as wild and rough as a tropical wilderness.

"Only a little farther," rose Bates' voice ahead of me; and then: "There's the light, sir,"—and, lifting my eyes, as I stumbled over the roots of a great tree, I saw for the first time the dark outlines of Glenarm House.

"Here we are, sir!" exclaimed Bates, stamping his feet upon a walk. I followed him to what I assumed to be the front door of the house, where a lamp shone brightly at either side of a massive entrance. Bates flung it open without ado, and I stepped quickly into a great hall that was lighted dimly by candles fastened into brackets on the walls.

"I hope you've not expected too much, Mr. Glenarm," said Bates, with a tone of mild apology. "It's very incomplete for living purposes."

"Well, we've got to make the best of it," I answered, though without much cheer. The sound of our steps reverberated and echoed in the well of a great staircase. There was not, as far as I could see, a single article of furniture in the place.

"Here's something you'll like better, sir,"—and Bates paused far down the hall and opened a door.

A single candle made a little pool of light in what I felt to be a large room. I was prepared for a disclosure of barren ugliness, and waited, in heartsick foreboding, for the silent guide to reveal a dreary prison.

"Please sit here, sir," said Bates, "while I make a better light."

He moved through the dark room with perfect ease, struck a match, lighted a taper and went swiftly and softly about. He touched the taper to one candle after another,—they seemed to be everywhere,—and won from the dark a faint twilight, that yielded slowly to a growing mellow splendor of light. I have often watched the acolytes in dim cathedrals of the Old World set countless candles ablaze on magnificent altars,—always with awe for the beauty of the spectacle; but in this unknown house the austere serving-man summoned from the shadows a lovelier and more bewildering enchantment. Youth alone, of beautiful things, is lovelier than light.

The lines of the walls receded as the light increased, and the raftered ceiling drew away, luring the eyes upward. I rose with a smothered exclamation on my lips and stared about, snatching off my hat in reverence as the spirit of the place wove its spell about me. Everywhere there were books; they covered the walls to the ceiling, with only long French windows and an enormous fireplace breaking the line. Above the fireplace a massive dark oak chimney-breast further emphasized the grand scale of the room. From every conceivable place—from shelves built for the purpose, from brackets that thrust out long arms among the books, from a great crystal chandelier suspended from the ceiling, and from the breast of the chimney—innumerable candles blazed with dazzling brilliancy. I exclaimed in wonder and pleasure as Bates paused, his sorcerer's wand in hand.

"Mr. Glenarm was very fond of candle-light; he liked to gather up candlesticks, and his collection is very fine. He called his place 'The House of a Thousand Candles.' There's only about a hundred here; but it was one of his conceits that when the house was finished there would be a thousand lights. He had quite a joking way, your grandfather. It suited his humor to call it a thousand. He enjoyed his own pleasantries, sir."

"I fancy he did," I replied, staring in bewilderment.

"Oil lamps might be more suited to your own taste, sir. But your grandfather would not have them. Old brass and copper were specialties with him, and he had a particular taste, Mr. Glenarm had, in glass candlesticks. He held that the crystal was most effective of all. I'll go and let in the baggageman and then serve you some supper."

He went somberly out and I examined the room with amazed and delighted eyes. It was fifty feet long and half as wide. The hard-wood floor was covered with handsome rugs; every piece of furniture was quaint or interesting. Carved in the heavy oak paneling above the fireplace, in large Old English letters, was the inscription:

𝕿𝖍𝖊 𝕾𝖕𝖎𝖗𝖎𝖙 𝖔𝖋 𝕸𝖆𝖓 𝖎𝖘 𝖙𝖍𝖊 𝕮𝖆𝖓𝖉𝖑𝖊 𝖔𝖋 𝖙𝖍𝖊 𝕷𝖔𝖗𝖉

and on either side great candelabra sent long arms across the hearth. All the books seemed related to architecture; German and French works stood side by side among those by English and American authorities. I found archæology represented in a division where all the titles were Latin or Italian. I opened several cabinets that contained sketches and drawings, all in careful order; and in another I found an elaborate card catalogue, evidently the work of a practised hand. The minute examination was too much for me; I threw myself into a great chair that might have been spoil from a cathedral, satisfied to enjoy the general effect. To find an apartment so handsome and so marked by good taste in the midst of an Indiana wood, staggered me. To be sure, in approaching the house I had seen only a dark bulk that conveyed no sense of its character or proportions; and certainly the entrance hall had not prepared me for the beauty of this room. I was so lost in contemplation that I did not hear a door open behind me. The respectful, mournful voice of Bates announced:

"There's a bite ready for you, sir."

I followed him through the hall to a small high-wainscoted room where a table was simply set.

"This is what Mr. Glenarm called the refectory. The dining-room, on the other side of the house, is unfinished. He took his own meals here. The library was the main thing with him. He never lived to finish the house, —more's the pity, sir. He would have made something very handsome of it if he'd had a few years more. But he hoped, sir, that you'd see it completed. It was his wish, sir."

"Yes, to be sure," I replied.

He brought cold fowl and a salad, and produced a bit of Stilton of unmistakable authenticity.

"I trust the ale is cooled to your liking. It's your grandfather's favorite, if I may say it, sir."

I liked the fellow's humility. He served me with a grave deference and an accustomed hand. Candles in crystal holders shed an agreeable light upon the table; the room was snug and comfortable, and hickory logs in a small fireplace crackled cheerily. If my grandfather had designed to punish me, with loneliness as his weapon, his shade, if it lurked near, must have been grievously disappointed. I had long been inured to my own society. I had often eaten my bread alone, and I found a pleasure in the quiet of the strange unknown house. There stole over me, too, the satisfaction that I was at last obeying a wish of my grandfather's, that I was doing something he would have me do. I was touched by the traces everywhere of his interest in what was to him the art of arts; there was something quite fine in his devotion to it. The little refectory had its air of distinction, though it was without decoration. There had been, we always said in the family, something whimsical or even morbid in my grandsire's devotion to architecture; but I felt that it had really appealed to something dignified and noble in his own mind and character, and a gentler mood than I had known in years possessed my heart. He had asked little of me, and I determined that in that little I would not fail.

Bates gave me my coffee, put matches within reach and left the room. I drew out my cigarette case and was holding it half-opened, when the glass in the window back of me cracked sharply, a bullet whistled over my head, struck the opposite wall and fell, flattened and marred, on the table under my hand.

CHAPTER IV

A VOICE FROM THE LAKE

I ran to the window and peered out into the night. The wood through which we had approached the house seemed to encompass it. The branches of a great tree brushed the panes. I was tugging at the fastening of the window when I became aware of Bates at my elbow.

"Did something happen, sir?"

His unbroken calm angered me. Some one had fired at me through a window and I had narrowly escaped being shot. I resented the unconcern with which this servant accepted the situation.

"Nothing worth mentioning. Somebody tried to assassinate me, that's all," I said, in a voice that failed to be calmly ironical. I was still fumbling at the catch of the window.

"Allow me, sir,"—and he threw up the sash with an ease that increased my irritation.

I leaned out and tried to find some clue to my assailant. Bates opened another window and surveyed the dark landscape with me.

47

"It was a shot from without, was it, sir?"

"Of course it was; you didn't suppose I shot at myself, did you?"

He examined the broken pane and picked up the bullet from the table.

"It's a rifle-ball, I should say."

The bullet was half-flattened by its contact with the wall. It was a cartridge ball of large caliber and might have been fired from either rifle or pistol.

"It's very unusual, sir!" I wheeled upon him angrily and found him fumbling with the bit of metal, a troubled look in his face. He at once continued, as though anxious to allay my fears. "Quite accidental, most likely. Probably boys on the lake are shooting at ducks."

I laughed out so suddenly that Bates started back in alarm.

"You idiot!" I roared, seizing him by the collar with both hands and shaking him fiercely. "You fool! Do the people around here shoot ducks at night? Do they shoot water-fowl with elephant guns and fire at people through windows just for fun?"

I threw him back against the table so that it leaped away from him, and he fell prone on the floor.

"Get up!" I commanded, "and fetch a lantern."

He said nothing, but did as I bade him. We traversed

the long cheerless hall to the front door, and I sent him before me into the woodland. My notions of the geography of the region were the vaguest, but I wished to examine for myself the premises that evidently contained a dangerous prowler. I was very angry and my rage increased as I followed Bates, who had suddenly retired within himself. We stood soon beneath the lights of the refectory window.

The ground was covered with leaves which broke crisply under our feet.

"What lies beyond here?" I demanded.

"About a quarter of mile of woods, sir, and then the lake."

"Go ahead," I ordered, "straight to the lake."

I was soon stumbling through rough underbrush similar to that through which we had approached the house. Bates swung along confidently enough ahead of me, pausing occasionally to hold back the branches. I began to feel, as my rage abated, that I had set out on a foolish undertaking. I was utterly at sea as to the character of the grounds; I was following a man whom I had not seen until two hours before, and whom I began to suspect of all manner of designs upon me. It was wholly unlikely that the person who had fired into the windows would lurk about, and, moreover, the light of the lantern, the crack of the leaves and the breaking of the boughs advertised our approach loudly. I am, however, a person given to steadfastness in error, if nothing else, and I plunged along behind my guide with a grim determination to reach the margin of the lake, if for no other reason than to exercise my authority over the custodian of this strange estate.

A bush slapped me sharply and I stopped to rub the sting from my face.

"Are you hurt, sir?" asked Bates solicitously, turning with the lantern.

"Of course not," I snapped. "I'm having the time of my life. Are there no paths in this jungle?"

"Not through here, sir. It was Mr. Glenarm's idea not to disturb the wood at all. He was very fond of walking through the timber."

"Not at night, I hope! Where are we now?"

"Quite near the lake, sir."

"Then go on."

I was out of patience with Bates, with the pathless woodland, and, I must confess, with the spirit of John Marshall Glenarm, my grandfather.

We came out presently upon a gravelly beach, and Bates stamped suddenly on planking.

"This is the Glenarm dock, sir; and that's the boat-house."

He waved his lantern toward a low structure that rose dark beside us. As we stood silent, peering out into the starlight, I heard distinctly the dip of a paddle and the soft gliding motion of a canoe.

"It's a boat, sir," whispered Bates, hiding the lantern under his coat.

I brushed past him and crept to the end of the dock. The paddle dipped on silently and evenly in the still water, but the sound grew fainter. A canoe is the most graceful, the most sensitive, the most inexplicable contrivance of man. With its paddle you may dip up stars along quiet shores or steal into the very harbor of dreams. I knew that furtive splash instantly, and knew that a trained hand wielded the paddle. My boyhood summers in the Maine woods were not, I frequently find, wholly wasted.

The owner of the canoe had evidently stolen close to the Glenarm dock, and had made off when alarmed by the noise of our approach through the wood.

"Have you a boat here?"

"The boat-house is locked and I haven't the key with me, sir," he replied without excitement.

"Of course you haven't it," I snapped, full of anger at his tone of irreproachable respect, and at my own helplessness. I had not even seen the place by daylight,

and the woodland behind me and the lake at my feet
were things of shadow and mystery. In my rage I
stamped my foot.

"Lead the way back," I roared.

I had turned toward the woodland when suddenly
there stole across the water a voice,—a woman's voice,
deep, musical and deliberate.

"Really, I shouldn't be so angry if I were you!" it
said, with a lingering note on the word angry.

"Who are you? What are you doing there?" I bawled.

"Just enjoying a little tranquil thought!" was the
drawling, mocking reply.

Far out upon the water I heard the dip and glide of
the canoe, and saw faintly its outline for a moment;
then it was gone. The lake, the surrounding wood, were
an unknown world,—the canoe, a boat of dreams. Then
again came the voice:

"Good night, merry gentlemen!"

"It was a lady, sir," remarked Bates, after we had
waited silently for a full minute.

"How clever you are!" I sneered. "I suppose ladies
prowl about here at night, shooting ducks or into people's houses."

"It would seem quite likely, sir."

I should have liked to cast him into the lake, but he
was already moving away, the lantern swinging at his

side. I followed him, back through the woodland to the house.

My spirits quickly responded to the cheering influence of the great library. I stirred the fire on the hearth into life and sat down before it, tired from my tramp. I was mystified and perplexed by the incident that had already marked my coming. It was possible, to be sure, that the bullet which narrowly missed my head in the little dining-room had been a wild shot that carried no evil intent. I dismissed at once the idea that it might have been fired from the lake; it had crashed through the glass with too much force to have come so far; and, moreover, I could hardly imagine even a rifle-ball's finding an unimpeded right of way through so dense a strip of wood. I found it difficult to get rid of the idea that some one had taken a pot-shot at me.

The woman's mocking voice from the lake added to my perplexity. It was not, I reflected, such a voice as one might expect to hear from a country girl; nor could I imagine any errand that would excuse a woman's presence abroad on an October night whose cool air inspired first confidences with fire and lamp. There was something haunting in that last cry across the water; it kept repeating itself over and over in my ears. It was a voice of quality, of breeding and charm.

"Good night, merry gentlemen!"

In Indiana, I reflected, rustics, young or old, men or women, were probably not greatly given to salutations of just this temper.

Bates now appeared.

"Beg pardon, sir; but your room's ready whenever you wish to retire."

I looked about in search of a clock.

"There are no timepieces in the house, Mr. Glenarm. Your grandfather was quite opposed to them. He had a theory, sir, that they were conducive, as he said, to idleness. He considered that a man should work by his conscience, sir, and not by the clock,—the one being more exacting than the other."

I smiled as I drew out my watch,—as much at Bates' solemn tones and grim lean visage as at his quotation from my grandsire. But the fellow puzzled and annoyed me. His unobtrusive black clothes, his smoothly-brushed hair, his shaven face, awakened an antagonism in me.

"Bates, if you didn't fire that shot through the window, who did—will you answer me that?"

"Yes, sir; if I didn't do it, it's quite a large question who did. I'll grant you that, sir."

I stared at him. He met my gaze directly without flinching; nor was there anything insolent in his tone or attitude. He continued:

"I didn't do it, sir. I was in the pantry when I heard the crash in the refectory window. The bullet came from out of doors, as I should judge, sir."

The facts and conclusions were undoubtedly with Bates, and I felt that I had not acquitted myself creditably in my effort to fix the crime on him. My abuse of him had been tactless, to say the least, and I now tried another line of attack.

"Of course, Bates, I was merely joking. What's your own theory of the matter?"

"I have no theory, sir. Mr. Glenarm always warned me against theories. He said—if you will pardon me—there was great danger in the speculative mind."

The man spoke with a slight Irish accent, which in itself puzzled me. I have always been attentive to the peculiarities of speech, and his was not the brogue of the Irish servant class. Larry Donovan, who was English-born, used on occasions an exaggerated Irish dialect that was wholly different from the smooth liquid tones of Bates. But more things than his speech were to puzzle me in this man.

"The person in the canoe? How do you account for her?" I asked.

"I haven't accounted for her, sir. There's no women on these grounds, or any sort of person except ourselves."

"But there are neighbors,—farmers, people of some kind must live along the lake."

"A few, sir; and then there's the school quite a bit beyond your own west wall."

His slight reference to my proprietorship, my own wall, as he put it, pleased me.

"Oh, yes; there is a school—girls?—yes; Mr. Pickering mentioned it. But the girls hardly paddle on the lake at night, at this season—hunting ducks—should you say, Bates?"

"I don't believe they do any shooting, Mr. Glenarm. It's a pretty strict school, I judge, sir, from all accounts."

"And the teachers—they are all women?"

"They're the Sisters of St. Agatha, I believe they call them. I sometimes see them walking abroad. They're very quiet neighbors, and they go away in the summer usually, except Sister Theresa. The school's her regular home, sir. And there's the little chapel quite near the wall; the young minister lives there; and the gardener's the only other man on the grounds."

So my immediate neighbors were Protestant nuns and school-girls, with a chaplain and gardener thrown in for variety. Still, the chaplain might be a social resource. There was nothing in the terms of my grandfather's will to prevent my cultivating the acquaintance

of a clergyman. It even occurred to me that this might
be a part of the game: my soul was to be watched over
by a rural priest, while, there being nothing else to do,
I was to give my attention to the study of architecture.
Bates, my guard and housekeeper, was brushing the
hearth with deliberate care.

"Show me my cell," I said, rising, "and I'll go to
bed."

He brought from somewhere a great brass candelabrum that held a dozen lights, and explained:

"This was Mr. Glenarm's habit. He always used this
one to go to bed with. I'm sure he'd wish you to have
it, sir."

I thought I detected something like a quaver in the
man's voice. My grandfather's memory was dear to him.
I reflected, and I was moved to compassion for him.

"How long were you with Mr. Glenarm, Bates?" I
inquired, as I followed him into the hall.

"Five years, sir. He employed me the year you went
abroad. I remember very well his speaking of it. He
greatly admired you, sir."

He led the way, holding the cluster of lights high for
my guidance up the broad stairway.

The hall above shared the generous lines of the whole
house, but the walls were white and hard to the eye.
Rough planks had been laid down for a floor, and be-

yond the light of the candles lay a dark region that gave out ghostly echoes as the loose boards rattled under our feet.

"I hope you'll not be too much disappointed, sir," said Bates, pausing a moment before opening a door. "It's all quite unfinished, but comfortable, I should say, quite comfortable."

"Open the door!"

He was not my host and I did not relish his apology. I walked past him into a small sitting-room that was, in a way, a miniature of the great library below. Open shelves filled with books lined the apartment to the ceiling on every hand, save where a small fireplace, a cabinet and table were built into the walls. In the center of the room was a long table with writing materials set in nice order. I opened a handsome case and found that it contained a set of draftsman's instruments.

I groaned aloud.

"Mr. Glenarm preferred this room for working. The tools were his very own, sir."

"The devil they were!" I exclaimed irascibly. I snatched a book from the nearest shelf and threw it open on the table. It was *The Tower: Its Early Use for Purposes of Defense. London: 1816.*

I closed it with a slam.

"The sleeping-room is beyond, sir. I hope—"

"Don't you hope any more!" I growled; "and it doesn't make any difference whether I'm disappointed or not."

"Certainly not, sir!" he replied in a tone that made me ashamed of myself.

The adjoining bedroom was small and meagerly furnished. The walls were untinted and were relieved only by prints of English cathedrals, French châteaux, and like suggestions of the best things known to architecture. The bed was the commonest iron type; and the other articles of furniture were chosen with a strict regard for utility. My trunks and bags had been carried in, and Bates asked from the door for my commands.

"Mr. Glenarm always breakfasted at seven-thirty, sir, as near as he could hit it without a timepiece, and he was quite punctual. His ways were a little odd, sir. He used to prowl about at night a good deal, and there was no following him."

"I fancy I shan't do much prowling," I declared. "And my grandfather's breakfast hour will suit me exactly, Bates."

"If there's nothing further, sir—"

"That's all;—and Bates—"

"Yes, Mr. Glenarm."

"Of course you understand that I didn't really mean to imply that you had fired that shot at me?"

"I beg you not to mention it, Mr. Glenarm."

"But it *was* a little queer. If you should gain any light on the subject, let me know."

"Certainly, sir."

"But I believe, Bates, that we'd better keep the shades down at night. These duck hunters hereabouts are apparently reckless. And you might attend to these now, —and every evening hereafter."

I wound my watch as he obeyed. I admit that in my heart I still half-suspected the fellow of complicity with the person who had fired at me through the dining-room window. It was rather odd, I reflected, that the shades should have been open, though I might account for this by the fact that this curious unfinished establishment was not subject to the usual laws governing orderly housekeeping. Bates was evidently aware of my suspicions, and he remarked, drawing down the last of the plain green shades:

"Mr. Glenarm never drew them, sir. It was a saying of his, if I may repeat his words, that he liked the open. These are eastern windows, and he took a quiet pleasure in letting the light waken him. It was one of his oddities, sir."

"To be sure. That's all, Bates."

He gravely bade me good night, and I followed him to the outer door and watched his departing figure, lighted by a single candle that he had produced from his pocket.

I stood for several minutes listening to his step, tracing it through the hall below—as far as my knowledge of the house would permit. Then, in unknown regions, I could hear the closing of doors and drawing of bolts. Verily, my jailer was a person of painstaking habits.

I opened my traveling-case and distributed its contents on the dressing-table. I had carried through all my adventures a folding leather photograph-holder, containing portraits of my father and mother and of John Marshall Glenarm, my grandfather, and this I set up on the mantel in the little sitting-room. I felt to-night as never before how alone I was in the world, and a need for companionship and sympathy stirred in me. It was with a new and curious interest that I peered into my grandfather's shrewd old eyes. He used to come and go fitfully at my father's house; but my father had displeased him in various ways that I need not recite, and my father's death had left me with an estrangement which I had widened by my own acts.

Now that I had reached Glenarm, my mind reverted to Pickering's estimate of the value of my grandfather's estate. Although John Marshall Glenarm was an eccentric man, he had been able to accumulate a large fortune; and yet I had allowed the executor to tell me that he had died comparatively poor. In so readily accepting the terms of the will and burying myself in a region of which I knew nothing, I had cut myself off from the usual channels of counsel. If I left the place to return to New York I should simply disinherit myself. At Glenarm I was, and there I must remain to the end of the year; I grew bitter against Pickering as I reflected upon the ease with which he had got rid of me. I had always satisfied myself that my wits were as keen as his, but I wondered now whether I had not stupidly put myself in his power.

CHAPTER V

A RED TAM-O'-SHANTER

I looked out on the bright October morning with a renewed sense of isolation. Trees crowded about my windows, many of them still wearing their festal colors, scarlet and brown and gold, with the bright green of some sulking companion standing out here and there with startling vividness. I put on an old corduroy outing suit and heavy shoes, ready for a tramp abroad, and went below.

The great library seemed larger than ever when I beheld it in the morning light. I opened one of the French windows and stepped out on a stone terrace, where I gained a fair view of the exterior of the house, which proved to be a modified Tudor, with battlements and two towers. One of the latter was only half-finished, and to it and to other parts of the house the workmen's scaffolding still clung. Heaps of stone and piles of lumber were scattered about in great disorder. The house extended partly along the edge of a ravine, through which a slender creek ran toward the lake. The terrace became a broad balcony immediately outside the library, and beneath it the water bubbled pleasantly around heavy stone pillars. Two pretty rustic bridges spanned the ravine, one near the front entrance, the other at the rear. My grandfather had begun his house on a generous plan, but, buried as it was among the trees, it suffered from lack of perspective. However, on one side toward the lake was a fair meadow, broken by a water-tower, and just beyond the west dividing wall I saw a little chapel; and still farther, in the same direction, the outlines of the buildings of St. Agatha's were vaguely perceptible in another strip of woodland.

The thought of gentle nuns and school-girls as neighbors amused me. All I asked was that they should keep to their own side of the wall.

I heard behind me the careful step of Bates.

"Good morning, Mr. Glenarm. I trust you rested quite well, sir."

His figure was as austere, his tone as respectful and colorless as by night. The morning light gave him a pallid cast. He suffered my examination coolly enough; his eyes were, indeed, the best thing about him.

"This is what Mr. Glenarm called the platform. I believe it's in *Hamlet,* sir."

I laughed aloud. *"Elsinore: A Platform Before the Castle."*

"It was one of Mr. Glenarm's little fancies, you might call it, sir."

"And the ghost,—where does the murdered majesty of Denmark lie by day?"

"I fear it wasn't provided, sir! As you see, Mr. Glenarm, the house is quite incomplete. My late master had not carried out all his plans."

Bates did not smile. I fancied he never smiled, and I wondered whether John Marshall Glenarm had played upon the man's lack of humor. My grandfather had been possessed of a certain grim, ironical gift at jesting, and quite likely he had amused himself by experimenting upon his serving man.

"You may breakfast when you like, sir,"—and thus admonished I went into the refectory.

A newspaper lay at my plate; it was the morning's issue of a Chicago daily. I was, then, not wholly out of the world, I reflected, scanning the head-lines.

"Your grandfather rarely examined the paper. Mr. Glenarm was more particularly interested in the old times. He wasn't what you might call up to date,—if you will pardon the expression, sir."

"You are quite right about that, Bates. He was a medievalist in his sympathies."

"Thank you for that word, sir; I've frequently heard

him apply it to himself. The plain omelette was a great
favorite with your grandfather. I hope it is to your liking, sir."

"It's excellent, Bates. And your coffee is beyond
praise."

"Thank you, Mr. Glenarm. One does what one can,
sir."

He had placed me so that I faced the windows, an
attention to my comfort and safety which I appreciated.
The broken pane told the tale of the shot that had so
narrowly missed me the night before.

"I'll repair that to-day, sir," Bates remarked, seeing
my eyes upon the window.

"You know that I'm to spend a year on this place;
I assume that you understand the circumstances," I
said, feeling it wise that we should understand each
other.

"Quite so, Mr. Glenarm."

"I'm a student, you know, and all I want is to be left
alone."

This I threw in to reassure myself rather than for
his information. It was just as well, I reflected, to as-
sert a little authority, even though the fellow undoubtedly represented Pickering and received orders from
him.

"In a day or two, or as soon as I have got used to the

place, I shall settle down to work in the library. You may give me breakfast at seven-thirty; luncheon at one-thirty and dinner at seven."

"Those were my late master's hours, sir."

"Very good. And I'll eat anything you please, except mutton broth, meat pie and canned strawberries. Strawberries in tins, Bates, are not well calculated to lift the spirit of man."

"I quite agree with you, sir, if you will pardon my opinion."

"And the bills—"

"They are provided for by Mr. Pickering. He sends me an allowance for the household expenses."

"So you are to report to him, are you, as heretofore?"

I blew out a match with which I had lighted a cigar and watched the smoking end intently.

"I believe that's the idea, sir."

It is not pleasant to be under compulsion,—to feel your freedom curtailed, to be conscious of espionage. I rose without a word and went into the hall.

"You may like to have the keys," said Bates, following me. "There's two for the gates in the outer wall and one for the St. Agatha's gate; they're marked, as you see. And here's the hall-door key and the boat-house key that you asked for last night."

After an hour spent in unpacking I went out into the

grounds. I had thought it well to wire Pickering of
my arrival, and I set out for Annandale to send him a
telegram. My spirit lightened under the influences of
the crisp air and cheering sunshine. What had seemed
strange and shadowy at night was clear enough by
day.

I found the gate through which we had entered the
grounds the night before without difficulty. The stone
wall was assuredly no flimsy thing. It was built in a
thoroughly workmanlike manner, and I mentally com-
puted its probable cost with amazement. There were,
I reflected, much more satisfactory ways of spending
money than in building walls around Indiana forests.
But the place was mine, or as good as mine, and there
was no manner of use in quarreling with the whims of
my dead grandfather. At the expiration of a year I
could tear down the wall if I pleased; and as to the incomplete house, that I should sell or remodel to my
liking.

On the whole, I settled into an amiable state of mind;
my perplexity over the shot of the night before was passing away under the benign influences of blue sky and
warm sunshine. A few farm-folk passed me in the
highway and gave me good morning in the fashion of
the country, inspecting my knickerbockers at the same

time with frank disapproval. I reached the lake and gazed out upon its quiet waters with satisfaction. At the foot of Annandale's main street was a dock where several small steam-craft and a number of catboats were being dismantled for the winter. As I passed, a man approached the dock in a skiff, landed and tied his boat. He started toward the village at a quick pace, but turned and eyed me with rustic directness.

"Good morning!" I said. "Any ducks about?"

He paused, nodded and fell into step with me.

"No,—not enough to pay for the trouble."

"I'm sorry for that. I'd hoped to pick up a few."

"I guess you're a stranger in these parts," he remarked, eying me again,—my knickerbockers no doubt marking me as an alien.

"Quite so. My name is Glenarm, and I've just come."

"I thought you might be him. We've rather been expecting you here in the village. I'm John Morgan, caretaker of the resorters' houses up the lake."

"I suppose you all knew my grandfather hereabouts."

"Well, yes; you might say as we did, or you might say as we didn't. He wasn't just the sort that you got next to in a hurry. He kept pretty much to himself. He built a wall there to keep us out, but he needn't have troubled himself. We're not the kind around here to meddle, and you may be sure the summer people never bothered him."

There was a tone of resentment in his voice, and I hastened to say:

"I'm sure you're mistaken about the purposes of that wall. My grandfather was a student of architecture. It was a hobby of his. The house and wall were in the line of his experiments, and to please his whims. I hope the people of the village won't hold any hard feelings against his memory or against me. Why, the labor there must have been a good thing for the people hereabouts."

"It ought to have been," said the man gruffly; "but that's where the trouble comes in. He brought a lot of queer fellows here under contract to work for him,— Italians, or Greeks, or some sort of foreigners. They built the wall, and he had them at work inside for half a year. He didn't even let them out for air; and when they finished his job he loaded 'em on to a train one day and hauled 'em away."

"That was quite like him, I'm sure," I said, remembering with amusement my grandfather's secretive ways.

"I guess he was a crank all right," said the man conclusively.

It was evident that he did not care to establish friendly relations with the resident of Glenarm. He was about forty, light, with a yellow beard and pale blue eyes. He was dressed roughly and wore a shabby soft hat.

"Well, I suppose I'll have to assume responsibility for him and his acts," I remarked, piqued by the fellow's surliness.

We had reached the center of the village, and he left me abruptly, crossing the street to one of the shops. I continued on to the railway station, where I wrote and paid for my message. The station-master inspected me carefully as I searched my pockets for change.

"You want your telegrams delivered at the house?" he asked.

"Yes, please," I answered, and he turned away to his desk of clicking instruments without looking at me again.

It seemed wise to establish relations with the post-office, so I made myself known to the girl who stood at the delivery window.

"You already have a box," she advised me. "There's a boy carries the mail to your house; Mr. Bates hires him."

Bates had himself given me this information, but the girl seemed to find pleasure in imparting it with a certain severity. I then bought a cake of soap at the principal drug store and purchased a package of smoking-tobacco, which I did not need, at a grocery.

News of my arrival had evidently reached the villagers; I was conceited enough to imagine that my presence was probably of interest to them; but the station-master, the girl at the post-office and the clerks in the shops treated me with an unmistakable cold reserve. There was a certain evenness of the chill which they visited upon me, as though a particular degree of frigidity had been determined in advance.

I shrugged my shoulders and turned toward Glenarm. My grandfather had left me a cheerful legacy of distrust among my neighbors, the result, probably, of importing foreign labor to work on his house. The surly Morgan had intimated as much; but it did not greatly matter. I had not come to Glenarm to cultivate the rustics, but to fulfil certain obligations laid down in my grandfather's will. I was, so to speak, on duty, and I much preferred that the villagers should let me alone. Comforting myself with these reflections I reached the wharf, where I saw Morgan sitting with his feet dangling over the water, smoking a pipe.

I nodded in his direction, but he feigned not to see me. A moment later he jumped into his boat and rowed out into the lake.

When I returned to the house Bates was at work in the kitchen. This was a large square room with heavy timbers showing in the walls and low ceiling. There

was a great fireplace having an enormous chimney and
fitted with a crane and bobs, but for practical purposes
a small range was provided.

Bates received me placidly.

"Yes; it's an unusual kitchen, sir. Mr. Glenarm
copied it from an old kitchen in England. He took
quite a pride in it. It's a pleasant place to sit in the
evening, sir."

He showed me the way below, where I found that the
cellar extended under every part of the house, and was
divided into large chambers. The door of one of them
was of heavy oak, bound in iron, with a barred opening
at the top. A great iron hasp with a heavy padlock and
grilled area windows gave further the impression of a
cell, and I fear that at this, as at many other things in
the curious house, I swore—if I did not laugh—thinking of the money my grandfather had expended in real-
izing his whims. The room was used, I noted with pleasure, as a depository for potatoes. I asked Bates whether
he knew my grandfather's purpose in providing a cell in
his house.

"That, sir, was another of the dead master's ideas.
He remarked to me once that it was just as well to have
a dungeon in a well-appointed house,—his humor again,
sir! And it comes in quite handy for the potatoes."

In another room I found a curious collection of lanterns of every conceivable description, grouped on shelves, and next door to this was a store-room filled with brass candlesticks of many odd designs. I shall not undertake to describe my sensations as, peering about with a candle in my hand, the vagaries of John Marshall Glenarm's mind were further disclosed to me. It was almost beyond belief that any man with such whims should ever have had the money to gratify them.

I returned to the main floor and studied the titles of the books in the library, finally smoking a pipe over a very tedious chapter in an exceedingly dull work on *Norman Revivals and Influences.* Then I went out, assuring myself that I should get steadily to work in a day or two. It was not yet eleven o'clock, and time was sure to move deliberately within the stone walls of my prison. The long winter lay before me in which I must study perforce, and just now it was pleasant to view the landscape in all its autumn splendor.

Bates was soberly chopping wood at a rough pile of timber at the rear of the house. His industry had already impressed me. He had the quiet ways of an ideal serving man.

"Well, Bates, you don't intend to let me freeze to death, do you? There must be enough in the pile there to last all winter."

"Yes, sir; I am just cutting a little more of the hickory, sir. Mr. Glenarm always preferred it to beech or maple. We only take out the old timber. The summer storms eat into the wood pretty bad, sir."

"Oh, hickory, to be sure! I've heard it's the best firewood. That's very thoughtful of you."

I turned next to the unfinished tower in the meadow, from which a windmill pumped water to the house. The iron frame was not wholly covered with stone, but material for the remainder of the work lay scattered at the base. I went on through the wood to the lake and inspected the boat-house. It was far more pretentious than I had imagined from my visit in the dark. It was of two stories, the upper half being a cozy lounging-room, with wide windows and a fine outlook over the water. The unplastered walls were hung with Indian blankets; lounging-chairs and a broad seat under the windows, colored matting on the floor and a few prints pinned upon the Navajoes gave further color to the place.

I followed the pebbly shore to the stone wall where it marked the line of the school-grounds. The wall, I observed, was of the same solid character here as along the road. I tramped beside it, reflecting that my grandfather's estate, in the heart of the Republic, would some day give the lie to foreign complaints that we have no ruins in America.

I had assumed that there was no opening in the wall, but half-way to the road I found an iron gate, fastened with chain and padlock, by means of which I climbed to the top. The pillars at either side of the gate were of huge dimensions and were higher than I could reach. An intelligent forester had cleared the wood in the school-grounds, which were of the same general character as the Glenarm estate. The little Gothic church near at hand was built of stone similar to that used in Glenarm House. As I surveyed the scene a number of young women came from one of the school-buildings and, forming in twos and fours, walked back and forth in a rough path that led to the chapel. A Sister clad in a brown habit lingered near or walked first with one and then another of the students. It was all very pretty and interesting and not at all the ugly school for paupers I had expected to find. The students were not the charity children I had carelessly pictured; they were not so young, for one thing, and they seemed to be appareled decently enough.

I smiled to find myself adjusting my scarf and straightening my collar as I beheld my neighbors for the first time.

As I sat thus on the wall I heard the sound of angry voices back of me on the Glenarm side, and a crash of underbrush marked a flight and pursuit. I crouched

down on the wall and waited. In a moment a man
plunged through the wood and stumbled over a low-
hanging vine and fell, not ten yards from where I lay.
To my great surprise it was Morgan, my acquaintance
of the morning. He rose, cursed his ill luck and, hug-
ging the wall close, ran toward the lake. Instantly the
pursuer broke into view. It was Bates, evidently much
excited and with an ugly cut across his forehead. He
carried a heavy club, and, after listening for a moment
for sounds of the enemy, he hurried after the caretaker.

It was not my row, though I must say it quickened
my curiosity. I straightened myself out, threw my legs
over the school side of the wall and lighted a cigar,
feeling cheered by the opportunity the stone barricade
offered for observing the world.

As I looked off toward the little church I found two
other actors appearing on the scene. A girl stood in a
little opening of the wood, talking to a man. Her hands
were thrust into the pockets of her covert coat; she wore
a red tam-o'-shanter, that made a bright bit of color in
the wood. They were not more than twenty feet away,
but a wild growth of young maples lay between us,
screening the wall. Their profiles were toward me, and
the tones of the girl's voice reached me clearly, as she
addressed her companion. He wore a clergyman's high
waistcoat, and I assumed that he was the chaplain whom

Bates had mentioned. I am not by nature an eavesdropper, but the girl was clearly making a plea of some
kind, and the chaplain's stalwart figure awoke in me an
antagonism that held me to the wall.

"If he comes here I shall go away, so you may as well
understand it and tell him. I shan't see him under any
circumstances, and I'm not going to Florida or California or anywhere else in a private car, no matter who
chaperones it."

"Certainly not, unless you want to—certainly not,"
said the chaplain. "You understand that I'm only giving you his message. He thought it best—"

"Not to write to me or to Sister Theresa!" interrupted the girl contemptuously. "What a clever man
he is!"

"And how unclever I am!" said the clergman, laughing. "Well, I thank you for giving me the opportunity
to present his message."

She smiled, nodded and turned swiftly toward the
school. The chaplain looked after her for a few moments, then walked away soberly toward the lake. He
was a young fellow, clean-shaven and dark, and with a
pair of shoulders that gave me a twinge of envy. I could
not guess how great a factor that vigorous figure was to
be in my own affairs. As I swung down from the wall
and walked toward Glenarm House, my thoughts were

not with the athletic chaplain, but with the girl, whose youth was, I reflected, marked by her short skirt, the unconcern with which her hands were thrust into the pockets of her coat, and the irresponsible tilt of the tam-o'-shanter. There is something jaunty, a suggestion of spirit and independence in a tam-o'-shanter, particularly a red one. If the red tam-o'-shanter expressed, so to speak, the key-note of St. Agatha's, the proximity of the school was not so bad a thing after all.

In high good-humor and with a sharp appetite I went in to luncheon.

CHAPTER VI

THE GIRL AND THE CANOE

"The persimmons are off the place, sir. Mr. Glenarm was very fond of the fruit."

I had never seen a persimmon before, but I was in a mood for experiment. The frost-broken rind was certainly forbidding, but the rich pulp brought a surprise of joy to my palate. Bates watched me with respectful satisfaction. His gravity was in no degree diminished by the presence of a neat strip of flesh-colored court-plaster over his right eye. A faint suggestion of arnica hung in the air.

"This is a quiet life," I remarked, wishing to give him an opportunity to explain his encounter of the morning.

"You are quite right, sir. As your grandfather used to say, it's a place of peace."

"When nobody shoots at you through a window," I suggested.

"Such a thing is likely to happen to any gentleman," he replied, "but not likely to happen more than once, if you'll allow the philosophy."

He did not refer to his encounter with the caretaker, and I resolved to keep my knowledge of it to myself. I always prefer to let a rascal hang himself, and here was a case, I reasoned, where, if Bates were disloyal to the duties Pickering had imposed upon him, the fact of his perfidy was bound to disclose itself eventually. Glancing around at him when he was off guard I surprised a look of utter dejection upon his face as he stood with folded arms behind my chair.

He flushed and started, then put his hand to his forehead.

"I met with a slight accident this morning, sir. The hickory's very tough, sir. A piece of wood flew up and struck me."

"Too bad!" I said with sympathy. "You'd better rest a bit this afternoon."

"Thank you, sir; but it's a small matter,—only, you might think it a trifle disfiguring."

He struck a match for my cigarette, and I left without looking at him again. But as I crossed the threshold of the library I formulated this note: "Bates is a liar, for one thing, and a person with active enemies for another; watch him."

All things considered, the day was passing well enough. I picked up a book, and threw myself on a comfortable divan to smoke and reflect before continuing my explorations. As I lay there, Bates brought me a telegram, a reply to my message to Pickering. It read:

"Yours announcing arrival received and filed."

It was certainly a queer business, my errand to Glenarm. I lay for a couple of hours dreaming, and counted the candles in the great crystal chandelier until my eyes ached. Then I rose, took my cap, and was soon tramping off toward the lake.

There were several small boats and a naphtha launch in the boat-house. I dropped a canoe into the water and paddled off toward the summer colony, whose gables and chimneys were plainly visible from the Glenarm shore.

I landed and roamed idly over leaf-strewn walks past nearly a hundred cottages, to whose windows and verandas the winter blinds gave a dreary and inhospitable air. There was, at one point, a casino, whose broad veranda hung over the edge of the lake, while beneath, on the water-side, was a boat-house. I had from this point a fine view of the lake, and I took advantage of it to fix in my mind the topography of the region. I could see the bold outlines of Glenarm House and its red-tile roofs; and the gray tower of the little chapel beyond the wall rose above the wood with a placid dignity. Above the trees everywhere hung the shadowy smoke of autumn.

I walked back to the wharf, where I had left my

canoe, and was about to step into it when I saw, rocking at a similar landing-place near-by, another slight
craft of the same type as my own, but painted dark
maroon. I was sure the canoe had not been there when
I landed. Possibly it belonged to Morgan, the caretaker. I walked over and examined it. I even lifted it
slightly in the water to test its weight. The paddle lay
on the dock beside me and it, too, I weighed critically,
deciding that it was a trifle light for my own taste.

"Please—if you don't mind—"

I turned to stand face to face with the girl in the red
tam-o'-shanter.

"I beg your pardon," I said, stepping away from the
canoe.

She did not wear the covert coat of the morning, but
a red knit jacket, buttoned tight about her. She was
young with every emphasis of youth. A pair of dark
blue eyes examined me with good-humored curiosity.
She was on good terms with the sun—I rejoiced in the
brown of her cheeks, so eloquent of companionship with
the outdoor world—a certificate indeed of the favor of
Heaven. Show me, in October, a girl with a face of
tan, whose hands have plied a paddle or driven a golf-
ball or cast a fly beneath the blue arches of summer,
and I will suffer her scorn in joy. She may vote me
dull and refute my wisest word with laughter, for hers

are the privileges of the sisterhood of Diana; and that soft bronze, those daring fugitive freckles beneath her eyes, link her to times when Pan whistled upon his reed and all the days were long.

She had approached silently and was enjoying, I felt sure, my discomfiture at being taken unawares.

I had snatched off my cap and stood waiting beside the canoe, feeling, I must admit, a trifle guilty at being caught in the unwarrantable inspection of another person's property—particularly a person so wholly pleasing to the eye.

"Really, if you don't need that paddle any more—"

I looked down and found to my annoyance that I held it in my hand,—was in fact leaning upon it with a cool air of proprietorship.

"Again, I beg your pardon," I said. "I hadn't expected—"

She eyed me calmly with the stare of the child that arrives at a drawing-room door by mistake and scrutinizes the guests without awe. I didn't know what I had expected or had not expected, and she manifested no intention of helping me to explain. Her short skirt suggested fifteen or sixteen—not more—and such being the case there was no reason why I should not be master of the situation. As I fumbled my pipe the hot coals of tobacco burned my hand and I cast the thing from me.

She laughed a little and watched the pipe bound from the dock into the water.

"Too bad!" she said, her eyes upon it; "but if you hurry you may get it before it floats away."

"Thank you for the suggestion," I said. But I did not relish the idea of kneeling on the dock to fish for a pipe before a strange school-girl who was, I felt sure, anxious to laugh at me.

She took a step toward the line by which her boat was fastened.

"Allow me."

"If you think you can,—safely," she said; and the laughter that lurked in her eyes annoyed me.

"The feminine knot is designed for the confusion of man," I observed, twitching vainly at the rope, which was tied securely in unfamiliar loops.

She was singularly unresponsive. The thought that she was probably laughing at my clumsiness did not make my fingers more nimble.

"The nautical instructor at St. Agatha's is undoubtedly a woman. This knot must come in the post-graduate course. But my gallantry is equal, I trust, to your patience."

The maid in the red tam-o'-shanter continued silent. The wet rope was obdurate, the knot more and more hopeless, and my efforts to make light of the situation awakened no response in the girl. I tugged away at the rope, attacking its tangle on various theories.

"A case for surgery, I'm afraid. A truly Gordian knot, but I haven't my knife."

"Oh, but you wouldn't!" she exclaimed. "I think I can manage."

She bent down—I was aware that the sleeve of her jacket brushed my shoulder—seized an end that I had ignored, gave it a sharp tug with a slim brown hand and pulled the knot free.

"There!" she exclaimed with a little laugh; "I might have saved you all the bother."

"How dull of me! But I didn't have the combination," I said, steadying the canoe carefully to mitigate the ignominy of my failure.

She scorned the hand I extended, but embarked with light confident step and took the paddle. It was growing late. The shadows in the wood were deepening; a chill crept over the water, and, beyond the tower of the chapel, the sky was bright with the splendor of sunset.

With a few skilful strokes she brought her little craft beside my pipe, picked it up and tossed it to the wharf.

"Perhaps you can pipe a tune upon it," she said, dipping the paddle tentatively.

"You put me under great obligations," I declared. "Are all the girls at St. Agatha's as amiable?"

"I should say not! I'm a great exception,—and—I really shouldn't be talking to you at all! It's against the rules! And we don't encourage smoking."

"The chaplain doesn't smoke, I suppose."

"Not in chapel; I believe it isn't done! And we rarely see him elsewhere."

She had idled with the paddle so far, but now lifted her eyes and drew back the blade for a long stroke.

"But in the wood—this morning—by the wall!"

I hate myself to this day for having so startled her. The poised blade dropped into the water with a splash; she brought the canoe a trifle nearer to the wharf with an almost imperceptible stroke, and turned toward me with wonder and dismay in her eyes.

"So you are an eavesdropper and detective, are you? I beg that you will give your master my compliments! I really owe you an apology; I *thought* you were a gentleman!" she exclaimed with withering emphasis, and dipped her blade deep in flight.

I called, stammering incoherently, after her, but her light argosy skimmed the water steadily. The paddle rose and fell with trained precision, making scarcely a ripple as she stole softly away toward the fairy towers of the sunset. I stood looking after her, goaded with self-contempt. A glory of yellow and red filled the west. Suddenly the wind moaned in the wood behind the line of cottages, swept over me and rippled the surface of the lake. I watched its flight until it caught her canoe and I marked the flimsy craft's quick response, as the shaken waters bore her alert figure upward on the swell, her blade still maintaining its regular dip, until she disappeared behind a little peninsula that made a harbor near the school grounds.

The red tam-o'-shanter seemed at last to merge in the red sky, and I turned to my canoe and paddled cheerlessly home.

CHAPTER VII

I was so thoroughly angry with myself that after idling along the shores for an hour I lost my way in the dark wood when I landed and brought up at the rear door used by Bates for communication with the villagers who supplied us with provender. I readily found my way to the kitchen and to a flight of stairs beyond, which connected the first and second floors. The house was dark, and my good spirits were not increased as I stumbled up the unfamiliar way in the dark, with, I fear, a malediction upon my grandfather, who had built and left incomplete a house so utterly preposterous. My unpardonable fling at the girl still rankled; and I was cold from the quick descent of the night chill on the water and anxious to get into more comfortable clothes. Once on the second floor I felt that I knew the way to my room, and I was feeling my way toward it over the rough floor when I heard low voices rising apparently from my sitting-room.

It was pitch dark in the hall. I stopped short and listened. The door of my room was open and a faint light flashed once into the hall and disappeared. I heard now a sound as of a hammer tapping upon wood-work.

Then it ceased, and a voice whispered:

"He'll kill me if he finds me here. I'll try again to-morrow. I swear to God I'll help you, but no more now—"

Then the sound of a scuffle and again the tapping of the hammer. After several minutes more of this there was a whispered dialogue which I could not hear.

Whatever was occurring, two or three points struck me on the instant. One of the conspirators was an unwilling party to an act as yet unknown; second, they had been unsuccessful and must wait for another opportunity; and third, the business, whatever it was, was clearly of some importance to myself, as my own apartments in my grandfather's strange house had been chosen for the investigation.

Clearly, I was not prepared to close the incident, but the idea of frightening my visitors appealed to my sense of humor. I tiptoed to the front stairway, ran lightly down, found the front door, and, from the inside, opened and slammed it. I heard instantly a hurried scamper above, and the heavy fall of one who had stumbled in the dark. I grinned with real pleasure at the sound of this mishap, hurried into the great library, which was as dark as a well, and, opening one of the long windows, stepped out on the balcony. At once from the rear of the house came the sound of a stealthy step, which increased to a run at the ravine bridge. I listened to the flight of the fugitive through the wood until the sounds died away toward the lake.

Then, turning to the library windows, I saw Bates, with a candle held above his head, peering about.

"Hello, Bates," I called cheerfully. "I just got home and stepped out to see if the moon had risen. I don't believe I know where to look for it in this country."

He began lighting the tapers with his usual deliberation.

"It's a trifle early, I think, sir. About seven o'clock, I should say, was the hour, Mr. Glenarm."

There was, of course, no doubt whatever that Bates had been one of the men I heard in my room. It was wholly possible that he had been compelled to assist in some lawless act against his will; but why, if he had been forced into aiding a criminal, should he not invoke my own aid to protect himself? I kicked the logs in the fireplace impatiently in my uncertainty. The man slowly lighted the many candles in the great apartment. He was certainly a deep one, and his case grew more puzzling as I studied it in relation to the rifle-shot of the night before, his collision with Morgan in the wood, which I had witnessed; and now the house itself had been invaded by some one with his connivance. The shot through the refectory window might have been innocent enough; but these other matters in connection with it could hardly be brushed aside.

Bates lighted me to the stairway, and said as I passed him:

"There's a baked ham for dinner. I should call it extra delicate, Mr. Glenarm. I suppose there's no change in the dinner hour, sir?"

"Certainly not," I said with asperity; for I am not a person to inaugurate a dinner hour one day and change it the next. Bates wished to make conversation,—the sure sign of a guilty conscience in a servant,—and I was not disposed to encourage him.

I closed the doors carefully and began a thorough examination of both the sitting-room and the little bed-chamber. I was quite sure that my own effects could not have attracted the two men who had taken advantage of my absence to visit my quarters. Bates had helped unpack my trunk and undoubtedly knew every item of my simple wardrobe. I threw open the doors of the three closets in the rooms and found them all in the good order established by Bates. He had carried my trunks and bags to a store-room, so that everything I owned must have passed under his eye. My money even, the remnant of my fortune that I had drawn from the

New York bank, I had placed carelessly enough in the drawer of a chiffonnier otherwise piled with collars. It took but a moment to satisfy myself that this had not been touched. And, to be sure, a hammer was not necessary to open a drawer that had, from its appearance, never been locked. The game was deeper than I had imagined; I had scratched the crust without result, and my wits were busy with speculations as I changed my clothes, pausing frequently to examine the furniture, even the bricks on the hearth.

One thing only I found—the slight scar of a hammer-head on the oak paneling that ran around the bedroom. The wood had been struck near the base and at the top of every panel, for though the mark was not perceptible on all, a test had evidently been made systematically. With this as a beginning, I found a moment later a spot of tallow under a heavy table in one corner. Evidently the furniture had been moved to permit of the closest scrutiny of the paneling. Even behind the bed I found the same impress of the hammer-head; the test had undoubtedly been thorough, for a pretty smart tap on oak is necessary to leave an impression. My visitors had undoubtedly been making soundings in search of a recess of some kind in the wall, and as they had failed of their purpose they were likely, I assumed, to pursue their researches further.

I pondered these things with a thoroughly-awakened interest in life. Glenarm House really promised to prove exciting. I took from a drawer a small revolver, filled its chambers with cartridges and thrust it into my hip pocket, whistling meanwhile Larry Donovan's favorite air, the *Marche Funèbre d'une Marionnette*. My heart went out to Larry as I scented adventure, and I wished him with me; but speculations as to Larry's whereabouts were always profitless, and quite likely he was in jail somewhere.

The ham of whose excellence Bates had hinted was no disappointment. There is, I have always held, nothing better in this world than a baked ham, and the specimen Bates placed before me was a delight to the eye,—so adorned was it with spices, so crisply brown its outer coat; and a taste—that first tentative taste, before the sauce was added—was like a dream of Lucullus come true. I could forgive a good deal in a cook with that touch,—anything short of arson and assassination!

"Bates," I said, as he stood forth where I could see him, "you cook amazingly well. Where did you learn the business?"

"Your grandfather grew very captious, Mr. Glenarm. I had to learn to satisfy him, and I believe I did it, sir, if you'll pardon the conceit."

"He didn't die of gout, did he? I can readily imagine it."

"No, Mr. Glenarm. It was his heart. He had his
warning of it."

"Ah, yes; to be sure. The heart or the stomach,—one
may as well fail as the other. I believe I prefer to keep
my digestion going as long as possible. Those grilled
sweet potatoes again, if you please, Bates."

The game that he and I were playing appealed to me
strongly. It was altogether worth while, and as I ate
guava jelly with cheese and toasted crackers, and then
lighted one of my own cigars over a cup of Bates' unfailing coffee, my spirit was livelier than at any time
since a certain evening on which Larry and I had
escaped from Tangier with our lives and the curses of
the police. It is a melancholy commentary on life that
contentment comes more easily through the stomach
than along any other avenue. In the great library, with
its rich store of books and its eternal candles, I sprawled
upon a divan before the fire and smoked and indulged
in pleasant speculations. The day had offered much
material for fireside reflection, and I reviewed its history calmly.

There was, however, one incident that I found unpleasant in the retrospect. I had been guilty of most

unchivalrous conduct toward one of the girls of St. Agatha's. It had certainly been unbecoming in me to sit on the wall, however unwillingly, and listen to the words—few though they were—that passed between her and the chaplain. I forgot the shot through the window; I forgot Bates and the interest my room possessed for him and his unknown accomplice; but the sudden distrust and contempt I had awakened in the girl by my clownish behavior annoyed me increasingly.

I rose presently, found my cap in a closet under the stairs, and went out into the moon-flooded wood toward the lake. The tangle was not so great when you knew the way, and there was indeed, as I had found, the faint suggestion of a path. The moon glorified a broad highway across the water; the air was sharp and still. The houses in the summer colony were vaguely defined, but the sight of them gave me no cheer. The tilt of her tam-o'-shanter as she paddled away into the sunset had conveyed an impression of spirit and dignity that I could not adjust to any imaginable expiation.

These reflections carried me to the borders of St. Agatha's, and I followed the wall to the gate, climbed up, and sat down in the shadow of the pillar farthest from the lake. Lights shone scatteringly in the buildings of St. Agatha's, but the place was wholly silent. I drew out a cigarette and was about to light it when

I heard a sound as of a tread on stone. There was, I knew, no stone pavement at hand, but peering toward the lake I saw a man walking boldly along the top of the wall toward me. The moonlight threw his figure into clear relief. Several times he paused, bent down and rapped upon the wall with an object he carried in his hand.

Only a few hours before I had heard a similar sound rising from the wainscoting of my own roòm in Glenarm House. Evidently the stone wall, too, was under suspicion!

Tap, tap, tap! The man with the hammer was examining the farther side of the gate, and very likely he would carry his investigations beyond it. I drew up my legs and crouched in the shadow of the pillar, revolver in hand. I was not anxious for an encounter; I much preferred to wait for a disclosure of the purpose that lay behind this mysterious tapping upon walls on my grandfather's estate.

But the matter was taken out of my own hands before I had a chance to debate it. The man dropped to the ground, sounded the stone base under the gate, likewise the pillars, evidently without results, struck a spiteful crack upon the iron bars, then stood up abruptly and looked me straight in the eyes. It was Morgan, the caretaker of the summer colony.

"Good evening, Mr. Morgan," I said, settling the revolver into my hand.

There was no doubt about his surprise; he fell back, staring at me hard, and instinctively drawing the hammer over his shoulder as though to fling it at me.

"Just stay where you are a moment, Morgan," I said pleasantly, and dropped to a sitting position on the wall for greater ease in talking to him.

He stood sullenly, the hammer dangling at arm's length, while my revolver covered his head.

"Now, if you please, I'd like to know what you mean by prowling about here and rummaging my house!"

"Oh, it's you, is it, Mr. Glenarm? Well, you certainly gave me a bad scare."

His air was one of relief and his teeth showed pleasantly through his beard.

"It certainly is I. But you haven't answered my question. What were you doing in my house to-day?"

He smiled again, shaking his head.

"You're really fooling, Mr. Glenarm. I wasn't in your house to-day; I never was in it in my life!"

His white teeth gleamed in his light beard; his hat was pushed back from his forehead so that I saw his eyes, and he wore unmistakably the air of a man whose conscience is perfectly clear. I was confident that he lied, but without appealing to Bates I was not prepared to prove it.

"But you can't deny that you're on my grounds now, can you?" I had dropped the revolver to my knee, but I raised it again.

"Certainly not, Mr. Glenarm. If you'll allow me to explain—"

"That's precisely what I want you to do."

"Well, it may seem strange,"—he laughed, and I felt the least bit foolish to be pointing a pistol at the head of a fellow of so amiable a spirit.

"Hurry," I commanded.

"Well, as I was saying, it may seem strange; but I was just examining the wall to determine the character of the work. One of the cottagers on the lake left me with the job of building a fence on his place, and I've been expecting to come over to look at this all fall. You see, Mr. Glenarm, your honored grandfather was a master in such matters, as you may know, and I didn't see any harm in getting the benefit—to put it so—of his experience."

I laughed. He had denied having entered the house with so much assurance that I had been prepared for some really plausible explanation of his interest in the wall.

"Morgan—you said it was Morgan, didn't you?—you are undoubtedly a scoundrel of the first water. I make the remark with pleasure."

"Men have been killed for saying less," he said.

"And for doing less than firing through windows at a man's head. It wasn't friendly of you."

"I don't see why you center all your suspicions on me. You exaggerate my importance, Mr. Glenarm. I'm only the man-of-all-work at a summer resort."

"I wouldn't believe you, Morgan, if you swore on a stack of Bibles as high as this wall."

"Thanks!" he ejaculated mockingly.

Like a flash he swung the hammer over his head and drove it at me, and at the same moment I fired. The hammer-head struck the pillar near the outer edge and in such a manner that the handle flew around and smote me smartly in the face. By the time I reached the ground the man was already running rapidly through the park, darting in and out among the trees, and I made after him at hot speed.

The hammer-handle had struck slantingly across my forehead, and my head ached from the blow. I abused myself roundly for managing the encounter so stupidly, and in my rage fired twice with no aim whatever after the flying figure of the caretaker. He clearly had the advantage of familiarity with the wood, striking off

Like a flash he swung the hammer, and at the same moment I fired.

Page 100

boldly into the heart of it, and quickly widening the distance between us; but I kept on, even after I ceased to hear him threshing through the undergrowth, and came out presently at the margin of the lake about fifty feet from the boat-house. I waited in the shadow for some time, expecting to see the fellow again, but he did not appear.

I found the wall with difficulty and followed it back to the gate. It would be just as well, I thought, to possess myself of the hammer; and I dropped down on the St. Agatha side of the wall and groped about among the leaves until I found it.

Then I walked home, went into the library, alight with its many candles just as I had left it, and sat down before the fire to meditate. I had been absent from the house only forty-five minutes.

CHAPTER VIII

A STRING OF GOLD BEADS

A moment later Bates entered with a fresh supply of wood. I watched him narrowly for some sign of perturbation, but he was not to be caught off guard. Possibly he had not heard the shots in the wood; at any rate, he tended the fire with his usual gravity, and after brushing the hearth paused respectfully.

"Is there anything further, sir?"

"I believe not, Bates. Oh! here's a hammer I picked up out in the grounds a bit ago. I wish you'd see if it belongs to the house."

He examined the implement with care and shook his head.

"It doesn't belong here, I think, sir. But we sometimes find tools left by the carpenters that worked on the house. Shall I put this in the tool-chest, sir?"

"Never mind. I need such a thing now and then and I'll keep it handy."

"Very good, Mr. Glenarm. It's a bit sharper to-night, but we're likely to have sudden changes at this season."

"I dare say."

We were not getting anywhere; the fellow was certainly an incomparable actor.

"You must find it pretty lonely here, Bates. Don't hesitate to go to the village when you like."

"I thank you, Mr. Glenarm; but I am not much for idling. I keep a few books by me for the evenings. Annandale is not what you would exactly call a diverting village."

"I fancy not. But the caretaker over at the summer resort has even a lonelier time, I suppose. That's what I'd call a pretty cheerless job,—watching summer cottages in the winter."

"That's Morgan, sir. I meet him occasionally when I go to the village; a very worthy person, I should call him, on slight acquaintance."

"No doubt of it, Bates. Any time through the winter you want to have him in for a social glass, it's all right with me."

He met my gaze without flinching, and lighted me to the stair with our established ceremony. I voted him an interesting knave and really admired the cool way in which he carried off difficult situations. I had no intention of being killed, and now that I had due warning of danger, I resolved to protect myself from foes without and within. Both Bates and Morgan, the caretaker, were liars of high attainment. Morgan was, moreover, a cheerful scoundrel, and experience taught me long ago that a knave with humor is doubly dangerous.

Before going to bed I wrote a long letter to Larry Donovan, giving him a full account of my arrival at Glenarm House. The thought of Larry always cheered me, and as the pages slipped from my pen I could feel his sympathy and hear him chuckling over the lively beginning of my year at Glenarm. The idea of being fired upon by an unseen foe would, I knew, give Larry a real lift of the spirit.

The next morning I walked into the village, mailed my letter, visited the railway station with true rustic instinct and watched the cutting out of a freight car for Annandale with a pleasure I had not before taken in that proceeding. The villagers stared at me blankly as on my first visit. A group of idle laborers stopped talking to watch me; and when I was a few yards past them they laughed at a remark by one of the number which I could not overhear. But I am not a particularly sensitive person; I did not care what my Hoosier neighbors said of me; all I asked was that they should refrain from shooting at the back of my head through the windows of my own house.

On this day I really began to work. I mapped out

a course of reading, set up a draftsman's table I found
put away in a closet, and convinced myself that I was
beginning a year of devotion to architecture. Such was,
I felt, the only honest course. I should work every day
from eight until one, and my leisure I should give to
recreation and a search for the motives that lay behind
the crafts and assaults of my enemies.

When I plunged into the wood in the middle of the
afternoon it was with the definite purpose of returning
to the upper end of the lake for an interview with Morgan, who had, so Bates informed me, a small house back
of the cottages.

I took the canoe I had chosen for my own use from
the boat-house and paddled up the lake. The air was
still warm, but the wind that blew out of the south
tasted of rain. I scanned the water and the borders of
the lake for signs of life,—more particularly, I may as
well admit, for a certain maroon-colored canoe and a
girl in a red tam-o'-shanter, but lake and summer cottages were mine alone. I landed and began at once my
search for Morgan. There were many paths through
the woods back of the cottages, and I followed several
futilely before I at last found a small house snugly
hid away in a thicket of young maples.

The man I was looking for came to the door quickly
in response to my knock.

"Good afternoon, Morgan."

"Good afternoon, Mr. Glenarm," he said, taking the pipe from his mouth the better to grin at me. He showed no sign of surprise, and I was nettled by his cool reception. There was, perhaps, a certain element of recklessness in my visit to the house of a man who had shown so singular an interest in my affairs, and his cool greeting vexed me.

"Morgan—" I began.

"Won't you come in and rest yourself, Mr. Glenarm?" he interrupted. "I reckon you're tired from your trip over—"

"Thank you, no," I snapped.

"Suit yourself, Mr. Glenarm." He seemed to like my name and gave it a disagreeable drawling emphasis.

"Morgan, you are an infernal blackguard. You have tried twice to kill me—"

"We'll call it that, if you like,"—and he grinned. "But you'd better cut off one for this."

He lifted the gray fedora hat from his head, and poked his finger through a hole in the top.

"You're a pretty fair shot, Mr. Glenarm. The fact about me is,"—and he winked,—"the honest truth is, I'm all out of practice. Why, sir, when I saw you paddling out on the lake this afternoon I sighted you from the casino half a dozen times with my gun, but I was afraid to risk it." He seemed to be shaken with inner mirth. "If I'd missed, I wasn't sure you'd be scared to death!"

For a novel diversion I heartily recommend a meeting with the assassin who has, only a few days or hours before, tried to murder you. I know of nothing in the way of social adventure that is quite equal to it. Morgan was a fellow of intelligence and, whatever lay back of his designs against me, he was clearly a foe to reckon with. He stood in the doorway calmly awaiting my next move. I struck a match on my box and lighted a cigarette.

"Morgan, I hope you understand that I am not responsible for any injury my grandfather may have inflicted on you. I hadn't seen him for several years before he died. I was never at Glenarm before in my life, so it's a little rough for you to visit your displeasure on me."

He smiled tolerantly as I spoke. I knew—and he knew that I did—that no ill feeling against my grandfather lay back of his interest in my affairs.

"You're not quite the man your grandfather was, Mr. Glenarm. You'll excuse my bluntness, but I take it that you're a frank man. He was a very keen person, and, I'm afraid,"—he chuckled with evident satisfaction to himself,—"I'm really afraid, Mr. Glenarm, that you're not!"

"There you have it, Morgan! I fully agree with you! I'm as dull as an oyster; that's the reason I've called on you for enlightenment. Consider that I'm here under a flag of truce, and let's see if we can't come to an agreement."

"It's too late, Mr. Glenarm; too late. There was a time when we might have done some business; but that's past now. You seem like a pretty decent fellow, too, and I'm sorry I didn't see you sooner; but better luck next time."

He stroked his yellow beard reflectively and shook his head a little sadly. He was not a bad-looking fellow; and he expressed himself well enough with a broad western accent.

"Well," I said, seeing that I should only make myself ridiculous by trying to learn anything from him, "I hope our little spats through windows and on walls won't interfere with our pleasant social relations. And I don't hesitate to tell you,"—I was exerting myself to keep down my anger,—"that if I catch you on my grounds again I'll fill you with lead and sink you in the lake."

"Thank you, sir," he said, with so perfect an imitation of Bates' voice and manner that I smiled in spite of myself.

"And now, if you'll promise not to fire into my back I'll wish you good day. Otherwise—"

He snatched off his hat and bowed profoundly. "It'll suit me much better to continue handling the case on your grounds," he said, as though he referred to a business matter. "Killing a man on your own property requires some explaining—you may have noticed it?"

"Yes; I commit most of my murders away from home," I said. "I formed the habit early in life. Good day, Morgan."

As I turned away he closed his door with a slam,—a delicate way of assuring me that he was acting in good faith, and not preparing to puncture my back with a rifle-ball. I regained the lake-shore, feeling no great discouragement over the lean results of my interview, but rather a fresh zest for the game, whatever the game might be. Morgan was not an enemy to trifle with; he was, on the other hand, a clever and daring foe; and the promptness with which he began war on me the night of my arrival at Glenarm House, indicated that there was method in his hostility.

The sun was going his ruddy way beyond St. Agatha's as I drove my canoe into a little cove near which the

girl in the tam-o'-shanter had disappeared the day before. The shore was high here and at the crest was a
long curved bench of stone reached by half a dozen
steps, from which one might enjoy a wide view of the
country, both across the lake and directly inland. The
bench was a pretty bit of work, boldly reminiscential of
Alma Tadema, and as clearly the creation of John
Marshall Glenarm as though his name had been carved
upon it.

It was assuredly a spot for a pipe and a mood, and
as the shadows crept through the wood before me and
the water, stirred by the rising wind, began to beat below, I invoked the one and yielded to the other. Something in the withered grass at my feet caught my eye.
I bent and picked up a string of gold beads, dropped
there, no doubt, by some girl from the school or a careless member of the summer colony. I counted the separate beads—they were round and there were fifty of
them. The proper length for one turn about a girl's
throat, perhaps; not more than that! I lifted my eyes
and looked off toward St. Agatha's.

"Child of the red tam-o'-shanter, I'm very sorry I
was rude to you yesterday, for I liked your steady stroke
with the paddle; and I admired, even more, the way you
spurned me when you saw that among all the cads in
the world I am number one in Class A. And these

golden bubbles (O girl of the red tam-o'-shanter!), if they are not yours you shall help me find the owner, for we are neighbors, you and I, and there must be peace between our houses."

With this foolishness I rose, thrust the beads into my pocket, and paddled home in the waning glory of the sunset.

That night, as I was going quite late to bed, bearing a candle to light me through the dark hall to my room, I heard a curious sound, as of some one walking stealthily through the house. At first I thought Bates was still abroad, but I waited, listening for several minutes, without being able to mark the exact direction of the sound or to identify it with him. I went on to the door of my room, and still a muffled step seemed to follow me,—first it had come from below, then it was much like some one going up stairs,—but where? In my own room I still heard steps, light, slow, but distinct. Again there was a stumble and a hurried recovery,—ghosts, I reflected, do not fall down stairs!

The sound died away, seemingly in some remote part of the house, and though I prowled about for an hour it did not recur that night.

CHAPTER IX

THE GIRL AND THE RABBIT

Wind and rain rioted in the wood, and occasionally both fell upon the library windows with a howl and a splash. The tempest had wakened me; it seemed that every chimney in the house held a screaming demon. We were now well-launched upon December, and I was growing used to my surroundings. I had offered myself frequently as a target by land and water; I had sat on the wall and tempted fate; and I had roamed the house constantly expecting to surprise Bates in some act of treachery; but the days were passing monotonously. I saw nothing of Morgan—he had gone to Chicago on some errand, so Bates reported—but I continued to walk abroad every day, and often at night, alert for a reopening of hostilities. Twice I had seen the red tam-o'-shanter far through the wood, and once I had passed my young acquaintance with another girl, a dark, laughing youngster, walking in the highway, and she had bowed to me coldly. Even the ghost in the wall proved inconstant, but I had twice heard the steps without being able to account for them.

Memory kept plucking my sleeve with reminders of

my grandfather. I was touched at finding constantly
his marginal notes in the books he had collected with so
much intelligence and loving care. It occurred to me
that some memorial, a tablet attached to the outer wall,
or perhaps, more properly placed in the chapel, would
be fitting; and I experimented with designs for it, covering many sheets of drawing-paper in an effort to set
forth in a few words some hint of his character. On this
gray morning I produced this:

1835

**The life of John Marshall Glenarm
was a testimony to the virtue of
generosity, forbearance and gentleness
The beautiful things he loved
were not nobler than his own days
His grandson (who served him ill)
writes this of him**

1901

I had drawn these words on a piece of cardboard and
was studying them critically when Bates came in with
wood.

"Those are unmistakable snowflakes, sir," said Bates
from the window. "We're in for winter now."

It was undeniably snow; great lazy flakes of it were
crowding down upon the wood.

Bates had not mentioned Morgan or referred even remotely to the pistol-shot of my first night, and he had

certainly conducted himself as a model servant. The man-of-all-work at St. Agatha's, a Scotchman named Ferguson, had visited him several times, and I had surprised them once innocently enjoying their pipes and whisky and water in the kitchen.

"They are having trouble · at the school, sir," said Bates from the hearth.

"The young ladies running a little wild, eh?"

"Sister Theresa's ill, sir. Ferguson told me last night!"

"No doubt Ferguson knows," I declared, moving the papers about on my desk, conscious, and not ashamed of it, that I enjoyed these dialogues with Bates. I occasionally entertained the idea that he would some day brain me as I sat dining upon the viands which he prepared with so much skill; or perhaps he would poison me, that being rather more in his line of business and perfectly easy of accomplishment; but the house was bare and lonely and he was a resource.

"So Sister Theresa's ill!" I began, seeing that Bates had nearly finished, and glancing with something akin to terror upon the open pages of a dreary work on English cathedrals that had put me to sleep the day before.

"She's been quite uncomfortable, sir; but they hope to see her out in a few days!"

"That's good; I'm glad to hear it."

"Yes, sir. I think we naturally feel interested, being neighbors. And Ferguson says that Miss Devereux's devotion to her aunt is quite touching."

I stood up straight and stared at Bates' back—he was trying to stop the rattle which the wind had set up in one of the windows.

"Miss Devereux!" I laughed outright.

"That's the name, sir,—rather odd, I should call it."

"Yes, it is rather odd," I said, composed again, but not referring to the name. My mind was busy with a certain paragraph in my grandfather's will:

Should he fail to comply with this provision, said property shall revert to my general estate, and become, without reservation, and without necessity for any process of law, the property, absolutely, of Marian Devereux, of the County and State of New York.

"Your grandfather was very fond of her, sir. She and Sister Theresa were abroad at the time he died. It was my sorrowful duty to tell them the sad news in New York, sir, when they landed."

"The devil it was!" It irritated me to remember that Bates probably knew exactly the nature of my grandfather's will; and the terms of it were not in the least creditable to me. Sister Theresa and her niece were doubtless calmly awaiting my failure to remain at Glenarm House during the disciplinary year,—Sister

Theresa, a Protestant nun, and the niece who probably taught drawing in the school for her keep! I was sure it was drawing; nothing else would, I felt, have brought the woman within the pale of my grandfather's beneficence.

I had given no thought to Sister Theresa since coming to Glenarm. She had derived her knowledge of me from my grandfather, and, such being the case, she would naturally look upon me as a blackguard and a menace to the peace of the neighborhood. I had, therefore, kept rigidly to my own side of the stone wall. A suspicion crossed my mind, marshaling a host of doubts and questions that had lurked there since my first night at Glenarm.

"Bates!"

He was moving toward the door with his characteristic slow step.

"If your friend Morgan, or any one else, should shoot me, or if I should tumble into the lake, or otherwise end my earthly career—Bates!"

His eyes had slipped from mine to the window and I spoke his name sharply.

"Yes, Mr. Glenarm."

"Then Sister Theresa's niece would get this property and everything else that belonged to Mr. Glenarm."

"That's my understanding of the matter, sir."

"Morgan, the caretaker, has tried to kill me twice since I came here. He fired at me through the window the night I came,—Bates!"

I waited for his eyes to meet mine again. His hands opened and shut several times, and alarm and fear convulsed his face for a moment.

"Bates, I'm trying my best to think well of you; but I want you to understand"—I smote the table with my clenched hand—"that if these women, or your employer, Mr. Pickering, or that damned hound, Morgan, or you— damn you, I don't know who or what you are!—think you can scare me away from here, you've waked up the wrong man, and I'll tell you another thing,—and you may repeat it to your school-teachers and to Mr. Pickering, who pays you, and to Morgan, whom somebody has hired to kill me,—that I'm going to keep faith with my dead grandfather, and that when I've spent my year here and done what that old man wished me to do, I'll give them this house and every acre of ground and every damned dollar the estate carries with it. And now one other thing! I suppose there's a sheriff or some kind of a constable with jurisdiction over this place, and I could have the whole lot of you put into jail for conspiracy, but I'm going to stand out against you alone,—do you understand me, you hypocrite, you stupid, slinking spy? Answer me, quick, before I throw you out of the room!"

I had worked myself into a great passion and fairly roared my challenge, pounding the table in my rage.

"Yes, sir; I quite understand you, sir. But I'm afraid, sir—"

"Of course you're afraid!" I shouted, enraged anew by his halting speech. "You have every reason in the world to be afraid. You've probably heard that I'm a bad lot and a worthless adventurer; but you can tell Sister Theresa or Pickering or anybody you please that I'm ten times as bad as I've ever been painted. Now clear out of here!"

He left the room without looking at me again. During the morning I strolled through the house several times to make sure he had not left it to communicate with some of his fellow plotters, but I was, I admit, disappointed to find him in every instance busy at some wholly proper task. Once, indeed, I found him cleaning my storm boots! To find him thus humbly devoted to my service after the raking I had given him dulled the edge of my anger. I went back to the library and planned a cathedral in seven styles of architecture, all unrelated and impossible, and when this began to bore me I designed a crypt in which the wicked should be buried standing on their heads and only the very good might lie and sleep in peace. These diversions and several black cigars won me to a more amiable mood. I felt better, on the whole, for having announced myself to the delectable Bates, who gave me for luncheon a brace of quails, done in a manner that stripped criticism of all weapons.

We did not exchange a word, and after knocking about in the library for several hours I went out for a tramp. Winter had indeed come and possessed the earth, and it had given me a new landscape. The snow continued to fall in great, heavy flakes, and the ground was whitening fast.

A rabbit's track caught my eye and I followed it, hardly conscious that I did so. Then the clear print of two small shoes mingled with the rabbit's trail. A few moments later I picked up an overshoe, evidently lost in the chase by one of Sister Theresa's girls, I reflected. I remembered that while at Tech I had collected diverse memorabilia from school-girl acquaintances, and here I was beginning a new series with a string of beads and an overshoe!

A rabbit is always an attractive quarry. Few things besides riches are so elusive, and the little fellows have, I am sure, a shrewd humor peculiar to themselves. I rather envied the school-girl who had ventured forth for a run in the first snow-storm of the season. I recalled Aldrich's turn on Gautier's lines as I followed the double trail:

"Howe'er you tread, a tiny mould
  Betrays that light foot all the same;
Upon this glistening, snowy fold
  At every step it signs your name."

A pretty autograph, indeed! The snow fell steadily and I tramped on over the joint signature of the girl and the rabbit. Near the lake they parted company, the rabbit leading off at a tangent, on a line parallel with the lake, while his pursuer's steps pointed toward the boat-house.

There was, so far as I knew, only one student of adventurous blood at St. Agatha's, and I was not in the least surprised to see, on the little sheltered balcony of the boat-house, the red tam-o'-shanter. She wore, too, the covert coat I remembered from the day I saw her first from the wall. Her back was toward me as I drew near; her hands were thrust into her pockets. She was evidently enjoying the soft mingling of the snow with the still, blue waters of the lake, and a girl and a snowstorm are, if you ask my opinion, a pretty combination. The fact of a girl's facing a winter storm argues mightily in her favor,—testifies, if you will allow me, to a serene and dauntless spirit, for one thing, and a sound constitution, for another.

I ran up the steps, my cap in one hand, her overshoe

in the other. She drew back a trifle, just enough to bring my conscience to its knees.

"I didn't mean to listen that day. I just happened to be on the wall and it was a thoroughly underbred trick—my twitting you about it—and I should have told you before if I'd known how to see you—"

"May I trouble you for that shoe?" she said with a great deal of dignity.

They taught that cold disdain of man, I supposed, as a required study at St. Agatha's.

"Oh, certainly! Won't you allow me?"

"Thank you, no!"

I was relieved, to tell the truth, for I had been out of the world for most of that period in which a youngster perfects himself in such graces as the putting on of a girl's overshoes. She took the damp bit of rubber—a wet overshoe, even if small and hallowed by associations, isn't pretty—as Venus might have received a soft-shell crab from the hand of a fresh young merman. I was between her and the steps to which her eyes turned longingly.

"Of course, if you won't accept my apology I can't do anything about it; but I hope you understand that I'm sincere and humble, and anxious to be forgiven."

"You seem to be making a good deal of a small matter—"

"I wasn't referring to the overshoe!" I said.

She did not relent.

"If you'll only go away—"

She rested one hand against the corner of the boat-house while she put on the overshoe. She wore, I noticed, brown gloves with cuffs.

"How can I go away! You children are always leaving things about for me to pick up. I'm perfectly worn out carrying some girl's beads about with me; and I spoiled a good glove on your overshoe."

"I'll relieve you of the beads, too, if you please." And her tone measurably reduced my stature.

She thrust her hands into the pockets of her coat and shook the tam-o'-shanter slightly, to establish it in a more comfortable spot on her head. The beads had been in my corduroy coat since I found them. I drew them out and gave them to her.

"Thank you; thank you very much."

"Of course they are yours, Miss—"

She thrust them into her pocket.

"Of course they're mine," she said indignantly, and turned to go.

"We'll waive proof of property and that sort of thing," I remarked, with, I fear, the hope of detaining her. "I'm sorry not to establish a more neighborly feeling with St. Agatha's. The stone wall may seem formi-

dable, but it's not of my building. I must open the gate.
That wall's a trifle steep for climbing."

I was amusing myself with the idea that my identity
was a dark mystery to her. I had read English novels
in which the young lord of the manor is always mistaken for the game-keeper's son by the pretty daughter
of the curate who has come home from school to be the
belle of the county. But my lady of the red tam-o'-
shanter was not a creature of illusions.

"It serves a very good purpose—the wall, I mean—
Mr. Glenarm."

She was walking down the steps and I followed. I
am not a man to suffer a lost school-girl to cross my
lands unattended in a snow-storm; and the piazza of a
boat-house is not, I submit, a pleasant loafing-place on
a winter day. She marched before me, her hands in her
pockets—I liked her particularly that way—with an
easy swing and a light and certain step. Her remark
about the wall did not encourage further conversation
and I fell back upon the poets.

> "Stone walls do not a prison make,
>   Nor iron bars a cage,"

I quoted. Quoting poetry in a snow-storm while you
stumble through a woodland behind a girl who shows
no interest in either your prose or your rhymes has its

embarrassments, particularly when you are breathing a trifle hard from the swift pace your auditor is leading you.

"I have heard that before," she said, half-turning her face, then laughing as she hastened on.

Her brilliant cheeks were a delight to the eye. The snow swirled about her, whitened the crown of her red cap and clung to her shoulders. Have you ever seen snow-crystals gleam, break, dissolve in fair, soft, storm-blown hair? Do you know how a man will pledge his soul that a particular flake will never fade, never cease to rest upon a certain flying strand over a girlish temple? And he loses—his heart and his wager—in a breath! If you fail to understand these things, and are furthermore unfamiliar with the fact that the color in the cheeks of a girl who walks abroad in a driving snow-storm marks the favor of Heaven itself, then I waste time, and you will do well to rap at the door of another inn.

"I'd rather missed you," I said; "and, really, I should have been over to apologize if I hadn't been afraid."

"Sister Theresa is rather fierce," she declared. "And we're not allowed to receive gentlemen callers,—it says so in the catalogue."

"So I imagined. I trust Sister Theresa is improving."

She marched before me, her hands in her pockets. *Page 123*

"Yes; thank you."

"And Miss Devereux,—she is quite well, I hope?"

She turned her head as though to listen more carefully, and her step slackened for a moment; then she hurried blithely forward.

"Oh, she's always well, I believe."

"You know her, of course."

"Oh, rather! She gives us music lessons."

"So Miss Devereux is the music-teacher, is she? Should you call her a popular teacher?"

"The girls call her"—she seemed moved to mirth by the recollection—"Miss Prim and Prosy."

"Ugh!" I exclaimed sympathetically. "Tall and hungry-looking, with long talons that pound the keys with grim delight. I know the sort."

"She's a sight!"—and my guide laughed approvingly. "But we have to take her; she's part of the treatment."

"You speak of St. Agatha's as though it were a sanatorium."

"Oh, it's not so bad! I've seen worse."

"Where do most of the students come from,—all what you call Hoosiers?"

"Oh, no! They're from all over—Cincinnati, Chicago, Cleveland, Indianapolis."

"What the magazines call the Middle West."

"I believe that is so. The bishop addressed us once

as the flower of the Middle West, and made us really
wish he'd come again."

We were approaching the gate. Her indifference to
the storm delighted me. Here, I thought in my admiration, is a real product of the western world. I felt that
we had made strides toward such a comradeship as it is
proper should exist between a school-girl in her teens
and a male neighbor of twenty-seven. I was—going
back to English fiction—the young squire walking home
with the curate's pretty young daughter and conversing
with fine condescension.

"We girls all wish we could come over and help hunt
the lost treasure. It must be simply splendid to live in
a house where there's a mystery,—secret passages and
chests of doubloons and all that sort of thing! My!
Squire Glenarm, I suppose you spend all your nights exploring secret passages."

This free expression of opinion startled me, though
she seemed wholly innocent of impertinence.

"Who says there's any secret about the house?" I demanded.

"Oh, Ferguson, the gardener, and all the girls!"

"I fear Ferguson is drawing on his imagination."

"Well, all the people in the village think so. I've
heard the candy-shop woman speak of it often."

"She'd better attend to her taffy," I retorted.

"Oh, you mustn't be sensitive about it! All us girls
think it ever so romantic, and we call you sometimes the
lord of the realm, and when we see you walking through
the darkling wood at evenfall we say, 'My lord is brood-
ing upon the treasure chests.'"

This, delivered in the stilted tone of one who is half-
quoting and half-improvising, was irresistibly funny,
and I laughed with good will.

"I hope you've forgiven me—" I began, kicking the
gate to knock off the snow, and taking the key from my
pocket.

"But I haven't, Mr. Glenarm. Your assumption is,
to say the least, unwarranted,—I got that from a book!"

"It isn't fair for you to know my name and for me not
to know yours," I said leadingly.

"You are perfectly right. You are Mr. John Glenarm—the gardener told me—and I am just Olivia.
They don't allow me to be called Miss yet. I'm very
young, sir!"

"You've only told me half,"—and I kept my hand on
the closed gate. The snow still fell steadily and the
short afternoon was nearing its close. I did not like to
lose her,—the life, the youth, the mirth for which she
stood. The thought of Glenarm House amid the snow-
hung wood and of the long winter evening that I must
spend alone moved me to delay. Lights already gleamed

in the school-buildings straight before us and the sight of them smote me with loneliness.

"Olivia Gladys Armstrong," she said, laughing, brushed past me through the gate and ran lightly over the snow toward St. Agatha's.

CHAPTER X

AN AFFAIR WITH THE CARETAKER

I read in the library until late, hearing the howl of
the wind outside with satisfaction in the warmth and
comfort of the great room.   Bates brought in some sand-
wiches and a bottle of ale at midnight.

"If there's nothing more, sir——"

"That is all, Bates."   And he went off sedately to his
own quarters.

I was restless and in no mood for bed and mourned
the lack of variety in my grandfather's library.   I moved
about from shelf to shelf, taking down one book after
another, and while thus engaged came upon a series of
large volumes extra-illustrated in water-colors of unusual beauty.   They occupied a lower shelf, and I
sprawled on the floor, like a boy with a new picture-book,
in my absorption, piling the great volumes about me.
They were on related subjects pertaining to the French
châteaux.

In the last volume I found a sheet of white note-
paper no larger than my hand, a forgotten book-mark,

129

I assumed, and half-crumpled it in my fingers before I noticed the lines of a pencil sketch on one side of it. I carried it to the table and spread it out.

It was not the bit of idle penciling it had appeared to be at first sight. A scale had evidently been followed and the lines drawn with a ruler. With such trifles my grandfather had no doubt amused himself. There was a long corridor indicated, but of this I could make nothing. I studied it for several minutes, thinking it might have been a tentative sketch of some part of the house. In turning it about under the candelabrum I saw that in several places the glaze had been rubbed from the paper by an eraser, and this piqued my curiosity. I brought a magnifying glass to bear upon the sketch. The drawing had been made with a hard pencil and the eraser had removed the lead, but a well-defined imprint remained.

I was able to make out the letters N. W. ¾ to C.— a reference clearly enough to points of the compass and a distance. The word *ravine* was scrawled over a rough outline of a doorway or opening of some sort, and then the phrase:

THE DOOR OF BEWILDERMENT

Now I am rather an imaginative person; that is why engineering captured my fancy. It was through his trying to make an architect (a person who quarrels with women about their kitchen sinks!) of a boy who wanted to be an engineer that my grandfather and I failed to hit it off. From boyhood I have never seen a great bridge or watched a locomotive climb a difficult hillside without a thrill; and a lighthouse still seems to me quite the finest monument a man can build for himself. My grandfather's devotion to old churches and medieval houses always struck me as trifling and unworthy of a grown man. And fate was busy with my affairs that night, for, instead of lighting my pipe with the little sketch, I was strangely impelled to study it seriously.

I drew for myself rough outlines of the interior of Glenarm House as it had appeared to me, and then I tried to reconcile the little sketch with every part of it.

"The Door of Bewilderment" was the charm that held me. The phrase was in itself a lure. The man who had built a preposterous house in the woods of Indiana and called it "The House of a Thousand Candles" was quite capable of other whims; and as I bent over this scrap of paper in the candle-lighted library it occurred to me that possibly I had not done justice to my grandfather's genius. My curiosity was thoroughly aroused as to the hidden corners of the queer old house, round which the wind shrieked tormentingly.

I went to my room, put on my corduroy coat for its greater warmth in going through the cold halls, took a candle and went below. One o'clock in the morning is not the most cheering hour for exploring the dark recesses of a strange house, but I had resolved to have a look at the ravine-opening and determine, if possible, whether it bore any relation to "The Door of Bewilderment."

All was quiet in the great cellar; only here and there an area window rattled dolorously. I carried a tapeline with me and made measurements of the length and depth of the corridor and of the chambers that were set off from it. These figures I entered in my note-book for further use, and sat down on an empty nail-keg to reflect. The place was certainly substantial; the candle at my feet burned steadily with no hint of a draft; but I saw no solution of my problem. All the doors along the corridor were open, or yielded readily to my hand. I was losing sleep for nothing; my grandfather's sketch was meaningless, and I rose and picked up my candle, yawning.

Then a curious thing happened. The candle, whose thin flame had risen unwaveringly, sputtered and went out as a sudden gust swept the corridor.

I had left nothing open behind me, and the outer

doors of the house were always locked and barred. But some one had gained ingress to the cellar by an opening of which I knew nothing.

I faced the stairway that led up to the back hall of the house, when to my astonishment, steps sounded behind me and, turning, I saw, coming toward me, a man carrying a lantern. I marked his careless step; he was undoubtedly on familiar ground. As I watched him he paused, lifted the lantern to a level with his eyes and began sounding the wall with a hammer.

Here, undoubtedly, was my friend Morgan,—again! There was the same periodicity in the beat on the wall that I had heard in my own rooms. He began at the top and went methodically to the floor. I leaned against the wall where I stood and watched the lantern slowly coming toward me. The small revolver with which I had fired at his flying figure in the wood was in my pocket. It was just as well to have it out with the fellow now. My chances were as good as his, though I confess I did not relish the thought of being found dead the next morning in the cellar of my own house. It pleased my humor to let him approach in this way, unconscious that he was watched, until I should thrust my pistol into his face.

His arms grew tired when he was about ten feet from

me and he dropped the lantern and hammer to his side, and swore under his breath impatiently.

Then he began again, with greater zeal. As he came nearer I studied his face in the lantern's light with interest. His hat was thrust back, and I could see his jaw hard-set under his blond beard.

He took a step nearer, ran his eyes over the wall and resumed his tapping. The ceiling was something less than eight feet, and he began at the top. In settling himself for the new series of strokes he swayed toward me slightly, and I could hear his hard breathing. I was deliberating how best to throw myself upon him, but as I wavered he stepped back, swore at his ill-luck and flung the hammer to the ground.

"Thanks!" I shouted, leaping forward and snatching the lantern. "Stand just where you are!"

With the revolver in my right hand and the lantern held high in my left, I enjoyed his utter consternation, as my voice roared in the corridor.

"It's too bad we meet under such strange circumstances, Morgan," I said. "I'd begun to miss you; but I suppose you've been sleeping in the daytime to gather strength for your night prowling."

"You're a fool," he growled. He was recovering from his fright,—I knew it by the gleam of his teeth in his yellow beard. His eyes, too, were moving restlessly about. He undoubtedly knew the house better than I did, and was considering the best means of escape. I did not know what to do with him now that I had him at the point of a pistol; and in my ignorance of his motives and my vague surmise as to the agency back of him, I was filled with uncertainty.

"You needn't hold that thing quite so near," he said, staring at me coolly.

"I'm glad it annoys you, Morgan," I said. "It may help you to answer some questions I'm going to put to you."

"So you want information, do you, Mr. Glenarm? I should think it would be beneath the dignity of a great man like you to ask a poor devil like me for help."

"We're not talking of dignity," I said. "I want you to tell me how you got in here."

He laughed.

"You're a very shrewd one, Mr. Glenarm. I came in by the kitchen window, if you must know. I got in before your solemn jack-of-all-trades locked up, and I walked down to the end of the passage there"—he indicated the direction with a slight jerk of his head—"and slept until it was time to go to work. You can see how easy it was!"

I laughed now at the sheer assurance of the fellow.

"If you can't lie better than that you needn't try again. Face about now, and march!"

I put new energy into my tone, and he turned and walked before me down the corridor in the direction from which he had come. We were, I dare say, a pretty pair,—he tramping doggedly before me, I following at his heels with his lantern and my pistol. The situation had played prettily into my hands, and I had every intention of wresting from him the reason for his interest in Glenarm House and my affairs.

"Not so fast," I admonished sharply.

"Excuse me," he replied mockingly.

He was no common rogue; I felt the quality in him with a certain admiration for his scoundrelly talents— a fellow, I reflected, who was best studied at the point of a pistol.

I continued at his heels, and poked the muzzle of the revolver against his back from time to time to keep him assured of my presence,—a device that I was to regret a second later.

We were about ten yards from the end of the corridor when he flung himself backward upon me, threw his arms over his head and seized me about the neck, turning himself lithely until his fingers clasped my throat.

I fired blindly once, and felt the smoke of the revolver hot in my own nostrils. The lantern fell from my hand, and one or the other of us smashed it with our feet.

A wrestling match in that dark hole was not to my liking. I still held on to the revolver, waiting for a chance to use it, and meanwhile he tried to throw me, forcing me back against one side and then the other of the passage.

With a quick rush he flung me away, and in the same second I fired. The roar of the shot in the narrow corridor seemed interminable. I flung myself on the floor, expecting a return shot, and quickly enough a flash broke upon the darkness dead ahead, and I rose to my feet, fired again and leaped to the opposite side of the corridor and crouched there. We had adopted the same tactics, firing and dodging to avoid the target made by the flash of our pistols, and watching and listening after the roar of the explosions. It was a very pretty game, but destined not to last long. He was slowly retreating toward the end of the passage, where there was, I remembered, a dead wall. His only chance was to crawl through an area window I knew to be there, and this would, I felt sure, give him into my hands.

After five shots apiece there was a truce. The pungent smoke of the powder caused me to cough, and he laughed.

"Have you swallowed a bullet, Mr. Glenarm?" he called.

I could hear his feet scraping on the cement floor; he was moving away from me, doubtless intending to fire when he reached the area window and escape before I could reach him. I crept warily after him, ready to fire on the instant, but not wishing to throw away my last cartridge. That I resolved to keep for close quarters at the window.

He was now very near the end of the corridor; I heard his feet strike some boards that I remembered lay on the floor there, and I was nerved for a shot and a hand-to-hand struggle, if it came to that.

I was sure that he sought the window; I heard his hands on the wall as he felt for it. Then a breath of cold air swept the passage, and I knew he must be drawing himself up to the opening. I fired and dropped to the floor. With the roar of the explosion I heard him yell, but the expected return shot did not follow.

The pounding of my heart seemed to mark the passing of hours. I feared that my foe was playing some trick, creeping toward me, perhaps, to fire at close range, or to grapple with me in the dark. The cold air still whistled into the corridor, and I began to feel the chill of it. Being fired upon is disagreeable enough, but waiting in the dark for the shot is worse.

I rose and walked toward the end of the passage.

Then his revolver flashed and roared directly ahead, the flame of it so near that it blinded me. I fell forward confused and stunned, but shook myself together in a moment and got upon my feet. The draft of air no longer blew into the passage. Morgan had taken himself off through the window and closed it after him. I made sure of this by going to the window and feeling of it with my hands.

I went back and groped about for my candle, which I found without difficulty and lighted. I then returned to the window to examine the catch. To my utter astonishment it was fastened with staples, driven deep into the sash, in such way that it could not possibly have been opened without the aid of tools. I tried it at every point. Not only was it securely fastened, but it could not possibly be opened without an expenditure of time and labor.

There was no doubt whatever that Morgan knew more about Glenarm House than I did. It was possible, but not likely, that he had crept past me in the corridor and gone out through the house, or by some other cellar window. My eyes were smarting from the smoke of the last shot, and my cheek stung where the burnt powder had struck my face. I was alive, but in my vexa-

tion and perplexity not, I fear, grateful for my safety.
It was, however, some consolation to feel sure I had
winged the enemy.

I gathered up the fragments of Morgan's lantern and
went back to the library. The lights in half the candlesticks had sputtered out. I extinguished the remainder
and started to my room.

Then, in the great dark hall, I heard a muffled tread
as of some one following me,—not on the great staircase, nor in any place I could identify,—yet unmistakably on steps of some sort beneath or above me. My
nerves were already keyed to a breaking pitch, and the
ghost-like tread in the hall angered me—Morgan, or his
ally, Bates, I reflected, at some new trick. I ran into my
room, found a heavy walking-stick and set off for Bates'
room on the third floor. It was always easy to attribute
any sort of mischief to the fellow, and undoubtedly he
was crawling through the house somewhere on an errand
that boded no good to me.

It was now past two o'clock and he should have been
asleep and out of the way long ago. I crept to his room
and threw open the door without, I must say, the slightest idea of finding him there. But Bates, the enigma,
Bates, the incomparable cook, the perfect servant, sat at
a table, the light of several candles falling on a book

over which he was bent with that maddening gravity
he had never yet in my presence thrown off.

He rose at once, stood at attention, inclining his head
slightly.

"Yes, Mr. Glenarm."

"Yes, the devil!" I roared at him, astonished at
finding him,—sorry, I must say, that he was there. The
stick fell from my hands. I did not doubt he knew
perfectly well that I had some purpose in breaking in
upon him. I was baffled and in my rage floundered
for words to explain myself.

"I thought I heard some one in the house. I don't
want you prowling about in the night, do you hear?"

"Certainly not, sir," he replied in a grieved tone.

I glanced at the book he had been reading. It was a
volume of Shakespeare's comedies, open at the first
scene of the last act of *The Winter's Tale.*

"Quite a pretty bit of work that, I should say," he
remarked. "It was one of my late master's favorites."

"Go to the devil!" I bawled at him, and went down
to my room and slammed the door in rage and chagrin.

CHAPTER XI

Going to bed at three o'clock on a winter morning in
a house whose ways are disquieting, after a duel in
which you escaped whole only by sheer good luck, does
not fit one for sleep. When I finally drew the covers
over me it was to lie and speculate upon the events of
the night in connection with the history of the few
weeks I had spent at Glenarm. Larry had suggested
in New York that Pickering was playing some deep
game, and I, myself, could not accept Pickering's state-
ment that my grandfather's large fortune had proved
to be a myth. If Pickering had not stolen or dissipated
it, where was it concealed? Morgan was undoubtedly
looking for something of value or he would not risk
his life in the business; and it was quite possible that he
was employed by Pickering to search for hidden property. This idea took strong hold of me, the more readily, I fear, since I had always been anxious to see evil
in Pickering. There was, to be sure, the unknown al-

142

ternative heir, but neither she nor Sister Theresa was, I imagined, a person capable of hiring an assassin to kill me.

On reflection I dismissed the idea of appealing to the county authorities, and I never regretted that resolution. The seat of Wabana County was twenty miles away, the processes of law were unfamiliar, and I wished to avoid publicity. Morgan might, of course, have been easily disposed of by an appeal to the Annandale constable, but now that I suspected Pickering of treachery the caretaker's importance dwindled. I had waited all my life for a chance at Arthur Pickering, and in this affair I hoped to draw him into the open and settle with him.

I slept presently, but woke at my usual hour, and after a tub felt ready for another day. Bates served me, as usual, a breakfast that gave a fair aspect to the morning. I was alert for any sign of perturbation in him; but I had already decided that I might as well look for emotion in a stone wall as in this placid, colorless serving man. I had no reason to suspect him of complicity in the night's affair, but I had no faith in him, and merely waited until he should throw himself more boldly into the game.

By my plate next morning I found this note, written in a clear, bold, woman's hand:

The Sisters of St. Agatha trust that the intrusion upon his grounds by Miss Armstrong, one of their students, has caused Mr. Glenarm no annoyance. The Sisters beg that this infraction of their discipline will be overlooked, and they assure Mr. Glenarm that it will not recur.

An unnecessary apology! The note-paper was of the best quality. At the head of the page "St. Agatha's, Annandale" was embossed in purple. It was the first note I had received from a woman for a long time, and it gave me a pleasant emotion. One of the Sisters I had seen beyond the wall undoubtedly wrote it—possibly Sister Theresa herself. A clever woman, that! Thoroughly capable of plucking money from guileless old gentlemen! Poor Olivia! born for freedom, but doomed to a pent-up existence with a lot of nuns! I resolved to send her a box of candy sometime, just to annoy her grim guardians. Then my own affairs claimed attention.

"Bates," I asked, "do you know what Mr. Glenarm did with the plans for the house?"

He started slightly. I should not have noticed it if I had not been keen for his answer.

"No, sir. I can't put my hand upon them, sir."

"That's all very well, Bates, but you didn't answer my question. Do you know where they are? *I'll* put *my* hand on them if you will kindly tell me where they're kept."

"Mr. Glenarm, I fear very much that they have been destroyed. I tried to find them before you came, to tell you the whole truth, sir; but they must have been made 'way with."

"That's very interesting, Bates. Will you kindly tell me whom you suspect of destroying them? The toast again, please."

His hand shook as he passed the plate.

"I hardly like to say, sir, when it's only a suspicion."

"Of course I shouldn't ask you to incriminate yourself, but I'll have to insist on my question. It may have occurred to you, Bates, that I'm in a sense—in a sense, mind you—the master here."

"Well, I should say, if you press me, that I fear Mr. Glenarm, your grandfather, burned the plans when he left here the last time. I hope you will pardon me, sir, for seeming to reflect upon him."

"Reflect upon the devil! What was his idea, do you suppose?"

"I think, sir, if you will pardon—"

"Don't be so fussy!" I snapped. "Damn your pardon, and go on!"

"He wanted you to study out the place for yourself, sir. It was dear to his heart, this house. He set his heart upon having you enjoy it—"

"I like the word—go ahead."

"And I suppose there are things about it that he wished you to learn for yourself."

"*You* know them, of course, and are watching me to see when I'm hot or cold, like kids playing hide the handkerchief."

The fellow turned and faced me across the table.

"Mr. Glenarm, as I hope God may be merciful to me in the last judgment, I don't know any more than you do."

"You were here with Mr. Glenarm all the time he was building the house, but you never saw walls built that weren't what they appeared to be, or doors made that didn't lead anywhere."

I summoned all my irony and contempt for this arraignment. He lifted his hand, as though making oath.

"As God sees me, that is all true. I was here to care for the dead master's comfort and not to spy on him."

"And Morgan, your friend, what about him?"

"I wish I knew, sir."

"I wish to the devil you did," I said, and flung out of the room and into the library.

At eleven o'clock I heard a pounding at the great front door and Bates came to announce a caller, who was now audibly knocking the snow from his shoes in the outer hall.

"The Reverend Paul Stoddard, sir."

The chaplain of St. Agatha's was a big fellow, as I had remarked on the occasion of his interview with Olivia Gladys Armstrong by the wall. His light brown hair was close-cut; his smooth-shaven face was bright with the freshness of youth. Here was a sturdy young apostle without frills, but with a vigorous grip that left my hand tingling. His voice was deep and musical,—a voice that suggested sincerity and inspired confidence.

"I'm afraid I haven't been neighborly, Mr. Glenarm. I was called away from home a few days after I heard of your arrival, and I have just got back. I blew in yesterday with the snow-storm."

He folded his arms easily and looked at me with cheerful directness, as though politely interested in what manner of man I might be.

"It was a fine storm; I got a great day out of it," I said. "An Indiana snow-storm is something I have never experienced before."

"This is my second winter. I came out here because I wished to do some reading, and thought I'd rather do it alone than in a university."

"Studious habits are rather forced on one out here, I should say. In my own case my course of reading is all cut out for me."

He ran his eyes over the room.

"The Glenarm collection is famous,—the best in the country, easily. Mr. Glenarm, your grandfather, was certainly an enthusiast. I met him several times; he was a trifle hard to meet,"—and the clergyman smiled.

I felt rather uncomfortable, assuming that he probably knew I was undergoing discipline, and why my grandfather had so ordained it. The Reverend Paul Stoddard was so simple, unaffected and manly a fellow that I shrank from the thought that I must appear to him an ungrateful blackguard whom my grandfather had marked with obloquy.

"My grandfather had his whims; but he was a fine, generous-hearted old gentleman," I said.

"Yes; in my few interviews with him he surprised me by the range of his knowledge. He was quite able to instruct me in certain curious branches of church history that had appealed to him."

"You were here when he built the house, I suppose?" My visitor laughed cheerfully.

"I was on my side of the barricade for a part of the time. You know there was a great deal of mystery about the building of this house. The country-folk hereabouts can't quite get over it. They have a superstition that there's treasure buried somewhere on the place. You see, Mr. Glenarm wouldn't employ any local labor. The work was done by men he brought from afar,—none of them, the villagers say, could speak English. They were all Greeks or Italians."

"I have heard something of the kind," I remarked, feeling that here was a man who with a little cultivating might help me to solve some of my riddles.

"You haven't been on our side of the wall yet? Well, I promise not to molest your hidden treasure if you'll be neighborly."

"I fear there's a big joke involved in the hidden treasure," I replied. "I'm so busy staying at home to guard it that I have no time for social recreation."

He looked at me quickly to see whether I was joking. His eyes were steady and earnest. The Reverend Paul Stoddard impressed me more and more agreeably. There was a suggestion of a quiet strength about him that drew me to him.

"I suppose every one around here thinks of nothing but that I'm at Glenarm to earn my inheritance. My residence here must look pretty sordid from the outside."

"Mr. Glenarm's will is a matter of record in the county, of course. But you are too hard on yourself. It's nobody's business if your grandfather wished to visit his whims on you. I should say, in my own case, that I don't consider it any of my business what you are here for. I didn't come over to annoy you or to pry into your affairs. I get lonely now and then, and thought I'd like to establish neighborly relations."

"Thank you; I appreciate your coming very much," —and my heart warmed under the manifest kindness of the man.

"And I hope"—he spoke for the first time with restraint—"I hope nothing may prevent your knowing Sister Theresa and Miss Devereux. They are interesting and charming—the only women about here of your own social status."

My liking for him abated slightly. He might be a detective, representing the alternative heir, for all I knew, and possibly Sister Theresa was a party to the conspiracy.

"In time, no doubt, in time, I shall know them," I answered evasively.

"Oh, quite as you like!"—and he changed the subject. We talked of many things,—of outdoor sports, with which he showed great familiarity, of universities, of travel and adventure. He was a Columbia man and had spent two years at Oxford.

"Well," he exclaimed, "this has been very pleasant, but I must run. I have just been over to see Morgan, the caretaker at the resort village. The poor fellow accidentally shot himself yesterday, cleaning his gun or something of that sort, and he has an ugly hole in his arm that will shut him in for a month or worse. He gave me an errand to do for him. He's a conscientious fellow and wished me to wire for him to Mr. Pickering that he'd been hurt, but was attending to his duties. Pickering owns a cottage over there, and Morgan has charge of it. You know Pickering, of course?"

I looked my clerical neighbor straight in the eye, a trifle coldly perhaps. I was wondering why Morgan, with whom I had enjoyed a duel in my own cellar only a few hours before, should be reporting his injury to Arthur Pickering.

"I think I have seen Morgan about here," I said.

"Oh, yes! He's a woodsman and a hunter—our Nimrod of the lake."

"A good sort, very likely!"

"I dare say. He has sometimes brought me ducks during the season."

"To be sure! They shoot ducks at night,—these Hoosier hunters,—so I hear!"

He laughed as he shook himself into his greatcoat.

"That's possible, though unsportsmanlike. But we don't have to look a gift mallard in the eye."

We laughed together. I found that it was easy to laugh with him.

"By the way, I forgot to get Pickering's address from Morgan. If you happen to have it—"

"With pleasure," I said. "Alexis Building, Broadway, New York."

"Good! That's easy to remember," he said, smiling and turning up his coat collar. "Don't forget me; I'm quartered in a hermit's cell back of the chapel, and I believe we can find many matters of interest to talk about."

"I'm confident of it," I said, glad of the sympathy and cheer that seemed to emanate from his stalwart figure.

I threw on my overcoat and walked to the gate with him, and saw him hurry toward the village with long strides.

CHAPTER XII

I EXPLORE A PASSAGE

"Bates!"—I found him busy replenishing the candle-sticks in the library,—it seemed to me that he was always poking about with an armful of candles,—"there are a good many queer things in this world, but I guess you're one of the queerest. I don't mind telling you that there are times when I think you a thoroughly bad lot, and then again I question my judgment and don't give you credit for being much more than a doddering fool."

He was standing on a ladder beneath the great crystal chandelier that hung from the center of the ceiling, and looked down upon me with that patient injury that is so appealing in a dog—in, say, the eyes of an Irish setter, when you accidentally step on his tail. That look is heartbreaking in a setter, but, seen in a man, it arouses the direst homicidal feelings of which I am capable.

"Yes, Mr. Glenarm," he replied humbly.

"Now, I want you to grasp this idea that I'm going

153

to dig into this old shell top and bottom; I'm going to blow it up with dynamite, if I please; and if I catch you spying on me or reporting my doings to my enemies, or engaging in any questionable performances whatever, I'll hang you between the posts out there in the school-wall—do you understand?—so that the sweet Sisters of St. Agatha and the dear little school-girls and the chaplain and all the rest will shudder through all their lives at the very thought of you."

"Certainly, Mr. Glenarm,"—and his tone was the same he would have used if I had asked him to pass me the matches, and under my breath I consigned him to the harshest tortures of the fiery pit.

"Now, as to Morgan—"

"Yes, sir."

"What possible business do you suppose he has with Mr. Pickering?" I demanded.

"Why, sir, that's clear enough. Mr. Pickering owns a house up the lake,—he got it through your grandfather. Morgan has the care of it, sir."

"Very plausible, indeed!"—and I sent him off to his work.

After luncheon I went below and directly to the end of the corridor, and began to sound the walls. To the eye they were all alike, being of cement, and substantial enough. Through the area window I saw the solid earth and snow; surely there was little here to base hope upon, and my wonder grew at the ease with which Morgan had vanished through a barred window and into frozen ground.

The walls at the end of the passage were as solid as rock, and they responded dully to the stroke of the hammer. I sounded them on both sides, retracing my steps to the stairway, becoming more and more impatient at my ill-luck or stupidity. There was every reason why I should know my own house, and yet a stranger and an outlaw ran through it with amazing daring.

After an hour's idle search I returned to the end of the corridor, repeated all my previous soundings, and, I fear, indulged in language unbecoming a gentleman. Then, in my blind anger, I found what patient search had not disclosed.

I threw the hammer from me in a fit of temper; it struck upon a large square in the cement floor which gave forth a hollow sound. I was on my knees in an instant, my fingers searching the cracks, and drawing down close I could feel a current of air, slight but unmistakable, against my face.

The cement square, though exactly like the others in the cellar floor, was evidently only a wooden imitation, covering an opening beneath.

The block was fitted into its place with a nicety that

certified to the skill of the hand that had adjusted it. I broke a blade of my pocket-knife trying to pry it up, but in a moment I succeeded, and found it to be in reality a trap-door, hinged to the substantial part of the floor.

A current of cool fresh air, the same that had surprised me in the night, struck my face as I lay flat and peered into the opening. The lower passage was as black as pitch, and I lighted a lantern I had brought with me, found that wooden steps gave safe conduct below and went down.

I stood erect in the passage and had several inches to spare. It extended both ways, running back under the foundations of the house. This lower passage cut squarely under the park before the house and toward the school wall. No wonder my grandfather had brought foreign laborers who could speak no English to work on his house! There was something delightful in the largeness of his scheme, and I hurried through the tunnel with a hundred questions tormenting my brain.

The air grew steadily fresher, until, after I had gone about two hundred yards, I reached a point where the wind seemed to beat down on me from above. I put up my hands and found two openings about two yards apart, through which the air sucked steadily. I moved out of the current with a chuckle in my throat and a grin on my face. I had passed under the gate in the school-wall, and I knew now why the piers that held it had been built so high,—they were hollow and were the means of sending fresh air into the tunnel.

I had traversed about twenty yards more when I felt a slight vibration accompanied by a muffled roar, and almost immediately came to a short wooden stair that marked the end of the passage. I had no means of judging directions, but I assumed I was somewhere near the chapel in the school-grounds.

I climbed the steps, noting still the vibration, and found a door that yielded readily to pressure. In a moment I stood blinking, lantern in hand, in a well-lighted, floored room. Overhead the tumult and thunder of an organ explained the tremor and roar I had heard below. I was in the crypt of St. Agatha's chapel. The inside of the door by which I had entered was a part of the wainscoting of the room, and the opening was wholly covered with a map of the Holy Land.

In my absorption I had lost the sense of time, and I was amazed to find that it was five o'clock, but I resolved to go into the chapel before going home.

The way up was clear enough, and I was soon in the vestibule. I opened the door, expecting to find a service in progress; but the little church was empty save where, at the right of the chancel, an organist was filling the church with the notes of a triumphant march. Cap in hand I stole forward and sank down in one of the pews.

A lamp over the organ keyboard gave the only light in the chapel, and made an aureole about her head,— about the uncovered head of Olivia Gladys Armstrong! I smiled as I recognized her and smiled, too, as I remembered her name. But the joy she brought to the music, the happiness in her face as she raised it in the minor harmonies, her isolation, marked by the little isle of light against the dark background of the choir,— these things touched and moved me, and I bent forward, my arms upon the pew in front of me, watching and listening with a kind of awed wonder. Here was a refuge of peace and lulling harmony after the disturbed life at Glenarm, and I yielded myself to its solace with an inclination my life had rarely known.

There was no pause in the outpouring of the melody. She changed stops and manuals with swift fingers and passed from one composition to another; now it was an august hymn, now a theme from Wagner, and finally Mendelssohn's *Spring Song* leaped forth exultant in the dark chapel.

She ceased suddenly with a little sigh and struck her hands together, for the place was cold. As she reached up to put out the lights I stepped forward to the chancel steps.

"Please allow me to do that for you?"

She turned toward me, gathering a cape about her.

"Oh, it's you, is it?" she asked, looking about quickly. "I don't remember—I don't *seem* to remember—that you were invited."

"I didn't know I was coming myself," I remarked truthfully, lifting my hand to the lamp.

"That is my opinion of you,—that you're a rather unexpected person. But thank you, very much."

She showed no disposition to prolong the interview, but hurried toward the door, and reached the vestibule before I came up with her.

"You can't go any further, Mr. Glenarm," she said, and waited as though to make sure I understood. Straight before us through the wood and beyond the school-buildings the sunset faded sullenly. The night was following fast upon the gray twilight and already the bolder planets were aflame in the sky. The path led straight ahead beneath the black boughs.

"I might perhaps walk to the dormitory, or whatever you call it," I said.

"Thank you, no! I'm late and haven't time to bother with you. It's against the rules, you know, for us to receive visitors."

She stepped out into the path.

"But I'm not a caller. I'm just a neighbor. And I owe you several calls, anyhow."

She laughed, but did not pause, and I followed a pace behind her.

"I hope you don't think for a minute that I chased a rabbit on your side of the fence just to meet you; do you, Mr. Glenarm?"

"Be it far from me! I'm glad I came, though, for I liked your music immensely. I'm in earnest; I think it quite wonderful, Miss Armstrong."

She paid no heed to me.

"And I hope I may promise myself the pleasure of hearing you often."

"You are positively flattering, Mr. Glenarm; but as I'm going away—"

I felt my heart sink at the thought of her going away. She was the only amusing person I had met at Glenarm, and the idea of losing her gave a darker note to the bleak landscape.

"That's really too bad! And just when we were getting acquainted! And I was coming to church every Sunday to hear you play and to pray for snow, so you'd come over often to chase rabbits!"

This, I thought, softened her heart. At any rate her tone changed.

"I don't play for services; they're afraid to let me for fear I'd run comic-opera tunes into the Te Deum!"

"How shocking!"

"Do you know, Mr. Glenarm,"—her tone became confidential and her pace slackened,—"we call you the squire, at St. Agatha's, and the lord of the manor, and names like that! All the girls are perfectly crazy about you. They'd be wild if they thought I talked with you, clandestinely,—is that the way you pronounce it?"

"Anything you say and any way you say it satisfies me," I replied.

"That's ever so nice of you," she said, mockingly again.

I felt foolish and guilty. She would probably get roundly scolded if the grave Sisters learned of her talks with me, and very likely I should win their hearty contempt. But I did not turn back.

"I hope the reason you're leaving isn't—" I hesitated.

"Ill conduct? Oh, yes; I'm *terribly* wicked, Squire Glenarm! They're sending me off."

"But I suppose they're awfully strict, the Sisters."

"They're hideous,—perfectly hideous."

"Where is your home?" I demanded. "Chicago, Indianapolis, Cincinnati, perhaps?"

"Humph, you *are* dull! You ought to know from my accent that I'm not from Chicago. And I hope I haven't a Kentucky girl's air of waiting to be flattered to death. And no Indianapolis girl would talk to a strange man at the edge of a deep wood in the gray twilight of a winter day,—that's from a book; and the Cincinnati girl is without my *élan, esprit,*—whatever you please to call it. She has more Teutonic repose,—more of Gretchen-of-the-Rhine-Valley about her. Don't you adore French, Squire Glenarm?" she concluded breathlessly, and with no pause in her quick step.

"I adore yours, Miss Armstrong," I asserted, yielding myself further to the joy of idiocy, and delighting in the mockery and changing moods of her talk. I did not make her out; indeed, I preferred not to! I was not then,—and I am not now, thank God,—of an analytical turn of mind. And as I grow older I prefer, even after many a blow, to take my fellow human beings a good deal as I find them. And as for women, old or young, I envy no man his gift of resolving them into elements. As well carry a spray of arbutus to the laboratory or subject the enchantment of moonlight upon running water to the flame and blow-pipe as try to analyze the heart of a girl,—particularly a girl who paddles a canoe with a sure stroke and puts up a good race with a rabbit.

A lamp shone ahead of us at the entrance of one of the houses, and lights appeared in all the buildings.

"If I knew your window I should certainly sing under it,—except that you're going home! You didn't tell me why they were deporting you."

"I'm really ashamed to! You would never—"

"Oh, yes, I would; I'm really an old friend!" I insisted, feeling more like an idiot every minute.

"Well, don't tell! But they caught me flirting—with the grocery boy! Now *aren't* you disgusted?"

"Thoroughly! I can't believe it! Why, you'd a lot better flirt with me," I suggested boldly.

"Well, I'm to be sent away for good at Christmas. I may come back then if I can square myself. My! That's slang,—isn't it horrid?"

"The Sisters don't like slang, I suppose?"

"They loathe it! Miss Devereux—you know who she is!—she spies on us and tells."

"You don't say so; but I'm not surprised at her. I've heard about *her!*" I declared bitterly.

We had reached the door, and I expected her to fly; but she lingered a moment.

"Oh, if you know her! Perhaps you're a spy, too! It's just as well we should never meet again, Mr. Glenarm," she declared haughtily.

"The memory of these few meetings will always linger with me, Miss Armstrong," I returned in an imitation of her own tone.

"I shall scorn to remember you!"—and she folded her arms under the cloak tragically.

"Our meetings have been all too few, Miss Armstrong. Three, exactly, I believe!"

"I see you prefer to ignore the first time I ever saw you," she said, her hand on the door.

"Out there in your canoe? Never! And you've forgiven me for overhearing you and the chaplain on the wall—please!"

She grasped the knob of the door and paused an instant as though pondering.

"I make it four times, not counting once in the road and other times when you didn't know, Squire Glenarm! I'm a foolish little girl to have remembered the first. I see now how b-l-i-n-d I have been."

She opened and closed the door softly, and I heard her running up the steps within.

I ran back to the chapel, roundly abusing myself for having neglected my more serious affairs for a bit of silly talk with a school-girl, fearful lest the openings I had left at both ends of the passage should have been discovered. The tunnel added a new and puzzling factor to the problem already before me, and I was eager for an opportunity to sit down in peace and comfort to study the situation.

At the chapel I narrowly escaped running into Stod-

"I shall scorn to remember you!"—and she folded her arms under
the cloak tragically.   *Page 164*

dard, but I slipped past him, pulled the hidden door into place, traversed the tunnel without incident, and soon climbed through the hatchway and slammed the false block securely into the opening.

CHAPTER XIII

A PAIR OF EAVESDROPPERS

When I came down after dressing for dinner, Bates called my attention to a belated mail. I pounced eagerly upon a letter in Laurance Donovan's well-known hand, bearing, to my surprise, an American stamp and postmarked New Orleans. It was dated, however, at Vera Cruz, Mexico, December fifteenth, 1901.

DEAR OLD MAN: I have had a merry time since I saw you in New York. Couldn't get away for a European port as I hoped when I left you, as the authorities seemed to be taking my case seriously, and I was lucky to get off as a deck-hand on a south-bound boat. I expected to get a slice of English prodigal veal at Christmas, but as things stand now, I am grateful to be loose even in this God-forsaken hole. The British bulldog is eager to insert its teeth in my trousers, and I was flattered to see my picture bulletined in a conspicuous place the day I struck Vera Cruz. You see, they're badgering the Government at home because I'm not apprehended, and they've got to catch and hang me to show that they've really got their hands on the Irish situation. I am not afraid of the Greasers—no people who gorge themselves with bananas and red peppers can be dangerous—but the British consul here has a bad eye and even as I write I am dimly con-

166

scious that a sleek person, who is ostensibly engaged in literary work at the next table, is really killing time while he waits for me to finish this screed.

No doubt you are peacefully settled on your ancestral estate with only a few months and a little patience between you and your grandfather's siller. You always were a lucky brute. People die just to leave you money, whereas I'll have to die to get out of jail.

I hope to land under the Stars and Stripes within a few days, either across country through El Paso or via New Orleans,—preferably the former, as a man's social position is rated high in Texas in proportion to the amount of reward that's out for him. They'd probably give me the freedom of the state if they knew my crimes had been the subject of debate in the House of Commons.

But the man across the table is casually looking over here for a glimpse of my signature, so I must give him a good one just for fun. With best wishes always,

Faithfully yours,

GEORGE WASHINGTON SMITH.

P. S.—I shan't mail this here, but give it to a red-haired Irishman on a steamer that sails north to-night. Pleasant, I must say, this eternal dodging! Wish I could share your rural paradise for the length of a pipe and a bottle! Have forgotten whether you said Indian Territory or Indiana, but will take chances on the latter as more remotely suggesting the aborigines.

Bates gave me my coffee in the library, as I wished to settle down to an evening of reflection without delay. Larry's report of himself was not reassuring. I knew that if he had any idea of trying to reach me he would not mention it in a letter which might fall into the hands of the authorities, and the hope that he might

join me grew. I was not, perhaps, entitled to a companion at Glenarm under the terms of my exile, but as
a matter of protection in the existing condition of affairs there could be no legal or moral reason why I
should not defend myself against my foes, and Larry
was an ally worth having.

In all my hours of questioning and anxiety at Glenarm I never doubted the amiable intentions of my
grandfather. His device for compelling my residence
at his absurd house was in keeping with his character,
and it was all equitable enough. But his dead hand had
no control over the strange issue, and I felt justified in
interpreting the will in the light of my experiences. I
certainly did not intend to appeal to the local police authorities, at least not until the animus of the attack on
me was determined.

My neighbor, the chaplain, had inadvertently given
me a bit of important news; and my mind kept revert-
ing to the fact that Morgan was reporting his injury to
the executor of my grandfather's estate in New York.
Everything else that had happened was tame and un-
important compared with this. Why had John Marshall
Glenarm made Arthur Pickering the executor of his
estate? He knew that I detested him, that Pickering's
noble aims and high ambitions had been praised by my
family until his very name sickened me; and yet my

own grandfather had thought it wise to intrust his fortune and my future to the man of all men who was
most repugnant to me. I rose and paced the floor in
anger.

Instead of accepting Pickering's word for it that the
will was all straight, I should have employed counsel
and taken legal advice before suffering myself to be
rushed away into a part of the world I had never visited
before, and cooped up in a dreary house under the eye
of a somber scoundrel who might poison me any day, if
he did not prefer to shoot me in my sleep. My rage
must fasten upon some one, and Bates was the nearest
target for it. I went to the kitchen, where he usually
spent his evenings, to vent my feelings upon him, only
to find him gone. I climbed to his room and found it
empty. Very likely he was off condoling with his friend
and fellow conspirator, the caretaker, and I fumed with
rage and disappointment. I was thoroughly tired, as
tired as on days when I had beaten my way through
tropical jungles without food or water; but I wished,
in my impotent anger against I knew not what agencies,
to punish myself, to induce an utter weariness that
would drag me exhausted to bed.

The snow in the highway was well beaten down and
I swung off countryward past St. Agatha's. A gray
mist hung over the fields in whirling clouds, breaking

away occasionally and showing the throbbing winter stars. The walk, and my interest in the alternation of star-lighted and mist-wrapped landscape won me to a better state of mind, and after tramping a couple of miles, I set out for home. Several times on my tramp I had caught myself whistling the air of a majestic old hymn, and smiled, remembering my young friend Olivia, and her playing in the chapel. She was an amusing child; the thought of her further lifted my spirit; and I turned into the school park as I passed the outer gate with a half-recognized wish to pass near the barracks where she spent her days.

At the school-gate the lamps of a carriage suddenly blurred in the mist. Carriages were not common in this region, and I was not surprised to find that this was the familiar village hack that met trains day and night at Glenarm station. Some parent, I conjectured, paying a visit to St. Agatha's; perhaps the father of Miss Olivia Gladys Armstrong had come to carry her home for a stricter discipline than Sister Theresa's school afforded.

The driver sat asleep on his box, and I passed him and went on into the grounds. A whim seized me to visit the crypt of the chapel and examine the opening to the tunnel. As I passed the little group of school-buildings a man came hurriedly from one of them and turned toward the chapel.

I first thought it was Stoddard, but I could not make him out in the mist and I waited for him to put twenty paces between us before I followed along the path that led from the school to the chapel.

He strode into the chapel porch with an air of assurance, and I heard him address some one who had been waiting. The mist was now so heavy that I could not see my hand before my face, and I stole forward until I could hear the voices of the two men distinctly.

"Bates!"

"Yes, sir."

I heard feet scraping on the stone floor of the porch.

"This is a devil of a place to talk in but it's the best we can do. Did the young man know I sent for you?"

"No, sir. He was quite busy with his books and papers."

"Humph! We can never be sure of him."

"I suppose that is correct, sir."

"Well, you and Morgan are a fine pair, I must say! I thought he had some sense, and that you'd see to it that he didn't make a mess of this thing. He's in bed now with a hole in his arm and you've got to go on alone."

"I'll do my best, Mr. Pickering."

"Don't call me by name, you idiot. We're not advertising our business from the housetops."

"Certainly not," replied Bates humbly.

The blood was roaring through my head, and my hands were clenched as I stood there listening to this colloquy.

Pickering's voice was—and is—unmistakable. There was always a purring softness in it. He used to remind me at school of a sleek, complacent cat, and I hate cats with particular loathing.

"Is Morgan lying or not when he says he shot himself accidentally?" demanded Pickering petulantly.

"I only know what I heard from the gardener here at the school. You'll understand, I hope, that I can't be seen going to Morgan's house."

"Of course not. But he says you haven't played fair with him, that you even attacked him a few days after Glenarm came."

"Yes, and he hit me over the head with a club. It was his indiscretion, sir. He wanted to go through the library in broad daylight, and it wasn't any use, anyhow. There's nothing there."

"But I don't like the looks of this shooting. Morgan's sick and out of his head. But a fellow like Morgan isn't likely to shoot himself accidentally, and now that it's done the work's stopped and the time is running on. What do you think Glenarm suspects?"

"I can't tell, sir, but mighty little, I should say. The

shot through the window the first night he was here seemed to shake him a trifle, but he's quite settled down now, I should say, sir."

"He probably doesn't spend much time on this side of the fence—doesn't haunt the chapel, I fancy?"

"Lord, no, sir! I hardly suspect the young gentleman of being a praying man."

"You haven't seen him prowling about analyzing the architecture—"

"Not a bit of it, sir. He hasn't, I should say, what his revered grandfather called the analytical mind."

Hearing yourself discussed in this frank fashion by your own servant is, I suppose, a wholesome thing for the spirit. The man who stands behind your chair may acquire, in time, some special knowledge of your mental processes by a diligent study of the back of your head. But I was not half so angry with these conspirators as with myself, for ever having entertained a single generous thought toward Bates. It was, however, consoling to know that Morgan was lying to Pickering, and that my own exploits in the house were unknown to the executor.

Pickering stamped his feet upon the paved porch floor in a way that I remembered of old. It marked a conclusion, and preluded serious statements.

"Now, Bates," he said, with a ring of authority and

speaking in a louder key than he had yet used, "it's your duty under all the circumstances to help discover the hidden assets of the estate. We've got to pluck the mystery from that architectural monster over there, and the time for doing it is short enough. Mr. Glenarm was a rich man. To my own knowledge he had a couple of millions, and he couldn't have spent it all on that house. He reduced his bank account to a few thousand dollars and swept out his safety-vault boxes with a broom before his last trip into Vermont. He didn't die with the stuff in his clothes, did he?"

"Lord bless me, no, sir! There was little enough cash to bury him, with you out of the country and me alone with him."

"He was a crank and I suppose he got a lot of satisfaction out of concealing his money. But this hunt for it isn't funny. I supposed, of course, we'd dig it up before Glenarm got here or I shouldn't have been in such a hurry to send for him. But it's over there somewhere, or in the grounds. There must be a plan of the house that would help. I'll give you a thousand dollars the day you wire me you have found any sort of clue."

"Thank you, sir."

"I don't want thanks, I want the money or securities or whatever it is. I've got to go back to my car now, and you'd better skip home. You needn't tell your young master that I've been here."

I was trying hard to believe, as I stood there with clenched hands outside the chapel porch, that Arthur Pickering's name was written in the list of directors of one of the greatest trust companies in America, and that he belonged to the most exclusive clubs in New York. I had run out for a walk with only an inverness over my dinner-jacket, and I was thoroughly chilled by the cold mist. I was experiencing, too, an inner cold as I reflected upon the greed and perfidy of man.

"Keep an eye on Morgan," said Pickering.

"Certainly, sir."

"And be careful what you write or wire."

"I'll mind those points, sir. But I'd suggest, if you please, sir—"

"Well?" demanded Pickering impatiently.

"That you should call at the house. It would look rather strange to the young gentleman if you'd come here and not see him."

"I haven't the slightest errand with him. And besides, I haven't time. If he learns that I've been here you may say that my business was with Sister Theresa and that I regretted very much not having an opportunity to call on him."

The irony of this was not lost on Bates, who chuckled softly. He came out into the open and turned away toward the Glenarm gate. Pickering passed me, so near that I might have put out my hand and touched him, and in a moment I heard the carriage drive off rapidly toward the village.

I heard Bates running home over the snow and listened to the clatter of the village hack as it bore Pickering back to Annandale.

Then out of the depths of the chapel porch—out of the depths of time and space, it seemed, so dazed I stood —some one came swiftly toward me, some one, light of foot like a woman, ran down the walk a little way into the fog and paused.

An exclamation broke from me.

"Eavesdropping for two!"—it was the voice of Olivia. "I'd take pretty good care of myself if I were you, Squire Glenarm. Good night!"

"Good-by!" I faltered, as she sped away into the mist toward the school.

CHAPTER XIV

THE GIRL IN GRAY

My first thought was to find the crypt door and return through the tunnel before Bates reached the house. The chapel was open, and by lighting matches I found my way to the map and panel. I slipped through and closed the opening; then ran through the passage with gratitude for the generous builder who had given it a clear floor and an ample roof. In my haste I miscalculated its length and pitched into the steps under the trap at a speed that sent me sprawling. In a moment more I had jammed the trap into place and was running up the cellar steps, breathless, with my cap smashed down over my eyes.

I heard Bates at the rear of the house and knew I had won the race by a scratch. There was but a moment in which to throw my coat and cap under the divan, slap the dust from my clothes and seat myself at the great table, where the candles blazed tranquilly.

Bates' step was as steady as ever—there was not the slightest hint of excitement in it—as he came and stood within the door.

"Beg pardon, Mr. Glenarm, did you wish anything, sir?"

"Oh, no, thank you, Bates."

"I had stepped down to the village, sir, to speak to the grocer. The eggs he sent this morning were not quite up to the mark. I have warned him not to send any of the storage article to this house."

"That's right, Bates." I folded my arms to hide my hands, which were black from contact with the passage, and faced my man servant. My respect for his rascally powers had increased immensely since he gave me my coffee. A contest with so clever a rogue was worth while.

"I'm grateful for your good care of me, Bates. I had expected to perish of discomfort out here, but you are treating me like a lord."

"Thank you, Mr. Glenarm. I do what I can, sir."

He brought fresh candles for the table candelabra, going about with his accustomed noiseless step. I felt a cold chill creep down my spine as he passed behind me on these errands. His transition from the rôle of conspirator to that of my flawless servant was almost too abrupt.

I dismissed him as quickly as possible, and listened to his step through the halls as he went about locking the doors. This was a regular incident, but I was aware

to-night that he exercised what seemed to me a particular care in settling the bolts. The locking-up process
had rather bored me before; to-night the snapping of
bolts was particularly trying.

When I heard Bates climbing to his own quarters I
quietly went the rounds on my own account and found
everything as tight as a drum.

In the cellar I took occasion to roll some barrels of
cement into the end of the corridor, to cover and block
the trap door. Bates had no manner of business in that
part of the house, as the heating apparatus was under
the kitchen and accessible by an independent stairway.
I had no immediate use for the hidden passage to the
chapel—and I did not intend that my enemies should
avail themselves of it. Morgan, at least, knew of it and,
while he was not likely to trouble me at once, I had resolved to guard every point in our pleasant game.

I was tired enough to sleep when I went to my room,
and after an eventless night, woke to a clear day and
keener air.

"I'm going to take a little run into the village, Bates,"
I remarked at breakfast.

"Very good, sir. The weather's quite cleared."

"If any one should call I'll be back in an hour or so."

"Yes, sir."

He turned his impenetrable face toward me as I rose.

There was, of course, no chance whatever that any one would call to see me; the Reverend Paul Stoddard was the only human being, except Bates, Morgan and the man who brought up my baggage, who had crossed the threshold since my arrival.

I really had an errand in the village. I wished to visit the hardware store and buy some cartridges, but Pickering's presence in the community was a disturbing factor in my mind. I wished to get sight of him,— to meet him, if possible, and see how a man, whose schemes were so deep, looked in the light of day.

As I left the grounds and gained the highway Stoddard fell in with me.

"Well, Mr. Glenarm, I'm glad to see you abroad so early. With that library of yours the temptation must be strong to stay within doors. But a man's got to subject himself to the sun and wind. Even a good wetting now and then is salutary."

"I try to get out every day," I answered. "But I've chiefly limited myself to the grounds."

"Well, it's a fine estate. The lake is altogether charming in summer. I quite envy you your fortune."

He walked with a long swinging stride, his hands thrust deep into his overcoat pockets. It was difficult to accept the idea of so much physical strength being wasted in the mere business of saying prayers in a girls'

school. Here was a fellow who should have been cap-
tain of a ship or a soldier, a leader of forlorn hopes. I
felt sure there must be a weakness of some sort in him.
Quite possibly it would prove to be a mild estheticism
that delighted in the savor of incense and the mournful
cadence of choral vespers. He declined a cigar and this
rather increased my suspicions.

The village hack, filled with young women, passed at
a gallop, bound for the station, and we took off our hats.

"Christmas holidays," explained the chaplain. "Practically all the students go home."

"Lucky kids, to have a Christmas to go home to!"

"I suppose Mr. Pickering got away last night?" he
observed, and my pulse quickened at the name.

"I haven't seen him yet," I answered guardedly.

"Then of course he hasn't gone!" and these words,
uttered in the big clergyman's deep tones, seemed wholly
plausible. There was, to be sure, nothing so unlikely as
that Arthur Pickering, executor of my grandfather's
estate, would come to Glenarm without seeing me.

"Sister Theresa told me this morning he was here.
He called on her and Miss Devereux last night. I
haven't seen him myself. I thought possibly I might
run into him in the village. His car's very likely on the
station switch."

"No doubt we shall find him there," I answered easily.

The Annandale station presented an appearance of unusual gaiety when we reached the main street of the village. There, to be sure, lay a private car on the siding, and on the platform was a group of twenty or more girls, with several of the brown-habited Sisters of St. Agatha. There was something a little foreign in the picture; the girls in their bright colors talking gaily, the Sisters in their somber garb hovering about, suggesting France or Italy rather than Indiana.

"I came here with the idea that St. Agatha's was a charity school," I remarked to the chaplain.

"Not a bit of it! Sister Theresa is really a swell, you know, and her school is hard to get into."

"I'm glad you warned me in time. I had thought of sending over a sack of flour occasionally, or a few bolts of calico to help on the good work. You've saved my life."

"I probably have. I might mention your good intentions to Sister Theresa."

"Pray don't. If there's any danger of meeting her on that platform—"

"No; she isn't coming down, I'm sure. But you ought to know her,—if you will pardon me. And Miss Devereux is charming,—but really I don't mean to be annoying."

"Not in the least. But under the circumstances,—

the will and my probationary year,—you can understand—"

"Certainly. A man's affairs are his own, Mr. Glenarm."

We stepped upon the platform. The private car was
on the opposite side of the station and had been
switched into a siding of the east and west road. Pickering was certainly getting on. The private car, even
more than the yacht, is the symbol of plutocracy, and
gaping rustics were evidently impressed by its grandeur.
As I lounged across the platform with Stoddard, Pickering came out into the vestibule of his car, followed by
two ladies and an elderly gentleman. They all descend-
ed and began a promenade of the plank walk.

Pickering saw me an instant later and came up hurriedly, with outstretched hand.

"This is indeed good fortune! We dropped off here
last night rather unexpectedly to rest a hot-box and
should have been picked up by the midnight express for
Chicago; but there was a miscarriage of orders somewhere and we now have to wait for the nine o'clock, and
it's late. If I'd known how much behind it was I
should have run out to see you. How are things going?"

"As smooth as a whistle! It really isn't so bad when
you face it. And the fact is I'm actually at work."

"That's splendid. The year will go fast enough, never fear. I suppose you pine for a little human society now and then. A man can never strike the right medium in such things. In New York we are all rushed to death. I sometimes feel that I'd like a little rustication myself. I get nervous, and working for corporations is wearing. The old gentleman there is Taylor, president of the Interstate and Western. The ladies are his wife and her sister. I'd like to introduce you." He ran his eyes over my corduroys and leggings amiably. He had not in years addressed me so pleasantly.

Stoddard had left me to go to the other end of the platform to speak to some of the students. I followed Pickering rather loathly to where the companions of his travels were pacing to and fro in the crisp morning air.

I laugh still whenever I remember that morning at Annandale station. As soon as Pickering had got me well under way in conversation with Taylor, he excused himself hurriedly and went off, as I assumed, to be sure the station agent had received orders for attaching the private car to the Chicago express. Taylor proved to be a supercilious person,—I believe they call him Chilly Billy at the Metropolitan Club,—and our efforts to con-

verse were pathetically unfruitful. He asked me the
value of land in my county, and as my ignorance on this
subject was vast and illimitable, I could see that he was
forming a low opinion of my character and intelligence.
The two ladies stood by, making no concealment of their
impatience. Their eyes were upon the girls from St.
Agatha's on the other platform, whom they could see
beyond me. I had jumped the conversation from Indiana farm-lands to the recent disorders in Bulgaria,
which interested me more, when Mrs. Taylor spoke
abruptly to her sister.

"That's she—the one in the gray coat, talking to the
clergyman. She came a moment ago in the carriage."

"The one with the umbrella? I thought you said—"

Mrs. Taylor glanced at her sister warningly, and
they both looked at me. Then they sought to detach
themselves and moved away. There was some one on
the farther side of the platform whom they wished to see,
and Taylor, not understanding their manœuver—he was
really anxious, I think, not to be left alone with me—
started down the platform after them, I following. Mrs.
Taylor and her sister walked to the end of the platform
and looked across, a biscuit-toss away, to where Stoddard stood talking to the girl I had already heard described as wearing a gray coat and carrying an umbrella.

The girl in gray crossed the track quickly and addressed the two women cordially. Taylor's back was to her and he was growing eloquent in a mild well-bred way over the dullness of our statesmen in not seeing the advantages that would accrue to the United States in fostering our shipping industry. His wife, her sister and the girl in gray were so near that I could hear plainly what they were saying. They were referring apparently to the girl's refusal of an invitation to ac· company them to California.

"So you can't go—it's too bad! We had hoped that when you really saw us on the way you would relent," said Mrs. Taylor.

"But there are many reasons; and above all Sister Theresa needs me."

It was the voice of Olivia, a little lower, a little more restrained than I had known it.

"But think of the rose gardens that are waiting for us out there!" said the other lady. They were showing her the deference that elderly women always have for pretty girls.

"Alas, and again alas!" exclaimed Olivia. "Please don't make it harder for me than necessary. But I gave my promise a year ago to spend these holidays in Cincinnati."

She ignored me wholly, and after shaking hands with the ladies returned to the other platform. I wondered whether she was overlooking Taylor on purpose to cut me.

Taylor was still at his lecture on the needs of our American merchant marine when Pickering passed hurriedly, crossed the track and began speaking earnestly to the girl in gray.

"The American flag should command the seas. What we need is not more battle-ships but more freight carriers—" Taylor was saying.

But I was watching Olivia Gladys Armstrong. In a long skirt, with her hair caught up under a gray toque that matched her coat perfectly, she was not my Olivia of the tam-o'-shanter, who had pursued the rabbit; nor yet the unsophisticated school-girl, who had suffered my idiotic babble; nor, again, the dreamy rapt organist of the chapel. She was a grown woman with at least twenty summers to her credit, and there was about her an air of knowing the world, and of not being at all a person one would make foolish speeches to. She spoke to Pickering gravely. Once she smiled dolefully and shook her head, and I vaguely strove to remember where I had seen that look in her eyes before. Her gold beads, which I had once carried in my pocket, were clasped tight about the close collar of her dress; and I was glad, very glad, that I had ever touched anything that belonged to her.

"As the years go by we are going to dominate trade more and more. Our manufactures already lead the world, and what we make we've got to sell, haven't we?" demanded Taylor.

"Certainly, sir," I answered warmly.

Who was Olivia Gladys Armstrong and what was Arthur Pickering's business with her? And what was it she had said to me that evening when I had found her playing on the chapel organ? So much happened that day that I had almost forgotten, and, indeed, I had tried to forget I had made a fool of myself for the edification of an amusing little school-girl. "I see you prefer to ignore the first time I ever saw you," she had said; but if I had thought of this at all it had been with righteous self-contempt. Or, I may have flattered my vanity with the reflection that she had eyed me—her hero, perhaps—with wistful admiration across the wall.

Meanwhile the Chicago express roared into Annandale and the private car was attached. Taylor watched the trainmen with the cool interest of a man for whom the proceeding had no novelty, while he continued to

dilate upon the nation's commercial opportunities. I
turned perforce, and walked with him back toward the
station, where Mrs. Taylor and her sister were talking
to the conductor.

Pickering came running across the platform with several telegrams in his hand. The express had picked up
the car and was ready to continue its westward journey.

"I'm awfully sorry, Glenarm, that our stop's so
short,"—and Pickering's face wore a worried look as he
addressed me, his eyes on the conductor.

"How far do you go?" I asked.

"California. We have interests out there and I have
to attend some stock-holders' meetings in Colorado in
January."

"Ah, you business men! You business men!" I said
reproachfully. I wished to call him a blackguard then
and there, and it was on my tongue to do so, but I concluded that to wait until he had shown his hand fully
was the better game.

The ladies entered the car and I shook hands with
Taylor, who threatened to send me his pamphlet on
The Needs of American Shipping, when he got back to
New York.

"It's too bad she wouldn't go with us. Poor girl!
this must be a dreary hole for her; she deserves wider

horizons," he said to Pickering, who helped him upon the platform of the car with what seemed to be unnecessary precipitation.

"You little know us," I declared, for Pickering's benefit. "Life at Annandale is nothing if not exciting. The people here are indifferent marksmen or there'd be murders galore."

"Mr. Glenarm is a good deal of a wag," explained Pickering dryly, swinging himself aboard as the train started.

"Yes; it's my humor that keeps me alive," I responded, and taking off my hat, I saluted Arthur Pickering with my broadest salaam.

CHAPTER XV

I MAKE AN ENGAGEMENT

The south-bound train had not arrived and as I turned away the station-agent again changed its time on the bulletin board. It was now due in ten minutes. A few students had boarded the Chicago train, but a greater number still waited on the farther platform. The girl in gray was surrounded by half a dozen students, all talking animatedly. As I walked toward them I could not justify my stupidity in mistaking a grown woman for a school-girl of fifteen or sixteen; but it was the tam-o'-shanter, the short skirt, the youthful joy in the outdoor world that had disguised her as effectually as Rosalind to the eyes of Orlando in the forest of Arden. She was probably a teacher,—quite likely the teacher of music, I argued, who had amused herself at my expense.

It had seemed the easiest thing in the world to approach her with an apology or a farewell, but those few inches added to her skirt and that pretty gray toque substituted for the tam-o'-shanter set up a barrier that did not yield at all as I drew nearer. At the last mo-

191

ment, as I crossed the track and stepped upon the other platform, it occurred to me that while I might have some claim upon the attention of Olivia Gladys Armstrong, a wayward school-girl of athletic tastes, I had none whatever upon a person whom it was proper to address as Miss Armstrong,—who was, I felt sure, quite capable of snubbing me if snubbing fell in with her mood.

She glanced toward me and bowed instantly. Her young companions withdrew to a conservative distance; and I will say this for the St. Agatha girls: their manners are beyond criticism, and an affable discretion is one of their most admirable traits.

"I didn't know they ever grew up so fast,—in a day and a night!"

I was glad I remembered the number of beads in her chain; the item seemed at once to become important.

"It's the air, I suppose. It's praised by excellent critics, as you may learn from the catalogue."

"But you are going to an ampler ether, a diviner air. You have attained the beatific state and at once take flight. If they confer perfection like an academic degree at St. Agatha's, then—"

I had never felt so stupidly helpless in my life. There were a thousand things I wished to say to her; there were countless questions I wished to ask; but her calmness and poise were disconcerting. She had not, apparently, the slightest curiosity about me; and there was no reason why she should have—I knew that well enough! Her eyes met mine easily; their azure depths puzzled me. She was almost, but not quite, some one I had seen before, and it was not my woodland Olivia. Her eyes, the soft curve of her cheek, the light in her hair,—but the memory of another time, another place, another girl, lured only to baffle me.

She laughed,—a little murmuring laugh.

"I'll never tell if you won't," she said.

"But I don't see how that helps me with you?"

"It certainly does not! That is a much more serious matter, Mr. Glenarm."

"And the worst of it is that I haven't a single thing to say for myself. It wasn't the not knowing that was so utterly stupid—"

"Certainly not! It was talking that ridiculous twaddle. It was trying to flirt with a silly school-girl. What will do for fifteen is somewhat vacuous for—"

She paused abruptly, colored and laughed.

"*I* am twenty-seven!"

"And *I* am just the usual age," she said.

"Ages don't count, but time is important. There are many things I wish you'd tell me,—you who hold the key of the gate of mystery."

"Then you'll have to pick the lock!"

She laughed lightly. The somber Sisters patrolling the platform with their charges heeded us little.

"I had no idea you knew Arthur Pickering—when you were just Olivia in the tam-o'-shanter."

"Maybe you think he wouldn't have cared for my acquaintance—as Olivia in the tam-o'-shanter. Men are very queer!"

"But Arthur Pickering is an old friend of mine."

"So he told me."

"We were neighbors in our youth."

"I believe I have heard him mention it."

"And we did our prep school together, and then parted!"

"You tell exactly the same story, so it must be true. He went to college and you went to Tech."

"And you knew him—?" I began, my curiosity thoroughly aroused.

"Not at college, any more than I knew you at Tech."

"The train's coming," I said earnestly, "and I wish you would tell me—when I shall see you again!"

"Before we part for ever?" There was a mischievous hint of the Olivia in short skirts in her tone.

"Please don't suggest it! Our times have been strange and few. There was that first night, when you called to me from the lake."

"How impertinent! How dare you—remember that?"

"And there was that other encounter at the chapel porch. Neither you nor I had the slightest business there. I admit my own culpability."

She colored again.

"But you spoke as though you understood what you must have heard there. It is important for me to know. I have a right to know just what you meant by that warning."

Real distress showed in her face for an instant. The agent and his helpers rushed the last baggage down the platform, and the rails hummed their warning of the approaching train.

"I was eavesdropping on my own account," she said hurriedly and with a note of finality. "I was there by intention, and"—there was another hint of the tam-o'-shanter in the mirth that seemed to bubble for a moment in her throat—"it's too bad you didn't see me, for I had on my prettiest gown, and the fog wasn't good for it. But you know as much of what was said there as I do. You are a man, and I have heard that you have had some experience in taking care of yourself, Mr. Glenarm."

"To be sure; but there are times—"

"Yes, there are times when the odds seem **rather heavy**. I have noticed that myself."

She smiled, but for an instant the sad look came into her eyes,—a look that vaguely but insistently suggested another time and place.

"I want you to come back," I said boldly, for the train was very near, and I felt that the eyes of the Sisters were upon us. "You can not go away where I shall not find you!"

I did not know who this girl was, her home, or her relation to the school, but I knew that her life and mine had touched strangely; that her eyes were blue, and that her voice had called to me twice through the dark, in mockery once and in warning another time, and that the sense of having known her before, of having looked into her eyes, haunted me. The youth in her was so luring; she was at once so frank and so guarded,—breeding and the taste and training of an ampler world than that of Annandale were so evidenced in the witchery of her voice, in the grace and ease that marked her every motion, in the soft gray tone of hat, dress and gloves, that a new mood, a new hope and faith sang in my pulses. There, on that platform, I felt again the sweet heartache I had known as a boy, when spring first warmed the Vermont hillsides and the mountains sent the last snows singing in joy of their release down through the brook-beds and into the wakened heart of youth.

She met my eyes steadily.

"If I thought there was the slightest chance of my ever seeing you again I shouldn't be talking to you here. But I thought, I thought it would be good fun to see how you really talked to a grown-up. So I am risking the displeasure of these good Sisters just to test your conversational powers, Mr. Glenarm. You see how perfectly frank I am."

"But you forget that I can follow you; I don't intend to sit down in this hole and dream about you. You can't go anywhere but I shall follow and find you."

"That is finely spoken, Squire Glenarm! But I imagine you are hardly likely to go far from Glenarm very soon. It isn't, of course, any of my affair; and yet I don't hesitate to say that I feel perfectly safe from pursuit!"—and she laughed her little low laugh that was delicious in its mockery.

I felt the blood mounting to my cheek. She knew, then, that I was virtually a prisoner at Glenarm, and for once in my life, at least, I was ashamed of my folly that had caused my grandfather to hold and check me from the grave, as he had never been able to control me in his life. The whole countryside knew why I was at Glenarm, and that did not matter; but my heart rebelled at the thought that this girl knew and mocked me with her knowledge.

"I shall see you Christmas Eve," I said, "wherever you may be."

"In three days? Then you will come to my Christmas Eve party. I shall be delighted to see you,—and flattered! Just think of throwing away a fortune to satisfy one's curiosity! I'm surprised at you, but gratified, on the whole, Mr. Glenarm!"

"I shall give more than a fortune, I shall give the honor I have pledged to my grandfather's memory to hear your voice again."

"That is a great deal,—for so small a voice; but money, fortune! A man will risk his honor readily enough, but his fortune is a more serious matter. I'm sorry we shall not meet again. It would be pleasant to discuss the subject further. It interests me particularly."

"In three days I shall see you," I said.

She was instantly grave.

"No! Please do not try. It would be a great mistake. And, anyhow, you can hardly come to my party without being invited."

"That matter is closed. Wherever you are on Christmas Eve I shall find you," I said, and felt my heart leap, knowing that I meant what I said.

"Good-by," she said, turning away. "I'm sorry I shan't ever chase rabbits at Glenarm any more."

"Or paddle a canoe, or play wonderful celestial music on the organ."

"Or be an eavesdropper or hear pleasant words from the master of Glenarm—"

"But I don't know where you are going—you haven't told me anything—you are slipping out into the world—"

She did not hear or would not answer. She turned away, and was at once surrounded by a laughing throng that crowded about the train. Two brown-robed Sisters stood like sentinels, one at either side, as she stepped into the car. I was conscious of a feeling that from the depths of their hoods they regarded me with un-Christian disdain. Through the windows I could see the students fluttering to seats, and the girl in gray seemed to be marshaling them. The gray hat appeared at a window for an instant, and a smiling face gladdened, I am sure, the guardians of the peace at St. Agatha's, for whom it was intended.

The last trunk crashed into the baggage car, every window framed for a moment a girl's face, and the train was gone.

CHAPTER XVI

THE PASSING OF OLIVIA

Bates brought a great log and rolled it upon exactly the right spot on the andirons, and a great constellation of sparks thronged up the chimney. The old relic of a house—I called the establishment by many names, but this was, I think, my favorite—could be heated in all its habitable parts, as Bates had demonstrated. The halls were of glacial temperature these cold days, but my room above, the dining-room and the great library were comfortable enough. I threw down a book and knocked the ashes from my pipe.

"Bates!"

"Yes, sir."

"I think my spiritual welfare is in jeopardy. I need counsel,—a spiritual adviser."

"I'm afraid that's beyond me, sir."

"I'd like to invite Mr. Stoddard to dinner so I may discuss my soul's health with him at leisure."

"Certainly, Mr. Glenarm."

--But it occurs to me that probably the terms of Mr. Glenarm's will point to my complete sequestration here. In other words, I may forfeit my rights by asking a guest to dinner."

He pondered the matter for a moment, then replied:

"I should think, sir,—as you ask my opinion,—that in the case of a gentleman in holy orders there would be no impropriety. Mr. Stoddard is a fine gentleman; I heard your late grandfather speak of him very highly."

"That, I imagine, is hardly conclusive in the matter. There is the executor—"

"To be sure; I hadn't considered him."

"Well, you'd better consider him. He's the court of last resort, isn't he?"

"Well, of course, that's one way of looking at it, sir."

"I suppose there's no chance of Mr. Pickering's dropping in on us now and then."

He gazed at me steadily, unblinkingly and with entire respect.

"He's a good deal of a traveler, Mr. Pickering is. He passed through only this morning, so the mail-boy told me. You may have met him at the station."

"Oh, yes; to be sure; so I did!" I replied. I was not

as good a liar as Bates; and there was nothing to be gained by denying that I had met the executor in the village. "I had a very pleasant talk with him. He was on the way to California with several friends."

"That is quite his way, I understand,—private cars and long journeys about the country. A very successful man is Mr. Pickering. Your grandfather had great confidence in him, did Mr. Glenarm."

"Ah, yes! A fine judge of character my grandfather was! I guess John Marshall Glenarm could spot a rascal about as far as any man in his day."

I felt like letting myself go before this masked scoundrel. The density of his mask was an increasing wonder to me. Bates was the most incomprehensible human being I had ever known. I had been torn with a thousand conflicting emotions since I overheard him discussing the state of affairs at Glenarm House with Pickering in the chapel porch; and Pickering's acquaintance with the girl in gray brought new elements into the affair that added to my uneasiness. But here was a treasonable dog on whom the stress of conspiracy had no outward effect whatever.

It was an amazing situation, but it called for calmness and eternal vigilance. With every hour my resolution grew to stand fast and fight it out on my own ac-

count without outside help. A thousand times during
the afternoon I had heard the voice of the girl in gray
saying to me: "You are a man, and I have heard that
you have had some experience in taking care of yourself,
Mr. Glenarm."

It was both a warning and a challenge, and the memory of the words was at once sobering and cheering.

Bates waited. Of him, certainly, I should ask no
questions touching Olivia Armstrong. To discuss her
with a blackguard servant even to gain answers to baf-
fling questions about her was not to my liking. And,
thank God! I taught myself one thing, if nothing
more, in those days at Glenarm House: I learned to
bide my time.

"I'll give you a note to Mr. Stoddard in the morning.
You may go now."

"Yes, sir."

The note was written and despatched. The chaplain
was not at his lodgings, and Bates reported that he had
left the message. The answer came presently by the
hand of the Scotch gardener, Ferguson, a short, wiry,
raw-boned specimen. I happened to open the door myself, and brought him into the library until I could read
Stoddard's reply. Ferguson had, I thought, an uneasy
eye, and his hair, of an ugly carrot color, annoyed me.

Mr. Paul Stoddard presented his compliments and would be delighted to dine with me. He wrote a large even hand, as frank and open as himself.

"That is all, Ferguson." And the gardener took himself off.

Thus it came about that Stoddard and I faced each other across the table in the refectory that same evening under the lights of a great candelabrum which Bates had produced from the store-room below. And I may say here, that while there was a slight hitch sometimes in the delivery of supplies from the village; while the fish which Bates caused to be shipped from Chicago for delivery every Friday morning failed once or twice, and while the grape-fruit for breakfast was not always what it should have been,—the supply of candles seemed inexhaustible. They were produced in every shade and size. There were enormous ones, such as I had never seen outside of a Russian church,—and one of the rooms in the cellar was filled with boxes of them. The House of a Thousand Candles deserved and proved its name.

Bates had certainly risen to the occasion. Silver and crystal of which I had not known before glistened on the table, and on the sideboard two huge candelabra added to the festival air of the little room.

Stoddard laughed as he glanced about.

"Here I have been feeling sorry for you, and yet you are living like a prince. I didn't know there was so much splendor in all Wabana County."

"I'm a trifle dazzled myself. Bates has tapped a new cellar somewhere. I'm afraid I'm not a good house-keeper, to speak truthfully. There are times when I hate the house; when it seems wholly ridiculous, the whim of an eccentric old man; and then again I'm actually afraid that I like its seclusion."

"Your seclusion is better than mine. You know my little two-room affair behind the chapel,—only a few books and a punching bag. That chapel also is one of your grandfather's whims. He provided that all the offices of the church must be said there daily or the endowment is stopped. Mr. Glenarm lived in the past, or liked to think he did. I suppose you know—or maybe you don't know—how I came to have this appointment?"

"Indeed, I should like to know."

We had reached the soup, and Bates was changing our plates with his accustomed light hand.

"It was my name that did the business,—Paul. A bishop had recommended a man whose given name was Ethelbert,—a decent enough name and one that you might imagine would appeal to Mr. Glenarm; but he rejected him because the name might too easily be cut down to Ethel, a name which, he said, was very distasteful to him."

"That is characteristic. The dear old gentleman!" I exclaimed with real feeling.

"But he reckoned without his host," Stoddard continued. "The young ladies, I have lately learned, call me Pauline, as a mark of regard or otherwise,—probably otherwise. I give two lectures a week on church history, and I fear my course isn't popular."

"But it is something, on the other hand, to be in touch with such an institution. They are a very sightly company, those girls. I enjoy watching them across the garden wall. And I had a closer view of them at the station this morning, when you ran off and deserted me."

He laughed,—his big wholesome cheering laugh.

"I take good care not to see much of them socially."

"Afraid of the eternal feminine?"

"Yes, I suppose I am. I'm preparing to go into a Brotherhood, as you probably don't know. And girls are distracting."

I glanced at my companion with a new inquiry and interest.

"I didn't know," I said.

"Yes; I'm spending my year in studies that I may never have a chance for hereafter. I'm going into an order whose members work hard."

He spoke as though he were planning a summer outing. I had not sat at meat with a clergyman since the death of my parents broke up our old home in Vermont, and my attitude toward the cloth was, I fear, one of antagonism dating from those days.

"Well, I saw Pickering after all," I remarked.

"Yes, I saw him, too. What is it in his case, genius or good luck?"

"I'm not a competent witness," I answered. "I'll be frank with you: I don't like him; I don't believe in him."

"Oh! I beg your pardon. I didn't know, of course."

"The subject is not painful to me," I hastened to add, "though he was always rather thrust before me as an ideal back in my youth, and you know how fatal that is. And then the gods of success have opened all the gates for him."

"Yes,—and yet—"

"And yet—" I repeated. Stoddard lifted a glass of sherry to the light and studied it for a moment. He did not drink wine, but was not, I found, afraid to look at it.

"And yet," he said, putting down the glass and speaking slowly, "when the gates of good fortune open too readily and smoothly, they may close sometimes rather too quickly and snap a man's coat-tails. Please don't think I'm going to afflict you with shavings of wisdom from the shop-floor, but life wasn't intended to be too easy. The spirit of man needs arresting and chastening. It doesn't flourish under too much fostering or too much of what we call good luck. I'm disposed to be afraid of good luck."

"I've never tried it," I said laughingly.

"I am not looking for it," and he spoke soberly.

I could not talk of Pickering with Bates—the masked beggar!—in the room, so I changed the subject.

"I suppose you impose penances, prescribe discipline for the girls at St. Agatha's,—an agreeable exercise of the priestly office, I should say!"

His laugh was pleasant and rang true. I was liking him better the more I saw of him.

"Bless you, no! I am not venerable enough. The Sisters attend to all that,—and a fine company of women they are!"

"But there must be obstinate cases. One of the young ladies confided to me—I tell you this in cloistral confidence—that she was being deported for insubordination."

"Ah, that must be Olivia! Well, her case is different. She is not one girl,—she is many kinds of a girl in one. I fear Sister Theresa lost her patience and hardened her heart."

"I should like to intercede for Miss Armstrong," I declared.

The surprise showed in his face, and I added:

"Pray don't misunderstand me. We met under rather curious circumstances, Miss Armstrong and I."

"She is usually met under rather unconventional circumstances, I believe," he remarked dryly. "My introduction to her came through the kitten she smuggled into the alms box of the chapel. It took me two days to find it."

He smiled ruefully at the recollection.

"She's a young woman of spirit," I declared defensively. "She simply must find an outlet for the joy of youth,—paddling a canoe, chasing rabbits through the snow, placing kittens in durance vile. But she's demure enough when she pleases,—and a satisfaction to the eye."

My heart warmed at the memory of Olivia. Verily the chaplain was right—she was many girls in one!

Stoddard dropped a lump of sugar into his coffee.

"Miss Devereux begged hard for her, but Sister Theresa couldn't afford to keep her. Her influence on the other girls was bad."

"That's to Miss Devereux's credit," I replied. "You needn't wait, Bates."

"Olivia was too popular. All the other girls indulged her. And I'll concede that she's pretty. That gipsy face of hers bodes ill to the hearts of men—if she ever grows up."

"I shouldn't exactly call it a gipsy face; and how much more should you expect her to grow? At twenty a woman's grown, isn't she?"

He looked at me quizzically.

"Fifteen, you mean! Olivia Armstrong—that little witch—the kid that has kept the school in turmoil all the fall?"

There was decided emphasis in his interrogations.

"I'm glad your glasses are full, or I should say—"

There was, I think, a little heat for a moment on both sides.

"The wires are evidently crossed somewhere," he said calmly. "*My* Olivia Armstrong is a droll child from Cincinnati, whose escapades caused her to be sent home for discipline to-day. She's a little mite who just about comes to the lapel of your coat, her eyes are as black as midnight—"

"Then she didn't talk to Pickering and his friends at the station this morning—the prettiest girl in the world—gray hat, gray coat, blue eyes? You can have *your* Olivia; but who, will you tell me, is mine?"

I pounded with my clenched hand on the table until the candles rattled and sputtered.

Stoddard stared at me for a moment as though he thought I had lost my wits. Then he lay back in his chair and roared. I rose, bending across the table toward him in my eagerness. A suspicion had leaped into my mind, and my heart was pounding as it roused a thousand questions.

"The blue-eyed young woman in gray? Bless your heart, man, Olivia is a child; I talked to her myself on the platform. *You* were talking to Miss Devereux. She isn't Olivia, she's Marian!"

"Then, who is Marian Devereux—where does she live—what is she doing here—?"

"Well," he laughed, "to answer your questions in order, she's a young woman; her home is New York; she has no near kinfolk except Sister Theresa, so she spends some of her time here."

"Teaches—music—"

"Not that I ever heard of! She does a lot of things well,—takes cups in golf tournaments and is the nimblest hand at tennis you ever saw. Also, she's a fine musician and plays the organ tremendously."

"Well, she *told* me she was Olivia!" I said.

"I should think she would, when you refused to meet her; when you had ignored her and Sister Theresa,—both of them among your grandfather's best friends, and your nearest neighbors here!"

"My grandfather be hanged! Of course I couldn't know her! We can't live on the same earth. I'm in her way, hanging on to this property here just to defeat her, when she's the finest girl alive!"

He nodded gravely, his eyes bent upon me with sympathy and kindness. The past events at Glenarm swept through my mind in kinetoscopic flashes, but the girl in gray talking to Arthur Pickering and his friends at the Annandale station, the girl in gray who had been an eavesdropper at the chapel,—the girl in gray with the eyes of blue! It seemed that a year passed before I broke the silence.

"Where has she gone?" I demanded.

He smiled, and I was cheered by the mirth that showed in his face.

"Why, she's gone to Cincinnati, with Olivia Gladys Armstrong," he said. "They're great chums, you know!"

CHAPTER XVII

SISTER THERESA

There was further information I wished to obtain, and I did not blush to pluck it from Stoddard before I let him go that night. Olivia Gladys Armstrong lived in Cincinnati; her father was a wealthy physician at Walnut Hills. Stoddard knew the family, and I asked questions about them, their antecedents and place of residence that were not perhaps impertinent in view of the fact that I had never consciously set eyes on their daughter in my life. As I look back upon it now my information secured at that time, touching the history and social position of the Armstrongs of Walnut Hills, Cincinnati, seems excessive, but the curiosity which the Reverend Paul Stoddard satisfied with so little trouble to himself was of immediate interest and importance. As to the girl in gray I found him far more difficult. She was Marian Devereux; she was a niece of Sister Theresa; her home was in New York, with another aunt, her parents being dead; and she was a frequent visitor at St. Agatha's.

213

The wayward Olivia and she were on excellent terms, and when it seemed wisest for that vivacious youngster to retire from school at the mid-year recess Miss Devereux had accompanied her home, ostensibly for a visit, but really to break the force of the blow. It was a pretty story, and enhanced my already high opinion of Miss Devereux, while at the same time I admired the unknown Olivia Gladys none the less.

When Stoddard left me I dug out of a drawer my copy of John Marshall Glenarm's will and re-read it for the first time since Pickering gave it to me in New York. There was one provision to which I had not given a single thought, and when I had smoothed the thin type-written sheets upon the table in my room I read it over and over again, construing it in a new light with every reading.

Provided, further, that in the event of the marriage of said John Glenarm to the said Marian Devereux, or in the event of any promise or contract of marriage between said persons within five years from the date of said John Glenarm's acceptance of the provisions of this will, the whole estate shall become the property absolutely of St. Agatha's School at Annandale, Wabana County, Indiana, a corporation under the laws of said state.

"Bully for the old boy!" I muttered finally, folding the copy with something akin to reverence for my grandfather's shrewdness in closing so many doors upon his heirs. It required no lawyer to interpret this paragraph. If I could not secure his estate by settling at Glenarm for a year I was not to gain it by marrying the alternative heir. Here, clearly, was not one of those situations so often contrived by novelists, in which the luckless heir presumptive, cut off without a cent, weds the pretty cousin who gets the fortune and they live happily together ever afterward. John Marshall Glenarm had explicitly provided against any such frustration of his plans.

"Bully for you, John Marshall Glenarm!" I rose and bowed low to his photograph.

On top of my mail next morning lay a small envelope, unstamped, and addressed to me in a free running hand.

"Ferguson left it," explained Bates.

I opened and read:

If convenient will Mr. Glenarm kindly look in at St. Agatha's some day this week at four o'clock. Sister Theresa wishes to see him.

I whistled softly. My feelings toward Sister Theresa had been those of utter repugnance and antagonism. I had been avoiding her studiously and was not a little surprised that she should seek an interview with me. Quite possibly she wished to inquire how soon I expected to abandon Glenarm House; or perhaps she wished to admonish me as to the perils of my soul. In any event I liked the quality of her note, and I was curious to know why she sent for me; moreover, Marian Devereux was her niece and that was wholly in the Sister's favor.

At four o'clock I passed into St. Agatha territory and rang the bell at the door of the building where I had left Olivia the evening I found her in the chapel. A Sister admitted me, led the way to a small reception-room where, I imagined, the visiting parent was received, and left me. I felt a good deal like a school-boy who has been summoned before a severe master for discipline. I was idly beating my hat with my gloves when a quick step sounded in the hall and instantly a brown-clad figure appeared in the doorway.

"Mr. Glenarm?"

It was a deep, rich voice, a voice of assurance, a voice, may I say? of the world,—a voice, too, may I add? of a woman who is likely to say what she means without ado. The white band at her forehead brought into relief two wonderful gray eyes that were alight with kindliness. She surveyed me a moment, then her lips parted in a smile.

"This room is rather forbidding; if you will come with me—"

She turned with an air of authority that was a part of her undeniable distinction, and I was seated a moment later in a pretty sitting-room, whose windows gave a view of the dark wood and frozen lake beyond.

"I'm afraid, Mr. Glenarm, that you are not disposed to be neighborly, and you must pardon me if I seem to be pursuing you."

Her smile, her voice, her manner were charming. I had pictured her a sour old woman, who had hidden away from a world that had offered her no pleasure.

"The apologies must all be on my side, Sister Theresa. I have been greatly occupied since coming here,— distressed and perplexed even."

"Our young ladies treasure the illusion that there are ghosts at your house," she said, with a smile that disposed of the matter.

She folded her slim white hands on her knees and spoke with a simple directness.

"Mr. Glenarm, there is something I wish to say to you, but I can say it only if we are to be friends. I have feared you might look upon us here as enemies."

"That is a strong word," I replied evasively.

"Let me say to you that I hope very much that nothing will prevent your inheriting all that Mr. Glenarm wished you to have from him."

"Thank you; that is both kind and generous," I said with no little surprise.

"Not in the least. I should be disloyal to your grandfather, who was my friend and the friend of my family, if I did not feel kindly toward you and wish you well. And I must say for my niece—"

"Miss Devereux." I found a certain pleasure in pronouncing her name.

"Miss Devereux is very greatly disturbed over the good intentions of your grandfather in placing her name in his will. You can doubtless understand how uncomfortable a person of any sensibility would be under the circumstances. I'm sorry you have never met her. She is a very charming young woman whose happiness does not, I may say, depend on other people's money."

She had never told, then! I smiled at the recollection of our interviews.

"I am sure that is true, Sister Theresa."

"Now I wish to speak to you about a matter of some delicacy. It is, I understand perfectly, no business of mine how much of a fortune Mr. Glenarm left. But this matter has been brought to my attention in a disagreeable way. Your grandfather established this school; he gave most of the money for these buildings. I had other friends who offered to contribute, but he insisted on doing it all. But now Mr. Pickering insists that the money—or part of it at least—was only a loan."

"Yes; I understand."

"Mr. Pickering tells me that he has no alternative in

the matter; that the law requires him to collect this money as a debt due the estate."

"That is undoubtedly true, as a general proposition. He told me in New York that he had a claim against you for fifty thousand dollars."

"Yes; that is the amount. I wish to say to you, Mr. Glenarm, that if it is necessary I can pay that amount."

"Pray do not trouble about it, Sister Theresa. There are a good many things about my grandfather's affairs that I don't understand, but I'm not going to see an old friend of his swindled. There's more in all this than appears. My grandfather seems to have mislaid or lost most of his assets before he died. And yet he had the reputation of being a pretty cautious business man."

"The impression is abroad, as you must know, that your grandfather concealed his fortune before his death. The people hereabouts believe so; and Mr. Pickering, the executor, has been unable to trace it."

"Yes, I believe Mr. Pickering has not been able to solve the problem," I said and laughed.

"But, of course, you and he will coöperate in an effort to find the lost property."

She bent forward slightly; her eyes, as they met mine, examined me with a keen interest.

"Why shouldn't I be frank with you, Sister Theresa?

I have every reason for believing Arthur Pickering a scoundrel. He does not care to coöperate with me in searching for this money. The fact is that he very much wishes to eliminate me as a factor in the settlement of the estate. I speak carefully; I know exactly what I am saying."

She bowed her head slightly and was silent for a moment. The silence was the more marked from the fact that the hood of her habit concealed her face.

"What you say is very serious."

"Yes, and his offense is equally serious. It may seem odd for me to be saying this to you when I am a stranger; when you may be pardoned for having no very high opinion of me."

She turned her face to me,—it was singularly gentle and refined,—not a face to associate with an idea of self-seeking or duplicity.

"I sent for you, Mr. Glenarm, because I had a very good opinion of you; because, for one reason, you are the grandson of your grandfather,"—and the friendly light in her gray eyes drove away any lingering doubt I may have had as to her sincerity. "I wished to warn you to have a care for your own safety. I don't warn you against Arthur Pickering alone, but against the countryside. The idea of a hidden fortune is alluring; a mysterious house and a lost treasure make a very en-

ticing combination. I fancy Mr. Glenarm did not realize that he was creating dangers for the people he wished to help."

She was silent again, her eyes bent meditatively upon me; then she spoke abruptly.

"Mr. Pickering wishes to marry my niece."

"Ah! I have been waiting to hear that. I am exceedingly glad to know that he has so noble an ambition. But Miss Devereux isn't encouraging him, as near as I can make out. She refused to go to California with his party—I happen to know that."

"That whole California episode would have been amusing if it had not been ridiculous. Marian never had the slightest idea of going with him; but she is sometimes a little—shall I say perverse?—"

"Please do! I like the word—and the quality!"

"—and Mr. Pickering's rather elaborate methods of wooing—"

"He's as heavy as lead!" I declared.

"—amuse Marian up to a certain point; then they annoy her. He has implied pretty strongly that the claim against me could be easily adjusted if Marian marries him. But she will never marry him, whether she benefits by your grandfather's will or however that may be!"

"I should say not," I declared with a warmth that caused Sister Theresa to sweep me warily with those wonderful gray eyes. "But first he expects to find this fortune and endow Miss Devereux with it. That is a part of the scheme. And my own interest in the estate must be eliminated before he can bring that condition about. But, Sister Theresa, I am not so easily got rid of as Arthur Pickering imagines. My staying qualities, which were always weak in the eyes of my family, have been braced up a trifle."

"Yes." I thought pleasure and hope were expressed in the monosyllable, and my heart warmed to her.

"Sister Theresa, you and I are understanding each other much better than I imagined we should,"—and we both laughed, feeling a real sympathy growing between us.

"Yes; I believe we are,"—and the smile lighted her face again.

"So I can tell you two things. The first is that Arthur Pickering will never find my grandfather's lost fortune, assuming that any exists. The second is that in no event will he marry your niece."

"You speak with a good deal of confidence," she said, and laughed a low murmuring laugh. I thought there was relief in it. "But I didn't suppose Marian's affairs interested you."

"They don't, Sister Theresa. Her affairs are not of the slightest importance,—but she is!"

There was frank inquiry in her eyes now.

"But you don't know her,—you have missed your opportunity."

"To be sure, I don't know her; but I know Olivia Gladys Armstrong. She's a particular friend of mine, —we have chased rabbits together, and she told me a great deal. I have formed a very good opinion of Miss Devereux in that way. Oh, that note you wrote about Olivia's intrusions beyond the wall! I should thank you for it,—but I really didn't mind."

"A note? I never wrote you a note until to-day!"

"Well, some one did!" I said; then she smiled.

"Oh, that must have been Marian. She was always Olivia's loyal friend!"

"I should say so!"

Sister Theresa laughed merrily.

"But you *shouldn't* have known Olivia,—it is unpardonable! If she played tricks upon you, you should not have taken advantage of them to make her acquaintance. That wasn't fair to me!"

"I suppose not! But I protest against this deportation. The landscape hereabouts is only so much sky, snow and lumber without her."

"We miss her, too," replied Sister Theresa. "We have less to do!"

"And still I protest!" I declared, rising. "Sister

Theresa, I thank you with all my heart for what you have said to me,—for the disposition to say it! And this debt to the estate is something, I promise you, that shall not trouble you."

"Then there's a truce between us! We are not enemies at all now, are we?"

"No; for Olivia's sake, at least, we shall be friends."

I went home and studied the time-table.

CHAPTER XVIII

GOLDEN BUTTERFLIES

If you are one of those captious people who must
verify by the calendar every new moon you read of in
a book, and if you are pained to discover the historian
lifting anchor and spreading sail contrary to the reck-
onings of the nautical almanac, I beg to call your attention to these items from the time-table of the Mid-
Western and Southern Railway for December, 1901.

The south-bound express passed Annandale at exactly
fifty-three minutes after four P. M.   It was scheduled
to reach Cincinnati at eleven o'clock sharp.   These
items are, I trust, sufficiently explicit.

To the student of morals and motives I will say a
further word.   I had resolved to practise deception in
running away from Glenarm House to keep my promise to Marian Devereux.   By leaving I should forfeit
my right to any part of my grandfather's estate; I
knew that and accepted the issue without regret; but I
had no intention of surrendering Glenarm House to
Arthur Pickering, particularly now that I realized how

completely I had placed myself in his trap. I felt, moreover, a duty to my dead grandfather ; and—not least—the attacks of Morgan and the strange ways of Bates had stirred whatever fighting blood there was in me. Pickering and I were engaged in a sharp contest, and I was beginning to enjoy it to the full, but I did not falter in my determination to visit Cincinnati, hoping to return without my absence being discovered ; so the next afternoon I began preparing for my journey.

"Bates, I fear that I'm taking a severe cold and I'm going to dose myself with whisky and quinine and go to bed. I shan't want any dinner,—nothing until you see me again."

I yawned and stretched myself with a groan.

"I'm very sorry, sir. Shan't I call a doctor?"

"Not a bit of it. I'll sleep it off and be as lively as a cricket in the morning."

At four o'clock I told him to carry some hot water and lemons to my room ; bade him an emphatic good night and locked the door as he left. Then I packed my evening clothes in a suit-case. I threw the bag and a heavy ulster from a window, swung myself out upon the limb of a big maple and let it bend under me to its harpest curve and then dropped lightly to the ground.

I passed the gate and struck off toward the village with a joyful sense of freedom. When I reached the station I sought at once the south-bound platform, not wishing to be seen buying a ticket. A few other passengers were assembling, but I saw no one I recognized. Number six, I heard the agent say, was on time; and in a few minutes it came roaring up. I bought a seat in the Washington sleeper and went into the dining-car for supper. The train was full of people hurrying to various ports for the holidays, but they had, I reflected, no advantage over me. I, too, was bound on a definite errand, though my journey was, I imagined, less commonplace in its character than the homing flight of most of my fellow travelers.

I made myself comfortable and dozed and dreamed as the train plunged through the dark. There was a wait, with much shifting of cars, where we crossed the Wabash, then we sped on. It grew warmer as we drew southward, and the conductor was confident we should reach Cincinnati on time. The through passengers about me went to bed, and I was left sprawled out in my open section, lurking on the shadowy frontier between the known world and dreamland.

"We're running into Cincinnati—ten minutes late," said the porter's voice; and in a moment I was in the vestibule and out, hurrying to a hotel. At the St. Botolph I ordered a carriage and broke all records changing my clothes. The time-table informed me that

the Northern express left at half-past one. There was
no reason why I should not be safe at Glenarm House
by my usual breakfast hour if all went well. To avoid
loss of time in returning to the station I paid the hotel
charge and carried my bag away with me.

"Doctor Armstrong's residence? Yes, sir; I've already taken one load there."

The carriage was soon climbing what seemed to be a
mountain to the heights above Cincinnati. To this day
I associate Ohio's most interesting city with a lonely
carriage ride that seemed to be chiefly uphill, through
a region that was as strange to me as a trackless jungle
in the wilds of Africa. And my heart began to perform
strange tattoos on my ribs. I was going to the house
of a gentleman who did not know of my existence, to
see a girl who was his guest, to whom I had never, as
the conventions go, been presented. It did not seem
half so easy, now that I was well launched upon the adventure.

I stopped the cabman just as he was about to enter
an iron gateway whose posts bore two great lamps.

"That is all right, sir. I can drive right in."

"But you needn't," I said, jumping out. "Wait here."

Doctor Armstrong's residence was brilliantly lighted,
and the strains of a waltz stole across the lawn cheerily.
Several carriages swept past me as I followed the walk.

I was arriving at a fashionable hour—it was nearly
twelve—and just how to effect an entrance without being thrown out as an interloper was a formidable problem, now that I had reached the house. I must catch
my train home, and this left no margin for explanation
to an outraged host whose first impulse would very
likely be to turn me over to the police.

I made a detour and studied the house, seeking a
door by which I could enter without passing the un-
friendly Gibraltar of a host and hostess on guard to
welcome belated guests.

A long conservatory filled with tropical plants gave
me my opportunity. Promenaders went idly through
and out into another part of the house by an exit I
could not see. A handsome, spectacled gentleman
opened a glass door within a yard of where I stood,
sniffed the air, and said to his companion, as he turned
back with a shrug into the conservatory:

"There's no sign of snow. It isn't Christmas weather
at all."

He strolled away through the palms, and I instantly
threw off my ulster and hat, cast them behind some
bushes, and boldly opened the door and entered.

The ball-room was on the third floor, but the guests
were straggling down to supper, and I took my stand
at the foot of the broad stairway and glanced up care-

lessly, as though waiting for some one. It was a large
and brilliant company and many a lovely face passed
me as I stood waiting. The very size of the gathering
gave me security, and I smoothed my gloves com-
placently.

The spectacled gentleman whose breath of night air
had given me a valued hint of the open conservatory
door came now and stood beside me. He even put his
hand on my arm with intimate friendliness.

There was a sound of mirth and scampering feet in
the hall above and then down the steps, between the
lines of guests arrested in their descent, came a dark
laughing girl in the garb of Little Red Riding Hood,
amid general applause and laughter.

"It's Olivia! She's won the wager!" exclaimed the
spectacled gentleman, and the girl, whose dark curls
were shaken about her face, ran up to us and threw
her arms about him and kissed him. It was a charming
picture,—the figures on the stairway, the pretty graceful child, the eager, happy faces all about. I was too
much interested by this scene of the comedy to be uncomfortable.

Then, at the top of the stair, her height accented by
her gown of white, stood Marian Devereux, hesitating
an instant, as a bird pauses before taking wing, and then
laughingly running between the lines to where Olivia

At the top of the stair, her height accented by her gown of white,
stood Marian Devereux.   *Page 230*

faced her in mock abjection. To the charm of the girl
in the woodland was added now the dignity of beautiful womanhood, and my heart leaped at the thought
that I had ever spoken to her, that I was there because
she had taunted me with the risk of coming.

Above, on the stair landing, a deep-toned clock began
to strike midnight and every one cried "Merry Christmas!" and "Olivia's won!" and there was more hand-
clapping, in which I joined with good will.

Some one behind me was explaining what had just
occurred. Olivia, the youngest daughter of the house,
had been denied a glimpse of the ball; Miss Devereux
had made a wager with her host that Olivia would appear before midnight; and Olivia had defeated the plot
against her, and gained the main hall at the stroke of
Christmas.

"Good night! Good night!" called Olivia—the real
Olivia—in derision to the company, and turned and ran
back through the applauding, laughing throng.

The spectacled gentleman was Olivia's father, and he
mockingly rebuked Marian Devereux for having en-
couraged an infraction of parental discipline, while she
was twitting him upon the loss of his wager. Then her
eyes rested upon me for the first time. She smiled
slightly, but continued talking placidly to her host.
The situation did not please me; I had not traveled so

far and burglariously entered Doctor Armstrong's house in quest of a girl with blue eyes merely to stand by while she talked to another man.

I drew nearer, impatiently; and was conscious that four other young men in white waistcoats and gloves quite as irreproachable as my own stood ready to claim her ,the instant she was free. I did not propose to be thwarted by the beaux of Cincinnati, so I stepped toward Doctor Armstrong.

"I beg your pardon, Doctor—," I said with an assurance for which I blush to this hour.

"All right, my boy; I, too, have been in Arcady!" he exclaimed in cheerful apology, and she put her hand on my arm and I led her away.

"He called me 'my boy,' so I must be passing muster," I remarked, not daring to look at her.

"He's afraid not to recognize you. His inability to remember faces is a town joke."

We reached a quiet corner of the great hall and I found a seat for her.

"You don't seem surprised to see me,—you knew I would come. I should have come across the world for this,—for just this."

Her eyes were grave at once.

"Why did you come? I did not think you were so

foolish. This is all—so wretched,—so unfortunate. You didn't know that Mr. Pickering—Mr. Pickering—"

She was greatly distressed and this name came from her chokingly.

"Yes; what of him?" I laughed. "He is well on his way to California,—and without you!"

She spoke hurriedly, eagerly, bending toward me.

"No—you don't know—you don't understand—he's here; he abandoned his California trip at Chicago; he telegraphed me to expect him—here—to-night! You must go at once,—at once!"

"Ah, but you can't frighten me," I said, trying to realize just what a meeting with Pickering in that house might mean.

"No,"—she looked anxiously about,—"they were to arrive late, he and the Taylors; they know the Armstrongs quite well. They may come at any moment now. Please go!"

"But I have only a few minutes myself,—you wouldn't have me sit them out in the station down town? There are some things I have come to say, and Arthur Pickering and I are not afraid of each other!"

"But you must not meet him here! Think what that would mean to me! You are very foolhardy, Mr. Glenarm. I had no idea you would come—"

"But you wished to try me,—you challenged me."

"That wasn't *me*,—it was Olivia," she laughed, more at ease, "I thought—"

"Yes, what did you think?" I asked. "That I was tied hand and foot by a dead man's money?"

"No, it wasn't that wretched fortune; but I enjoyed playing the child before you—I really love Olivia—and it seemed that the fairies were protecting me and that I could play being a child to the very end of the chapter without any real mischief coming of it. I wish I were Olivia!" she declared, her eyes away from me.

"That's rather idle. I'm not really sure yet what your name is, and I don't care. Let's imagine that we haven't any names,—I'm sure my name isn't of any use, and I'll be glad to go nameless all my days if only—"

"If only—" she repeated idly, opening and closing her fan. It was a frail blue trifle, painted in golden butterflies.

"There are so many 'if onlies' that I hesitate to choose; but I will venture one. If only you will come back to St. Agatha's! Not to-morrow, or the next day, but, say, with the first bluebirds. I believe they are the harbingers up there."

Her very ease was a balm to my spirit; she was now

a veritable daughter of repose. One arm in its long white sheath lay quiet in her lap; her right hand held the golden butterflies against the soft curve of her cheek. A collar of pearls clasped her throat and accented the clear girlish lines of her profile. I felt the appeal of her youth and purity. It was like a cry in my heart, and I forgot the dreary house by the lake, and Pickering and the weeks within the stone walls of my prison.

"The friends who know me best never expect me to promise to be anywhere at a given time. I can't tell; perhaps I shall follow the bluebirds to Indiana; but why should I, when I can't play being Olivia any more?"

"No! I am very dull. That note of apology you wrote from the school really fooled me. But I have seen the real Olivia now. I don't want you to go too far—not where I can't follow—this flight I shall hardly dare repeat."

Her lips closed—like a rose that had gone back to be a bud again—and she pondered a moment, slowly freeing and imprisoning the golden butterflies.

"You have risked a fortune, Mr. Glenarm, very, very foolishly,—and more—if you are found here. Why, Olivia must have recognized you! She must have seen you often across the wall."

"But I don't care—I'm not staying at that ruin up there for money. My grandfather meant more to me than that—"

"Yes; I believe that is so. He was a dear old gentleman; and he liked me because I thought his jokes adorable. My father and he had known each other. But there was—no expectation—no wish to profit by his friendship. My name in his will is a great embarrassment, a source of real annoyance. The newspapers have printed dreadful pictures of me. That is why I say to you, quite frankly, that I wouldn't accept a cent of Mr. Glenarm's money if it were offered me; and that is why,"—and her smile was a flash of spring,—"I want you to obey the terms of the will and earn your fortune."

She closed the fan sharply and lifted her eyes to mine.

"But there isn't any fortune! It's all a myth, a joke," I declared.

"Mr. Pickering doesn't seem to think so. He had every reason for believing that Mr. Glenarm was a very rich man. The property can't be found in the usual places,—banks, safety vaults, and the like. Then where do you think it is,—or better, where do you think Mr. Pickering thinks it is?"

"But assuming that it's buried up there by the lake like a pirate's treasure, it isn't Pickering's if he finds

it. There are laws to protect even the dead from rob-
bery!" I concluded hotly.

"How difficult you are! Suppose you should fall
from a boat, or be shot—accidentally—then I might
have to take the fortune after all; and Mr. Pickering
might think of an easier way of getting it than by—"

"Stealing it! Yes, but you wouldn't—!"

Half-past twelve struck on the stairway and I started
to my feet.

"You wouldn't—" I repeated.

"I might, you know!"

"I must go,—but not with that, not with any hint of
that,—please!"

"If you let him defeat you, if you fail to spend your
year there,—we'll overlook this one lapse,"—she looked
me steadily in the eyes, wholly guiltless of coquetry but
infinitely kind,—"then,—"

She paused, opened the fan, held it up to the light
and studied the golden butterflies.

"Yes—"

"Then—let me see—oh, I shall never chase another
rabbit as long as I live! Now go—quickly—quickly!"

"But you haven't told me when and where it was we
met the first time. Please!"

She laughed, but urged me away with her eyes.

"I shan't do it! It isn't proper for me to remember,

if your memory is so poor. I wonder how it would seem for us to meet just once—and be introduced! Good night! You really came. You are a gentleman of your word, Squire Glenarm!"

She gave me the tips of her fingers without looking at me.

A servant came in hurriedly.

"Miss Devereux, Mr. and Mrs. Taylor and Mr. Pickering are in the drawing-room."

"Yes; very well; I will come at once."

Then to me:

"They must not see you—there, that way!" and she stood in the door, facing me, her hands lightly toucning the frame as though to secure my way.

I turned for a last look and saw her waiting—her eyes bent gravely upon me, her arms still half-raised, barring the door; then she turned swiftly away into the hall.

Outside I found my hat and coat, and wakened my sleeping driver. He drove like mad into the city, and I swung upon the north-bound sleeper just as it was drawing out of the station.

CHAPTER XIX

I MEET AN OLD FRIEND

When I reached the house I found, to my astonishment, that the window I had left open as I scrambled out the night before was closed. I dropped my bag and crept to the front door, thinking that if Bates had discovered my absence it was useless to attempt any further deception. I was amazed to find the great doors of the main entrance flung wide, and in real alarm I ran through the hall and back to the library.

The nearest door stood open, and, as I peered in, a curious scene disclosed itself. A few of the large cathedral candles still burned brightly in several places, their flame rising strangely in the gray morning light. Books had been taken from the shelves and scattered everywhere, and sharp implements had cut ugly gashes in the shelving. The drawers containing sketches and photographs had been pulled out and their contents thrown about and trampled under foot.

The house was as silent as a tomb, but as I stood on the threshold trying to realize what had happened, something stirred by the fireplace and I crept forward, listening, until I stood by the long table beneath the great chandelier. Again I heard a sound as of some animal waking and stretching, followed by a moan that was undoubtedly human. Then the hands of a man clutched the farther edge of the table, and slowly and evidently with infinite difficulty a figure rose and the dark face of Bates, with eyes blurred and staring strangely, confronted me.

He drew his body to its height, and leaned heavily upon the table. I snatched a candle and bent toward him to make sure my eyes were not tricking me.

"Mr. Glenarm! Mr. Glenarm!" he exclaimed in broken whispers. "It is Bates, sir."

"What have you done; what has happened?" I demanded.

He put his hand to his head uncertainly and gaped as though trying to gather his wits.

He was evidently dazed by whatever had occurred, and I sprang around and helped him to a couch. He would not lie down but sat up, staring and passing his hand over his head. It was rapidly growing lighter, and I saw a purple and black streak across his temple where a bludgeon of some sort had struck him.

"What does this mean, Bates? Who has been in the house?"

"I can't tell you, Mr. Glenarm."

"Can't tell me! You will tell me or go to jail!

There's been mischief done here and I don't intend to have any nonsense about it from you. Well—?"

He was clearly suffering, but in my anger at the sight of the wreck of the room I grasped his shoulder and shook him roughly.

"It was early this morning," he faltered, "about two o'clock, I heard noises in the lower part of the house. I came down thinking likely it was you, and remembering that you had been sick yesterday—"

"Yes, go on."

The thought of my truancy was no balm to my conscience just then.

"As I came into the hall, I saw lights in the library. As you weren't down last night the room hadn't been lighted at all. I heard steps, and some one tapping with a hammer—"

"Yes; a hammer. Go on!"

It was, then, the same old story! The war had been carried openly into the house, but Bates,—just why should any one connected with the conspiracy injure Bates, who stood so near to Pickering, its leader? The fellow was undoubtedly hurt,—there was no mistaking the lump on his head. He spoke with a painful difficulty that was not assumed, I felt increasingly sure, as he went on.

"I saw a man pulling out the books and tapping the

inside of the shelves. He was working very fast. And the next thing I knew he let in another man through one of the terrace doors,—the one there that still stands a little open."

He flinched as he turned slightly to indicate it, and his face twitched with pain.

"Never mind that; tell the rest of your story."

"Then I ran in, grabbed one of the big candelabra from the table, and went for the nearest man. They were about to begin on the chimney-breast there,—it was Mr. Glenarm's pride in all the house,—and that accounts for my being there in front of the fireplace. They rather got the best of me, sir."

"Clearly; I see they did. You had a hand-to-hand fight with them, and being two to one—"

"No; there were two of *us*,—don't you understand, two of us! There was another man who came running in from somewhere, and he took sides with me. I thought at first it was you. The robbers thought so, too, for one of them yelled, 'Great God; it's Glenarm!' just like that. But it wasn't you, but quite another person."

"That's a good story so far; and then what happened?"

"I don't remember much more, except that some one soused me with water that helped my head considerably, and the next thing I knew I was staring across the table there at you."

"Who were these men, Bates? Speak up quickly!"

My tone was peremptory. Here was, I felt, a crucial moment in our relations.

"Well," he began deliberately, "I dislike to make charges against a fellow man, but I strongly suspect one of the men of being—"

"Yes! Tell the whole truth or it will be the worse for you."

"I very much fear one of them was Ferguson, the gardener over the way. I'm disappointed in him, sir."

"Very good; and now for the other one."

"I didn't get my eyes on him. I had closed with Ferguson and we were having quite a lively time of it when the other one came in; then the man who came to my help mixed us all up,—he was a very lively person,—and what became of Ferguson and the rest of it I don't know."

There was food for thought in what he said. He had taken punishment in defense of my property—the crack on his head was undeniable—and I could not abuse him or question his veracity with any grace; not, at least, without time for investigation and study. However, I ventured to ask him one question.

"If you were guessing, shouldn't you think it quite likely that Morgan was the other man?"

He met my gaze squarely.

"I think it wholly possible, Mr. Glenarm."

"And the man who helped you—who in the devil was he?"

"Bless me, I don't know. He disappeared. I'd like mightily to see him again."

"Humph! Now you'd better do something for your head. I'll summon the village doctor if you say so."

"No; thank you, sir. I'll take care of it myself."

"And now we'll keep quiet about this. Don't mention it or discuss it with any one."

"Certainly not, sir."

He rose, and staggered a little, but crossed to the broad mantel-shelf in the great chimney-breast, rested his arm upon it for a moment, passed his hand over the dark wood with a sort of caress, then bent his eyes upon the floor littered with books and drawings and papers torn from the cabinets and all splashed with tallow and wax from the candles. The daylight had increased until the havoc wrought by the night's visitors was fully apparent. The marauders had made a sorry mess of the room, and I thought Bates' lip quivered as he saw the wreck.

"It would have been a blow to Mr. Glenarm; the room was his pride,—his pride, sir."

He went out toward the kitchen, and I ran up stairs to my own room. I cursed the folly that had led me to leave my window open, for undoubtedly Morgan and his new ally, St. Agatha's gardener, had taken advantage of it to enter the house. Quite likely, too, they had observed my absence, and this would undoubtedly be communicated to Pickering. I threw open my door and started back with an exclamation of amazement.

Standing at my chiffonnier, between two windows, was a man, clad in a bath-gown—my own, I saw with fury—his back to me, the razor at his face, placidly shaving himself.

Without turning he addressed me, quite coolly and casually, as though his being there was the most natural thing in the world.

"Good morning, Mr. Glenarm! Rather damaging evidence, that costume. I suppose it's the custom of the country for gentlemen in evening clothes to go out by the window and return by the door. You might think the other way round preferable."

"Larry!" I shouted.

"Jack!"

"Kick that door shut and lock it," he commanded, in

a sharp, severe tone that I remembered well—and just now welcomed—in him.

"How, why and when—?"

"Never mind about me. I'm here—thrown the enemy off for a few days; and you give me lessons in current history first, while I climb into my armor. Pray pardon the informality—"

He seized a broom and began work upon a pair of trousers to which mud and briers clung tenaciously. His coat and hat lay on a chair, they, too, much the worse for rough wear.

There was never any use in refusing to obey Larry's orders, and as he got into his clothes I gave him in as few words as possible the chief incidents that had marked my stay at Glenarm House. He continued dressing with care, helping himself to a shirt and collar from my chiffonnier and choosing with unfailing eye the best tie in my collection. Now and then he asked a question tersely, or, again, he laughed or swore direly in Gaelic. When I had concluded the story of Pickering's visit, and of the conversation I overheard between the executor and Bates in the church porch, Larry wheeled round with the scarf half-tied in his fingers and surveyed me commiseratingly.

"And you didn't rush them both on the spot and have it out?"

"No. I was too much taken aback, for one thing—"

"I dare say you were !"

"And for another I didn't think the time ripe. I'm going to beat that fellow, Larry, but I want him to show his hand fully before we come to a smash-up. I know as much about the house and its secrets as he does, —that's one consolation. Sometimes I don't believe there's a shilling here, and again I'm sure there's a big stake in it. The fact that Pickering is risking so much to find what's supposed to be hidden here is pretty fair evidence that something's buried on the place."

"Possibly, but they're giving you a lively boycott. Now where in the devil have you been?"

"Well,—" I began and hesitated. I had not mentioned Marian Devereux and this did not seem the time for confidences of that sort.

He took a cigarette from his pocket and lighted it.

"Bah, these women! Under the terms of your revered grandfather's will you have thrown away all your rights. It looks to me, as a member of the Irish bar in bad standing, as though you had delivered yourself up to the enemy, so far as the legal situation is concerned. How does it strike you?"

"Of course I've forfeited my rights. But I don't mean that any one shall know it yet a while."

"My lad, don't deceive yourself. Everybody round

here will know it before night. You ran off, left your window open invitingly, and two gentlemen who meditated breaking in found that they needn't take the trouble. One came in through your own room, noting, of course, your absence, let in his friend below, and tore up the place regrettably."

"Yes, but how did you get here?—if you don't mind telling."

"It's a short story. That little chap from Scotland Yard, who annoyed me so much in New York and drove me to Mexico—for which may he dwell for ever in fiery torment—has never given up. I shook him off, though, at Indianapolis three days ago. I bought a ticket for Pittsburg with him at my elbow. I suppose he thought the chase was growing tame, and that the farther east he could arrest me the nearer I should be to a British consul and tide-water. I went ahead of him into the station and out to the Pittsburg sleeper. I dropped my bag into my section—if that's what they call it in your atrocious American language—looked out and saw him coming along the platform. Just then the car began to move,—they were shunting it about to attach a sleeper that had been brought in from Louisville, and my carriage, or whatever you call it, went skimming out of the sheds into a yard where everything seemed to be most noisy and complex. I dropped off in the dark

just before they began to haul the carriage back. A
long train of empty goods wagons was just pulling
out and I threw my bag into a wagon and climbed after
it. We kept going for an hour or so until I was thoroughly lost, then I took advantage of a stop at a place
that seemed to be the end of terrestrial things, got out
and started across country. I expressed my bag to you
the other day from a town that rejoiced in the cheering
name of Kokomo, just to get rid of it. I walked into
Annandale about midnight, found this medieval marvel
through the kindness of the station-master and was re-
connoitering with my usual caution when I saw a gentleman romantically entering through an open window."

Larry paused to light a fresh cigarette.

"You always did have a way of arriving opportunely.
Go on!"

"It pleased my fancy to follow him; and by the time
I had studied your diggings here a trifle, things began to happen below. It sounded like a St. Patrick's
Day celebration in an Irish village, and I went down at
a gallop to see if there was any chance of breaking in.
Have you seen the room? Well,"—he gave several
turns to his right wrist, as though to test it,—"we all
had a jolly time there by the fireplace. Another chap
had got in somewhere, so there were two of them. Your
man—I suppose it's your man—was defending himself

gallantly with a large thing of brass that looked like the pipes of a grand organ—and I sailed in with a chair. My presence seemed to surprise the attacking party, who evidently thought I was you,—flattering, I must say, to me!"

"You undoubtedly saved Bates' life and prevented the rifling of the house. And after you had poured water on Bates,—he's the servant,—you came up here—"

"That's the way of it."

"You're a brick, Larry Donovan. There's only one of you; and now—"

"And now, John Glenarm, we've got to get down to business,—or you must. As for me, after a few hours of your enlivening society—"

"You don't go a step until we go together,—no, by the beard of the prophet! I've a fight on here and I'm going to win if I die in the struggle, and you've got to stay with me to the end."

"But under the will you dare not take a boarder."

"Of course I dare! That will's as though it had never been as far as I'm concerned. My grandfather never expected me to sit here alone and be murdered. John Marshall Glenarm wasn't a fool exactly!"

"No, but a trifle queer, I should say. I don't have to tell you, old man, that this situation appeals to me.

It's my kind of a job. If it weren't that the hounds are at my heels I'd like to stay with you, but you have enough trouble on hands without opening the house to an attack by my enemies."

"Stop talking about it. I don't propose to be deserted by the only friend I have in the world when I'm up to my eyes in trouble. Let's go down and get some coffee."

We found Bates trying to remove the evidences of the night's struggle. He had fastened a cold pack about his head and limped slightly; otherwise he was the same— silent and inexplicable.

Daylight had not improved the appearance of the room. Several hundred books lay scattered over the floor, and the shelves which had held them were hacked and broken.

"Bates, if you can give us some coffee—? Let the room go for the present."

"Yes, sir."

"And Bates—"

He paused and Larry's keen eyes were bent sharply upon him.

"Mr. Donovan is a friend who will be with me for some time. We'll fix up his room later in the day."

He limped out, Larry's eyes following him.

"What do you think of that fellow?" I asked.

Larry's face wore a puzzled look.

"What do you call him,—Bates? He's a plucky fellow."

Larry picked up from the hearth the big candelabrum with which Bates had defended himself. It was badly bent and twisted, and Larry grinned.

"The fellow who went out through the front door probably isn't feeling very well to-day. Your man was swinging this thing like a windmill."

"I can't understand it," I muttered. "I can't, for the life of me, see why he should have given battle to the enemy. They all belong to Pickering, and Bates is the biggest rascal of the bunch."

"Humph! we'll consider that later. And would you mind telling me what kind of a tallow foundry this is? I never saw so many candlesticks in my life. I seem to taste tallow. I had no letters from you, and I supposed you were loafing quietly in a grim farm-house, dying of ennui, and here you are in an establishment that ought to be the imperial residence of an Eskimo chief. Possibly you have crude petroleum for soup and whipped salad-oil for dessert. I declare, a man living here ought to attain a high candle-power of luminosity. It's perfectly immense." He stared and laughed. "And hidden treasure, and night attacks, and young virgins in the middle distance,—yes, I'd really like to stay a while."

As we ate breakfast I filled in gaps I had left in my hurried narrative, with relief that I can not describe filling my heart as I leaned again upon the sympathy of an old and trusted friend.

As Bates came and went I marked Larry's scrutiny of the man. I dismissed him as soon as possible that we might talk freely.

"Take it up and down and all around, what do you think of all this?" I asked.

Larry was silent for a moment; he was not given to careless speech in personal matters.

"There's more to it than frightening you off or getting your grandfather's money. It's my guess that there's something in this house that somebody—Pickering supposedly—is very anxious to find."

"Yes; I begin to think so. He could come in here legally if it were merely a matter of searching for lost assets."

"Yes; and whatever it is it must be well hidden. As I remember, your grandfather died in June. You got a letter calling you home in October."

"It was sent out blindly, with not one chance in a hundred that it would ever reach me."

"To be sure. You were a wanderer on the face of the

earth, and there was nobody in America to look after your interests. You may be sure that the place was thoroughly ransacked while you were sailing home. I'll wager you the best dinner you ever ate that there's more at stake than your grandfather's money. The situation is inspiring. I grow interested. I'm almost persuaded to linger."

CHAPTER XX

Larry refused to share my quarters and chose a room for himself, which Bates fitted up out of the house stores. I did not know what Bates might surmise about Larry, but he accepted my friend in good part, as a guest who would remain indefinitely. He seemed to interest Larry, whose eyes followed the man inquiringly. When we went into Bates' room on our tour of the house, Larry scanned the books on a little shelf with something more than a casual eye. There were exactly four volumes,—Shakespeare's Comedies, *The Faerie Queen,* Sterne's *Sentimental Journey* and Yeats' *Land of Heart's Desire.*

"A queer customer, Larry. Nobody but my grandfather could ever have discovered him—he found him up in Vermont."

"I suppose his being a bloomin' Yankee naturally accounts for this," remarked Larry, taking from under the pillow of the narrow iron bed a copy of the Dublin *Freeman's Journal.*

"It is a little odd," I said. "But if you found a Yiddish newspaper or an Egyptian papyrus under his pillow I should not be surprised."

"Nor I," said Larry. "I'll wager that not another shelf in this part of the world contains exactly that collection of books, and nothing else. You will notice that there was once a book-plate in each of these volumes and that it's been scratched out with care."

On a small table were pen and ink and a curious much-worn portfolio.

"He always gets the mail first, doesn't he?" asked Larry.

"Yes, I believe he does."

"I thought so; and I'll swear he never got a letter from Vermont in his life."

When we went down Bates was limping about the library, endeavoring to restore order.

"Bates," I said to him, "you are a very curious person. I have had a thousand and one opinions about you since I came here, and I still don't make you out."

He turned from the shelves, a defaced volume in his hands.

"Yes, sir. It was a good deal that way with your lamented grandfather. He always said I puzzled him."

Larry, safe behind the fellow's back, made no attempt to conceal a smile.

"I want to thank you for your heroic efforts to protect the house last night. You acted nobly, and I must
confess, Bates, that I didn't think it was in you. You've
got the right stuff in you; I'm only sorry that there are
black pages in your record that I can't reconcile with
your manly conduct of last night. But we've got to
come to an understanding."

"Yes, sir."

"The most outrageous attacks have been made on me
since I came here. You know what I mean well enough.
Mr. Glenarm never intended that I should sit down in
his house and be killed or robbed. He was the gentlest
being that ever lived, and I'm going to fight for his
memory and to protect his property from the scoundrels
who have plotted against me. I hope you follow me."

"Yes, Mr. Glenarm." He was regarding me atten-
tively. His lips quavered, perhaps from weakness, for
he certainly looked ill.

"Now I offer you your choice,—either to stand loyally
by me and my grandfather's house or to join these
scoundrels Arthur Pickering has hired to drive me out.
I'm not going to bribe you,—I don't offer you a cent for
standing by me, but I won't have a traitor in the house,
and if you don't like me or my terms I want you to go
and go now."

He straightened quickly,—his eyes lighted and the

color crept into his face. I had never before seen him appear so like a human being.

"Mr. Glenarm, you have been hard on me; there have been times when you have been very unjust—"

"Unjust,—my God, what do you expect me to take from you! Haven't I known that you were in league with Pickering? I'm not as dull as I look, and after your interview with Pickering in the chapel porch you can't convince me that you were faithful to my interests at that time."

He started and gazed at me wonderingly. I had had no intention of using the chapel porch interview at this time, but it leaped out of me uncontrollably.

"I suppose, sir," he began brokenly, "that I can hardly persuade you that I meant no wrong on that occasion."

"You certainly can not,—and it's safer for you not to try. But I'm willing to let all that go as a reward for your work last night. Make your choice now; stay here and stop your spying or clear out of Annandale within an hour."

He took a step toward me; the table was between us and he drew quite near but stood clear of it, erect until there was something almost soldierly and commanding in his figure.

"By God, I will stand by *you*, John Glenarm!" he

said, and struck the table smartly with his clenched hand.

He flushed instantly, and I felt the blood mounting into my own face as we gazed at each other,—he, Bates, the servant, and I, his master! He had always addressed me so punctiliously with the "sir" of respect that his declaration of fealty, spoken with so sincere and vigorous an air of independence, and with the bold emphasis of the oath, held me spellbound, staring at him. The silence was broken by Larry, who sprang forward and grasped Bates' hand.

"I, too, Bates," I said, feeling my heart leap with liking, even with admiration for the real manhood that seemed to transfigure this hireling,—this fellow whom I had charged with most infamous treachery, this servant who had cared for my needs in so humble a spirit of subjection.

The knocker on the front door sounded peremptorily, and Bates turned away without another word, and admitted Stoddard, who came in hurriedly.

"Merry Christmas!" in his big hearty tones was hardly consonant with the troubled look on his face. I introduced him to Larry and asked him to sit down.

"Pray excuse our disorder,—we didn't do it for fun; it was one of Santa Claus' tricks."

He stared about wonderingly.

"So you caught it, too, did you?"

"To be sure. You don't mean to say that they raided the chapel?"

"That's exactly what I mean to say. When I went into the church for my early service I found that some one had ripped off the wainscoting in a half a dozen places and even pried up the altar. It's the most outrageous thing I ever knew. You've heard of the proverbial poverty of the church mouse,—what do you suppose anybody could want to raid a simple little country chapel for? And more curious yet, the church plate was untouched, though the closet where it's kept was upset, as though the miscreants had been looking for something they didn't find."

Stoddard was greatly disturbed, and gazed about the topsy-turvy library with growing indignation.

We drew together for a council of war. Here was an opportunity to enlist a new recruit on my side. I already felt stronger by reason of Larry's accession; as to Bates, my mind was still numb and bewildered.

"Larry, there's no reason why we shouldn't join forces with Mr. Stoddard, as he seems to be affected by this struggle. We owe it to him and the school to put him on guard, particularly since we know that Ferguson's with the enemy."

"Yes, certainly," said Larry.

He always liked or disliked new people unequivocally, and I was glad to see that he surveyed the big clergyman with approval.

"I'll begin at the beginning," I said, "and tell you the whole story."

He listened quietly to the end while I told him of my experience with Morgan, of the tunnel into the chapel crypt, and finally of the affair in the night and our interview with Bates.

"I feel like rubbing my eyes and accusing you of reading penny-horrors," he said. "That doesn't sound like the twentieth century in Indiana."

"But Ferguson,—you'd better have a care in his direction. Sister Theresa—"

"Bless your heart! Ferguson's gone—without notice. He got his traps and skipped without saying a word to any one."

"We'll hear from him again, no doubt. Now, gentlemen, I believe we understand one another. I don't like to draw you, either one of you, into my private affairs—"

The big chaplain laughed.

"Glenarm,"—prefixes went out of commission quickly that morning,—"if you hadn't let me in on this I should never have got over it. Why, this is a page out of the good old times! Bless me! I never appreciated your grandfather! I must run—I have another service. But I hope you gentlemen will call on me, day or night, for anything I can do to help you. Please don't forget me. I had the record once for putting the shot."

"Why not give our friend escort through the tunnel?" asked Larry. "I'll not hesitate to say that I'm dying to see it."

"To be sure!" We went down into the cellar, and poked over the lantern and candlestick collections, and I pointed out the exact spot where Morgan and I had indulged in our revolver duel. It was fortunate that the plastered walls of the cellar showed clearly the cuts and scars of the pistol-balls or I fear my story would have fallen on incredulous ears.

The debris I had piled upon the false block of stone in the cellar lay as I had left it, but the three of us quickly freed the trap. The humor of the thing took strong hold of my new allies, and while I was getting a lantern to light us through the passage Larry sat on the edge of the trap and howled a few bars of a wild Irish jig. We set forth at once and found the passage unchanged. When the cold air blew in upon us I paused.

"Have you gentlemen the slightest idea of where you are?"

"We must be under the school-grounds, I should say," replied Stoddard.

"We're exactly under the stone wall. Those tall posts at the gate are a scheme for keeping fresh air in the passage."

"You certainly have all the modern improvements," observed Larry, and I heard him chuckling all the way to the crypt door.

When I pushed the panel open and we stepped out into the crypt Stoddard whistled and Larry swore softly.

"It must be *for* something!" exclaimed the chaplain. "You don't suppose Mr. Glenarm built a secret passage just for the fun of it, do you? He must have had some purpose. Why, I sleep out here within forty yards of where we stand and I never had the slightest idea of this."

"But other people seem to know of it," observed Larry.

"To be sure; the curiosity of the whole countryside was undoubtedly piqued by the building of Glenarm House. The fact that workmen were brought from a distance was in itself enough to arouse interest. Morgan seems to have discovered the passage without any trouble."

"More likely it was Ferguson. He was the sexton of

the church and had a chance to investigate," said Stoddard. "And now, gentlemen, I must go to my service. I'll see you again before the day is over."

"And we make no confidences!" I admonished.

"'Sdeath!—I believe that is the proper expression under all the circumstances." And the Reverend Paul Stoddard laughed, clasped my hand and went up into the chapel vestry.

I closed the door in the wainscoting and hung the map back in place.

We went up into the little chapel and found a small company of worshipers assembled,—a few people from the surrounding farms, half a dozen Sisters sitting somberly near the chancel and the school servants.

Stoddard came out into the chancel, lighted the altar tapers and began the Anglican communion office. I had forgotten what a church service was like; and Larry, I felt sure, had not attended church since the last time his family had dragged him to choral vespers.

It was comforting to know that here was, at least, one place of peace within reach of Glenarm House. But I may be forgiven, I hope, if my mind wandered that morning, and my thoughts played hide-and-seek with memory. For it was here, in the winter twilight, that Marian Devereux had poured out her girl's heart in a great flood of melody. I was glad that the organ was closed; it would have wrung my heart to hear a note from it that her hands did not evoke.

When we came out upon the church porch and I stood on the steps to allow Larry to study the grounds, one of the brown-robed Sisterhood spoke my name.

It was Sister Theresa.

"Can you come in for a moment?" she asked.

"I will follow at once," I said.

She met me in the reception-room where I had seen her before.

"I'm sorry to trouble you on Christmas Day with my affairs, but I have had a letter from Mr. Pickering, saying that he will be obliged to bring suit for settlement of my account with Mr. Glenarm's estate. I needn't say that this troubles me greatly. In my position a lawsuit is uncomfortable; it would do a real harm to the school. Mr. Pickering implies in a very disagreeable way that I exercised an undue influence over Mr. Glenarm. You can readily understand that that is not a pleasant accusation."

"He is going pretty far," I said.

"He gives me credit for a degree of power over others that I regret to say I do not possess. He thinks, for instance, that I am responsible for Miss Devereux's attitude toward him,—something that I have had nothing whatever to do with."

"No, of course not."

"I'm glad you have no harsh feeling toward her. It was unfortunate that Mr. Glenarm saw fit to mention her in his will. It has given her a great deal of notoriety, and has doubtless strengthened the impression in some minds that she and I really plotted to get as much as possible of your grandfather's estate."

"No one would regret all this more than my grandfather,—I am sure of that. There are many inexplicable things about his affairs. It seems hardly possible that a man so shrewd as he, and so thoughtful of the feelings of others, should have left so many loose ends behind him. But I assure you I am giving my whole attention to these matters, and I am wholly at your service in anything I can do to help you."

"I sincerely hope that nothing may interfere to prevent your meeting Mr. Glenarm's wish that you remain through the year. That was a curious and whimsical provision, but it is not, I imagine, so difficult."

She spoke in a kindly tone of encouragement that made me feel uneasy and almost ashamed for having already forfeited my claim under the will. Her beautiful gray eyes disconcerted me; I had not the heart to deceive her.

"I have already made it impossible for me to inherit under the will," I said.

The disappointment in her face rebuked me sharply.

"I am sorry, very sorry, indeed," she said coldly. "But how, may I ask?"

"I ran away, last night. I went to Cincinnati to see Miss Devereux."

She rose, staring in dumb astonishment, and after a full minute in which I tried vainly to think of something to say, I left the house.

There is nothing in the world so tiresome as explanations, and I have never in my life tried to make them without floundering into seas of trouble.

CHAPTER XXI

PICKERING SERVES NOTICE

The next morning Bates placed a letter postmarked Cincinnati at my plate. I opened and read it aloud to Larry:

On Board the Heloise

December 25, 1901.

John Glenarm, Esq.,
        Glenarm House,
                Annandale, Wabana Co., Indiana:

DEAR SIR—I have just learned from what I believe to be a trustworthy source that you have already violated the terms of the agreement under which you entered into residence on the property near Annandale, known as Glenarm House. The provisions of the will of John Marshall Glenarm are plain and unequivocal, as you undoubtedly understood when you accepted them, and your absence, not only from the estate itself, but from Wabana County, violates beyond question your right to inherit.

I, as executor, therefore demand that you at once vacate said property, leaving it in as good condition as when received by you.   Very truly yours,

ARTHUR PICKERING,
Executor of the Estate of John Marshall Glenarm.

"Very truly the devil's," growled Larry, snapping his cigarette case viciously.

268

"How did he find out?" I asked lamely, but my heart sank like lead. Had Marian Devereux told him! How else could he know?

"Probably from the stars,—the whole universe undoubtedly saw you skipping off to meet your lady-love. Bah, these women!"

"Tut! They don't all marry the sons of brewers," I retorted. "You assured me once, while your affair with that Irish girl was on, that the short upper lip made Heaven seem possible, but unnecessary; then the next thing I knew she had shaken you for the bloated maltster. Take that for your impertinence. But perhaps it was Bates?"

I did not wait for an answer. I was not in a mood for reflection or nice distinctions. The man came in just then with a fresh plate of toast.

"Bates, Mr. Pickering has learned that I was away from the house on the night of the attack, and I'm ordered off for having broken my agreement to stay here. How do you suppose he heard of it so promptly?"

"From Morgan, quite possibly. I have a letter from Mr. Pickering myself this morning. Just a moment, sir."

He placed before me a note bearing the same date as my own. It was a sharp rebuke of Bates for his failure to report my absence, and he was ordered to prepare to leave on the first of February. "Close your accounts at the shopkeepers' and I will audit your bills on my arrival."

The tone was peremptory and contemptuous. Bates had failed to satisfy Pickering and was flung off like a smoked-out cigar.

"How much had he allowed you for expenses, Bates?"

He met my gaze imperturbably.

"He paid me fifty dollars a month as wages, sir, and I was allowed seventy-five for other expenses."

"But you didn't buy English pheasants and champagne on that allowance!"

He was carrying away the coffee tray and his eyes wandered to the windows.

"Not quite, sir. You see—"

"But I don't see!"

"It had occurred to me that as Mr. Pickering's allowance wasn't what you might call generous it was better to augment it— Well, sir, I took the liberty of advancing a trifle, as you might say, to the estate. Your grandfather would not have had you starve, sir."

He left hurriedly, as though to escape from the consequences of his words, and when I came to myself Larry was gloomily invoking his strange Irish gods.

"Larry Donovan, I've been tempted to kill that fel-

low a dozen times! This thing is too damned compli-
cated for me. I wish my lamented grandfather had left
me something easy. To think of it—that fellow, after
my treatment of him—my cursing and abusing him
since I came here! Great Scott, man, I've been enjoying his bounty, I've been living on his money! And
all the time he's been trusting in me, just because of
his dog-like devotion to my grandfather's memory.
Lord, I can't face the fellow again!"

"As I have said before, you're rather lacking at times
in perspicacity. Your intelligence is marred by large
opaque spots. Now that there's a woman in the case
you're less sane than ever. Bah, these women! And
now we've got to go to work."

Bah, these women! My own heart caught the words.
I was enraged and bitter. No wonder she had been
anxious for me to avoid Pickering after daring me to
follow her!

We called a council of war for that night that we
might view matters in the light of Pickering's letter.
His assuredness in ordering me to leave made prompt
and decisive action necessary on my part. I summoned
Stoddard to our conference, feeling confident of his
friendliness.

"Of course," said the broad-shouldered chaplain, "if

you could show that your absence was on business of very grave importance, the courts might construe in that you had not really violated the will."

Larry looked at the ceiling and blew rings of smoke languidly. I had not disclosed to either of them the cause of my absence. On such a matter I knew I should get precious little sympathy from Larry, and I had, moreover, a feeling that I could not discuss Marian Devereux with any one; I even shrank from mentioning her name, though it rang like the call of bugles in my blood.

She was always before me,—the charmed spirit of youth, linked to every foot of the earth, every gleam of the sun upon the ice-bound lake, every glory of the winter sunset. All the good impulses I had ever stifled were quickened to life by the thought of her. Amid the day's perplexities I started sometimes, thinking I heard her voice, her girlish laughter, or saw her again coming toward me down the stairs, or holding against the light her fan with its golden butterflies. I really knew so little of her; I could associate her with no home, only with that last fling of the autumn upon the lake, the snow-driven woodland, that twilight hour at the organ in the chapel, those stolen moments at the Armstrongs'. I resented the pressure of the hour's affairs, and chafed at the necessity for talking of my perplexities with the good friends who were there to help. I wished to be alone, to yield to the sweet mood that the thought of her brought me. The doubt that crept through my mind as to any possibility of connivance between her and Pickering was as vague and fleeting as the shadow of a swallow's wing on a sunny meadow.

"You don't intend fighting the fact of your absence, do you?" demanded Larry, after a long silence.

"Of course not!" I replied quietly. "Pickering was right on my heels, and my absence was known to his men here. And it would not be square to my grandfather,—who never harmed a flea, may his soul rest in blessed peace!—to lie about it. They might nail me for perjury besides."

"Then the quicker we get ready for a siege the better. As I understand your attitude, you don't propose to move out until you've found where the siller's hidden. Being a gallant gentleman and of a forgiving nature, you want to be sure that the lady who is now entitled to it gets all there is coming to her, and as you don't trust the executor, any further than a true Irishman trusts a British prime minister's promise, you're going to stand by to watch the boodle counted. Is that a correct analysis of your intentions?"

"That's as near one of my ideas as you're likely to get, Larry Donovan!"

"And if he comes with the authorities,—the sheriff and that sort of thing,—we must prepare for such an emergency," interposed the chaplain.

"So much the worse for the sheriff and the rest of them!" I declared.

"Spoken like a man of spirit. And now we'd better stock up at once, in case we should be shut off from our source of supplies. This is a lonely place here; even the school is a remote neighbor. Better let Bates raid the village shops to-morrow. I've tried being hungry, and I don't care to repeat the experience."

And Larry reached for the tobacco jar.

"I can't imagine, I really can't believe," began the chaplain, "that Miss Devereux will want to be brought into this estate matter in any way. In fact, I have heard Sister Theresa say as much. I suppose there's no way of preventing a man from leaving his property to a young woman, who has no claim on him,—who doesn't want anything from him."

"Bah, these women! People don't throw legacies to the birds these days. Of course she'll take it."

Then his eyes widened and met mine in a gaze that reflected the mystification and wonder that struck both of us. Stoddard turned from the fire suddenly:

"What's that? There's some one up stairs!"

Larry was already running toward the hall, and I heard him springing up the steps like a cat, while Stoddard and I followed.

"Where's Bates?" demanded the chaplain.

"I'll thank you for the answer," I replied.

Larry stood at the top of the staircase, holding a candle at arm's length in front of him, staring about.

We could hear quite distinctly some one walking on a stairway; the sounds were unmistakable, just as I had heard them on several previous occasions, without ever being able to trace their source.

The noise ceased suddenly, leaving us with no hint of its whereabouts.

I went directly to the rear of the house and found Bates putting the dishes away in the pantry.

"Where have you been?" I demanded.

"Here, sir; I have been clearing up the dinner things, Mr. Glenarm. Is there anything the matter, sir?"

"Nothing."

I joined the others in the library.

"Why didn't you tell me this feudal imitation was haunted?" asked Larry, in a grieved tone. "All it needed was a cheerful ghost, and now I believe it lacks absolutely nothing. I'm increasingly glad I came. How often does it walk?"

"It's not on a schedule. Just now it's the wind in the tower probably; the wind plays queer pranks up there sometimes."

"You'll have to do better than that, Glenarm," said Stoddard. "It's as still outside as a country grave-yard."

"Only the *slaugh sidhe,* the people of the faery hills, the cheerfulest ghosts in the world," said Larry. "You literal Saxons can't grasp the idea, of course."

But there was substance enough in our dangers without pursuing shadows. Certain things were planned that night. We determined to exercise every precaution to prevent a surprise from without, and we resolved upon a new and systematic sounding of walls and floors, taking our clue from the efforts made by Morgan and his ally to find hiding-places by this process. Pickering would undoubtedly arrive shortly, and we wished to anticipate his movements as far as possible.

We resolved, too, upon a day patrol of the grounds and a night guard. The suggestion came, I believe, from Stoddard, whose interest in my affairs was only equaled by the fertility of his suggestions. One of us should remain abroad at night, ready to sound the alarm in case of attack. Bates should take his turn with the rest—Stoddard insisted on it.

Within two days we were, as Larry expressed it, on a

war footing. We added a couple of shot-guns and several revolvers to my own arsenal, and piled the library table with cartridge boxes. Bates, acting as quartermaster, brought a couple of wagon-loads of provisions. Stoddard assembled a remarkable collection of heavy sticks; he had more confidence in them, he said, than in gunpowder, and, moreover, he explained, a priest might not with propriety bear arms.

It was a cheerful company of conspirators that now gathered around the big hearth. Larry, always restless, preferred to stand at one side, an elbow on the mantel-shelf, pipe in mouth; and Stoddard sought the biggest chair,—and filled it. He and Larry understood each other at once, and Larry's stories, ranging in subject from undergraduate experiences at Dublin to adventures in Africa and always including endless conflicts with the Irish constabulary, delighted the big boyish clergyman.

Often, at some one's suggestion of a new idea, we ran off to explore the house again in search of the key to the Glenarm riddle, and always we came back to the library with that riddle still unsolved.

CHAPTER XXII

THE RETURN OF MARIAN DEVEREUX

"Sister Theresa has left, sir."

Bates had been into Annandale to mail some letters, and I was staring out upon the park from the library windows when he entered. Stoddard, having kept watch the night before, was at home asleep, and Larry was off somewhere in the house, treasure-hunting. I was feeling decidedly discouraged over our failure to make any progress with our investigations, and Bates' news did not interest me.

"Well, what of it?" I demanded, without turning round.

"Nothing, sir; but Miss Devereux has come back!"

"The devil!"

I turned and took a step toward the door.

"I said Miss Devereux," he repeated in dignified rebuke. "She came up this morning, and the Sister left at once for Chicago. Sister Theresa depends particularly upon Miss Devereux,—so I've heard, sir. Miss Devereux quite takes charge when the Sister goes away.

A few of the students are staying in school through the holidays."

"You seem full of information," I remarked, taking another step toward my hat and coat.

"And I've learned something else, sir."

"Well?"

"They all came together, sir."

"Who came; if you please, Bates?"

"Why, the people who've been traveling with Mr. Pickering came back with him, and Miss Devereux came with them from Cincinnati. That's what I learned in the village. And Mr. Pickering is going to stay—"

"Pickering stay!"

"At his cottage on the lake for a while. The reason is that he's worn out with his work, and wishes quiet. The other people went back to New York in the car."

"He's opened a summer cottage in mid-winter, has he?"

I had been blue enough without this news. Marian Devereux had come back to Annandale with Arthur Pickering; my faith in her snapped like a reed at this astounding news. She was now entitled to my grandfather's property and she had lost no time in returning as soon as she and Pickering had discussed together at the Armstrongs' my flight from Annandale. Her return could have no other meaning than that there was a

strong tie between them, and he was now to stay on the
ground until I should be dispossessed and her rights
established. She had led me to follow her, and my for-
feiture had been sealed by that stolen interview at the
Armstrongs'. It was a black record, and the thought of
it angered me against myself and the world.

"Tell Mr. Donovan that I've gone to St. Agatha's,"
I said, and I was soon striding toward the school.

A Sister admitted me. I heard the sound of a piano,
somewhere in the building, and I consigned the in-
ventor of pianos to hideous torment as scales were
pursued endlessly up and down the keys. Two girls
passing through the hall made a pretext of looking for
a book and came in and exclaimed over their inability
to find it with much suppressed giggling.

The piano-pounding continued and I waited for what
seemed an interminable time. It was growing dark and
a maid lighted the oil lamps. I took a book from the
table. It was *The Life of Benvenuto Cellini* and "Marian Devereux" was written on the fly leaf, by unmistakably the same hand that penned the apology for
Olivia's performances. I saw in the clear flowing lines
of the signature, in their lack of superfluity, her own
ease, grace and charm; and, in the deeper stroke with
which the x was crossed, I felt a challenge, a readiness
to abide by consequences once her word was given.

Then my own inclination to think well of her angered me. It was only a pretty bit of chirography, and I dropped the book impatiently when I heard her step on the threshold.

"I am sorry to have kept you waiting, Mr. Glenarm. But this is my busy hour."

"I shall not detain you long. I came,"—I hesitated, not knowing why I had come.

She took a chair near the open door and bent forward with an air of attention that was disquieting. She wore black—perhaps to fit her the better into the house of a somber Sisterhood. I seemed suddenly to remember her from a time long gone, and the effort of memory threw me off guard. Stoddard had said there were several Olivia Armstrongs; there were certainly many Marian Devereuxs. The silence grew intolerable; she was waiting for me to speak, and I blurted:

"I suppose you have come to take charge of the property."

"Do you?" she asked.

"And you came back with the executor to facilitate matters. I'm glad to see that you lose no time."

"Oh!" she said lingeringly, as though she were find-ing with difficulty the note in which I wished to pitch the conversation. Her calmness was maddening.

"I suppose you thought it unwise to wait for the

bluebird when you had beguiled me into breaking a promise, when I was trapped, defeated,—"

Her elbow on the arm of the chair, her hand resting against her cheek, the light rippling goldenly in her hair, her eyes bent upon me inquiringly, mournfully,— mournfully, as I had seen them—where?—once before! My heart leaped in that moment, with that thought.

"I remember now the first time!" I exclaimed, more angry than I had ever been before in my life.

"That is quite remarkable," she said, and nodded her head ironically.

"It was at Sherry's; you were with Pickering—you dropped your fan and he picked it up, and you turned toward me for a moment. You were in black that night; it was the unhappiness in your face, in your eyes, that made me remember."

I was intent upon the recollection, eager to fix and establish it.

"You are quite right. It was at Sherry's. I was wearing black then; many things made me unhappy that night."

Her forehead contracted slightly and she pressed her lips together.

"I suppose that even then the conspiracy was thoroughly arranged," I said tauntingly, laughing a little perhaps, and wishing to wound her, to take vengeance upon her.

She rose and stood by her chair, one hand resting upon it. I faced her; her eyes were like violet seas. She spoke very quietly.

"Mr. Glenarm, has it occurred to you that when I talked to you there in the park, when I risked unpleasant gossip in receiving you in a house where you had no possible right to be, that I was counting upon something,—foolishly and stupidly,—yet counting upon it?"

"You probably thought I was a fool," I retorted.

"No;"—she smiled slightly—"I thought—I believe I have said this to you before!—you were a gentleman. I really did, Mr. Glenarm. I must say it to justify myself. I relied upon your chivalry; I even thought, when I played being Olivia, that you had a sense of honor. But you are not the one and you haven't the other. I even went so far, after you knew perfectly well who I was, as to try to help you—to give you another chance to prove yourself the man your grandfather wished you to be. And now you come to me in a shocking bad humor,—I really think you would like to be insulting, Mr. Glenarm, if you could."

"But Pickering,—you came back with him; he is here and he's going to stay! And now that the property belongs to you, there is not the slightest reason why we should make any pretense of anything but enmity. When you and Arthur Pickering stand together I take the other side of the barricade! I suppose chivalry would require me to vacate, so that you may enjoy at once the spoils of war."

"I fancy it would not be very difficult to eliminate you as a factor in the situation," she remarked icily.

"And I suppose, after the unsuccessful efforts of Mr. Pickering's allies to assassinate me, as a mild form of elimination, one would naturally expect me to sit calmly down and wait to be shot in the back. But you may tell Mr. Pickering that I throw myself upon your mercy. I have no other home than this shell over the way, and I beg to be allowed to remain until—at least—the blue-birds come. I hope it will not embarrass you to deliver the message."

"I quite sympathize with your reluctance to deliver it yourself," she said. "Is this all you came to say?"

"I came to tell you that you could have the house, and everything in its hideous walls," I snapped; "to tell you that my chivalry is enough for some situations and that I don't intend to fight a woman. I had accepted your own renouncement of the legacy in good part, but now, please believe me, it shall be yours to-morrow. I'll yield possession to you whenever you ask it,—but never to Arthur Pickering! As against him and his treasure-hunters and assassins I will hold out for a dozen years!"

"Nobly spoken, Mr. Glenarm! Yours is really an admirable, though somewhat complex character."

"My character is my own, whatever it is," I blurted.

"I shouldn't call that a debatable proposition," she replied, and I was angry to find how the mirth I had loved in her could suddenly become so hateful. She half-turned away so that I might not see her face. The thought that she should countenance Pickering in any way tore me with jealous rage.

"Mr. Glenarm, you are what I have heard called a quitter, defined in common Americanese as one who quits! Your blustering here this afternoon can hardly conceal the fact of your failure,—your inability to keep a promise. I had hoped you would really be of some help to Sister Theresa; you quite deceived her,—she told me as she left to-day that she thought well of you, —she really felt that her fortunes were safe in your hands. But, of course, that is all a matter of past history now."

Her tone, changing from cold indifference to the most severe disdain, stung me into self-pity for my stupidity in having sought her. My anger was not against her, but against Pickering, who had, I persuaded myself, always blocked my path. She went on.

"You really amuse me exceedingly. Mr. Pickering is decidedly more than a match for you, Mr. Glenarm, —even in humor."

She left me so quickly, so softly, that I stood staring like a fool at the spot where she had been, and then I went gloomily back to Glenarm House, angry, ashamed and crestfallen.

While we were waiting for dinner I made a clean breast of my acquaintance with her to Larry, omitting nothing,—rejoicing even to paint my own conduct as black as possible.

"You may remember her," I concluded, "she was the girl we saw at Sherry's that night we dined there. She was with Pickering, and you noticed her,—spoke of her, as she went out."

"That little girl who seemed so bored, or tired? Bless me! Why her eyes haunted me for days. Lord man, do you mean to say—"

A look of utter scorn came into his face, and he eyed me contemptuously.

"Of course I mean it!" I thundered at him.

He took the pipe from his mouth, pressed the tobacco

viciously into the bowl, and swore steadily in Gaelic until I was ready to choke him.

"Stop!" I bawled. "Do you think that's helping me? And to have you curse in your blackguardly Irish dialect! I wanted a little Anglo-Saxon sympathy, you fool! I didn't mean for you to invoke your infamous gods against the girl!"

"Don't be violent, lad. Violence is reprehensible," he admonished with maddening sweetness and patience. "What I was trying to inculcate was rather the fact, borne in upon me through years of acquaintance, that you are,—to be bold, my lad, to be bold,—a good deal of a damned fool."

The trilling of his r's was like the whirring rise of a flock of quails.

"Dinner is served," announced Bates, and Larry led the way, mockingly chanting an Irish love-song.

CHAPTER XXIII

THE DOOR OF BEWILDERMENT

We had established the practice of barring all the gates and doors at nightfall. There was no way of guarding against an attack from the lake, whose frozen surface increased the danger from without; but we counted on our night patrol to prevent a surprise from that quarter. I was well aware that I must prepare to resist the militant arm of the law, which Pickering would no doubt invoke to aid him, but I intended to exhaust the possibilities in searching for the lost treasure before I yielded. Pickering might, if he would, transfer the estate of John Marshall Glenarm to Marian Devereux and make the most he could of that service, but he should not drive me forth until I had satisfied myself of the exact character of my grandfather's fortune. If it had vanished, if Pickering had stolen it and outwitted me in making off with it, that was another matter.

The phrase, "The Door of Bewilderment," had never ceased to reiterate itself in my mind. We discussed a

thousand explanations of it as we pondered over the
scrap of paper I had found in the library, and every
book in the house was examined in the search for further
clues.

The passage between the house and the chapel seemed
to fascinate Larry. He held that it must have some
particular use and he devoted his time to exploring it.

He came up at noon—it was the twenty-ninth of
December—with grimy face and hands and a grin on his
face. I had spent my morning in the towers, where it
was beastly cold, to no purpose and was not in a mood
for the ready acceptance of new theories.

"I've found something," he said, filling his pipe.

"Not soap, evidently!"

"No, but I'm going to say the last word on the tunnel, and within an hour. Give me a glass of beer and a
piece of bread, and we'll go back and see whether we're
sold again or not."

"Let us explore the idea and be done with it. Wait
till I tell Stoddard where we're going."

The chaplain was trying the second-floor walls, and
I asked him to eat some luncheon and stand guard while
Larry and I went to the tunnel.

We took with us an iron bar, an ax and a couple of
hammers. Larry went ahead with a lantern.

"You see," he explained, as we dropped through the

trap into the passage, "I've tried a compass on this tunnel and find that we've been working on the wrong theory. The passage itself runs a straight line from the house under the gate to the crypt; the ravine is a rough crescent-shape and for a short distance the tunnel touches it. How deep does that ravine average—about thirty feet?"

"Yes; it's shallowest where the house stands. It drops sharply from there on to the lake."

"Very good; but the ravine is all on the Glenarm side of the wall, isn't it? Now when we get under the wall I'll show you something."

"Here we are," said Larry, as the cold air blew in through the hollow posts. "Now we're pretty near that sharp curve of the ravine that dips away from the wall. Take the lantern while I get out the compass. What do you think that C on the piece of paper means? Why, chapel, of course. I have measured the distance from the house, the point of departure, we may assume, to the chapel, and three-fourths of it brings us under those beautiful posts. The directions are as plain as daylight. The passage itself is your N. W., as the compass proves, and the ravine cuts close in here; therefore, our business is to explore the wall on the ravine side."

"Good! but this is just wall here—earth with a layer of brick and a thin coat of cement. A nice job it must have been to do the work,—and it cost the price of a tiger hunt," I grumbled.

"Take heart, lad, and listen,"—and Larry began pounding the wall with a hammer, exactly under the north gate-post. We had sounded everything in and about the house until the process bored me.

"Hurry up and get through with it," I jerked impatiently, holding the lantern at the level of his head. It was sharply cold under the posts and I was anxious to prove the worthlessness of his idea and be done.

Thump! thump!

"There's a place here that sounds a trifle off the key. You try it."

I snatched the hammer and repeated his soundings.

Thump! thump!

There was a space about four feet square in the wall that certainly gave forth a hollow sound.

"Stand back!" exclaimed Larry eagerly. "Here goes with the ax."

He struck into the wall sharply and the cement chipped off in rough pieces, disclosing the brick beneath. Larry paused when he had uncovered a foot of the inner layer, and examined the surface.

"They're loose—these bricks are loose, and there's something besides earth behind them!"

I snatched the hammer and drove hard at the wall.

The bricks were set up without mortar, and I plucked them out and rapped with my knuckles on a wooden surface.

Even Larry grew excited as we flung out the bricks.

"Ah, lad," he said, "the old gentleman had a way with him—he had a way with him!" A brick dropped on his foot and he howled in pain.

"Bless the old gentleman's heart! He made it as easy for us as he could. Now, for the Glenarm millions, —red money all piled up for the ease of counting it,— a thousand pounds in every pile."

"Don't be a fool, Larry," I coughed at him, for the brick dust and the smoke of Larry's pipe made breathing difficult.

"That's all the loose brick,—bring the lantern closer," —and we peered through the aperture upon a wooden door, in which strips of iron were deep-set. It was fastened with a padlock and Larry reached down for the ax.

"Wait!" I called, drawing closer with the lantern. What's this?"

The wood of the door was fresh and white, but burned deep on the surface, in this order, were the words:

THE DOOR
OF
BEWILDERMENT

"There are dead men inside, I dare say! Here, my lad, it's not for me to turn loose the family skeletons," —and Larry stood aside while I swung the ax and brought it down with a crash on the padlock. It was of no flimsy stuff and the remaining bricks cramped me, but half a dozen blows broke it off.

"The house of a thousand ghosts," chanted the irrepressible Larry, as I pushed the door open and crawled through.

Whatever the place was it had a floor and I set my feet firmly upon it and turned to take the lantern.

"Hold a bit," he exclaimed. "Some one's coming," —and bending toward the opening I heard the sound of steps down the corridor. In a moment Bates ran up, calling my name with more spirit than I imagined possible in him.

"What is it?" I demanded, crawling out into the tunnel.

"It's Mr. Pickering. The sheriff has come with him, sir."

As he spoke his glance fell upon the broken wall and open door. The light of Larry's lantern struck full upon him. Amazement, and, I thought, a certain satisfaction, were marked upon his countenance.

"Run along, Jack,—I'll be up a little later," said Larry. "If the fellow has come in daylight with the sheriff, he isn't dangerous. It's his friends that shoot in the dark that give us the trouble."

I crawled out and stood upright. Bates, staring at the opening, seemed reluctant to leave the spot.

"You seem to have found it, sir," he said,—I thought a little chokingly. His interest in the matter nettled me; for my first business was to go above for an inter-view with the executor, and the value of our discovery was secondary.

"Of course we have found it!" I ejaculated, brushing the dust from my clothes. "Is Mr. Stoddard in the library?"

"Oh, yes, sir; I left him entertaining the gentlemen."

"Their visit is certainly most inopportune," said Larry. "Give them my compliments and tell them I'll be up as soon as I've articulated the bones of my friend's ancestors."

Bates strode on ahead of me with his lantern, and I left Larry crawling through the new-found door as I hurried toward the house. I knew him well enough to be sure he would not leave the spot until he had found what lay behind the Door of Bewilderment.

"You didn't tell the callers where you expected to find me, did you?" I asked Bates, as he brushed me off in the kitchen.

"No, sir. Mr. Stoddard received the gentlemen. He

rang the bell for me and when I went into the library he was saying, 'Mr. Glenarm is at his studies. Bates,'— he says—'kindly tell Mr. Glenarm that I'm sorry to interrupt him, but won't he please come down?' I thought it rather neat, sir, considering his clerical office. I knew you were below somewhere, sir; the trap-door was open and I found you easily enough."

Bates' eyes were brighter than I had ever seen them. A certain buoyant note gave an entirely new tone to his voice. He walked ahead of me to the library door, threw it open and stood aside.

"Here you are, Glenarm," said Stoddard. Pickering and a stranger stood near the fireplace in their overcoats.

Pickering advanced and offered his hand, but I turned away from him without taking it. His companion, a burly countryman, stood staring, a paper in his hand.

"The sheriff," Pickering explained, "and our business is rather personal—"

He glanced at Stoddard, who looked at me.

"Mr. Stoddard will do me the kindness to remain," I said and took my stand beside the chaplain.

"Oh!" Pickering ejaculated scornfully. "I didn't understand that you had established relations with the neighboring clergy. Your taste is improving, Glenarm."

"Mr. Glenarm is a friend of mine," remarked Stoddard quietly. "A very particular friend," he added.

"I congratulate you—both."

I laughed. Pickering was surveying the room as he spoke,—and Stoddard suddenly stepped toward him, merely, I think, to draw up a chair for the sheriff; but Pickering, not hearing Stoddard's step on the soft rug until the clergyman was close beside him, started perceptibly and reddened.

It was certainly ludicrous, and when Stoddard faced me again he was biting his lip.

"Pardon me!" he murmured.

"Now, gentlemen, will you kindly state your business? My own affairs press me."

Pickering was studying the cartridge boxes on the library table. The sheriff, too, was viewing these effects with interest not, I think, unmixed with awe.

"Glenarm, I don't like to invoke the law to eject you from this property, but I am left with no alternative. I can't stay out here indefinitely, and I want to know what I'm to expect."

"That is a fair question," I replied. "If it were merely a matter of following the terms of the will I should not hesitate or be here now. But it isn't the will, or my grandfather, that keeps me, it's the determination to give you all the annoyance possible,—to make it

hard and mighty hard for you to get hold of this house
until I have found why you are so much interested
in it."

"You always had a grand way in money matters. As
I told you before you came out here, it's a poor stake.
The assets consist wholly of this land and this house,
whose quality you have had an excellent opportunity
to test. You have doubtless heard that the country
people believe there is money concealed here,—but I
dare say you have exhausted the possibilities. This is
not the first time a rich man has died leaving precious
little behind him."

"You seem very anxious to get possession of a property that you call a poor stake," I said. "A few acres
of land, a half-finished house and an uncertain claim
upon a school-teacher!"

"I had no idea you would understand it," he replied.
"The fact that a man may be under oath to perform
the solemn duties imposed upon him by the law would
hardly appeal to you. But I haven't come here to debate
this question. When are you going to leave?"

"Not till I'm ready,—thanks!"

"Mr. Sheriff, will you serve your writ?" he said, and
I looked to Stoddard for any hint from him as to what
I should do.

"I believe Mr. Glenarm is quite willing to hear whatever the sheriff has to say to him," said Stoddard. He stepped nearer to me, as though to emphasize the fact that he belonged to my side of the controversy, and the sheriff read an order of the Wabana County Circuit Court directing me, immediately, to deliver the house and grounds into the keeping of the executor of the will of the estate of John Marshall Glenarm.

The sheriff rather enjoyed holding the center of the stage, and I listened quietly to the unfamiliar phraseology. Before he had quite finished I heard a step in the hall and Larry appeared at the door, pipe in mouth. Pickering turned toward him frowning, but Larry paid not the slightest attention to the executor, leaning against the door with his usual tranquil unconcern.

"I advise you not to trifle with the law, Glenarm," said Pickering angrily. "You have absolutely no right whatever to be here. And these other gentlemen—your guests, I suppose—are equally trespassers under the law."

He stared at Larry, who crossed his legs for greater ease in adjusting his lean frame to the door.

"Well, Mr. Pickering, what is the next step?" asked the sheriff, with an importance that had been increased by the legal phrases he had been reading.

"Mr. Pickering," said Larry, straightening up and taking the pipe from his mouth, "I'm Mr. Glenarm's counsel. If you will do me the kindness to ask the sheriff to retire for a moment I should like to say a few words to you that you might prefer to keep between ourselves."

I had usually found it wise to take any cue Larry threw me, and I said:

"Pickering, this is Mr. Donovan, who has every authority to act for me in the matter."

Pickering looked impatiently from one to the other of us.

"You seem to have the guns, the ammunition and the numbers on your side," he observed dryly.

"The sheriff may wait within call," said Larry, and at a word from Pickering the man left the room.

"Now, Mr. Pickering,"—Larry spoke slowly,—"as my friend has explained the case to me, the assets of his grandfather's estate are all accounted for,—the land hereabouts, this house, the ten thousand dollars in securities and a somewhat vague claim against a lady known as Sister Theresa, who conducts St. Agatha's School. Is that correct?"

"I don't ask you to take my word for it, sir," rejoined Pickering hotly. "I have filed an inventory of the estate, so far as found, with the proper authorities."

"Certainly. But I merely wish to be sure of my facts for the purpose of this interview, to save me the trouble of going to the records. And, moreover, I am somewhat unfamiliar with your procedure in this country. I am a member, sir, of the Irish Bar. Pardon me, but I repeat my question."

"I have made oath—that, I trust, is sufficient even for a member of the Irish Bar."

"Quite so, Mr. Pickering," said Larry, nodding his head gravely.

He was not, to be sure, a presentable member of any bar, for a smudge detracted considerably from the appearance of one side of his face, his clothes were rumpled and covered with black dust, and his hands were black. But I had rarely seen him so calm. He recrossed his legs, peered into the bowl of his pipe for a moment, then asked, as quietly as though he were soliciting an opinion of the weather:

"Will you tell me, Mr. Pickering, whether you yourself are a debtor of John Marshall Glenarm's estate?"

Pickering's face grew white and his eyes stared, and when he tried suddenly to speak his jaw twitched. The room was so still that the breaking of a blazing log on the andirons was a pleasant relief. We stood, the three of us, with our eyes on Pickering, and in my own case I must say that my heart was pounding my ribs at an uncomfortable speed, for I knew Larry was not sparring for time.

The blood rushed into Pickering's face and he turned toward Larry stormily.

"This is unwarrantable and infamous! My relations with Mr. Glenarm are none of your business. When you remember that after being deserted by his own flesh and blood he appealed to me, going so far as to intrust all his affairs to my care at his death, your reflection is an outrageous insult. I am not accountable to you or any one else!"

"Really, there's a good deal in all that," said Larry. "We don't pretend to any judicial functions. We are perfectly willing to submit the whole business and all my client's acts to the authorities."

(I would give much if I could reproduce some hint of the beauty of that word authorities as it rolled from Larry's tongue!)

"Then, in God's name, do it, you blackguards!" roared Pickering.

Stoddard, sitting on a table, knocked his heels together gently. Larry recrossed his legs and blew a cloud of smoke. Then, after a quarter of a minute in which he gazed at the ceiling with his quiet blue eyes, he said:

"Yes; certainly, there are always the authorities. And as I have a tremendous respect for your American institutions I shall at once act on your suggestion. Mr.

Pickering, the estate is richer than you thought it was. It holds, or will hold, your notes given to the decedent for three hundred and twenty thousand dollars."

He drew from his pocket a brown envelope, walked to where I stood and placed it in my hands.

At the same time Stoddard's big figure grew active, and before I realized that Pickering had leaped toward the packet, the executor was sitting in a chair, where the chaplain had thrown him. He rallied promptly, stuffing his necktie into his waistcoat; he even laughed a little.

"So much old paper! You gentlemen are perfectly welcome to it."

"Thank you!" jerked Larry.

"Mr. Glenarm and I had many transactions together, and he must have forgotten to destroy those papers."

"Quite likely," I remarked. "It is interesting to know that Sister Theresa wasn't his only debtor."

Pickering stepped to the door and called the sheriff.

"I shall give you until to-morrow morning at nine o'clock to vacate the premises. The court understands this situation perfectly. These claims are utterly worthless, as I am ready to prove."

"Perfectly, perfectly," repeated the sheriff.

"I believe that is all," said Larry, pointing to the door with his pipe.

The sheriff was regarding him with particular attention.

"What did I understand your name to be?" he demanded.

"Laurance Donovan," Larry replied coolly.

Pickering seemed to notice the name now and his eyes lighted disagreeably.

"I think I have heard of your friend before," he said, turning to me. "I congratulate you on the international reputation of your counsel. He's esteemed so highly in Ireland that they offer a large reward for his return. Sheriff, I think we have finished our business for to-day."

He seemed anxious to get the man away, and we gave them escort to the outer gate where a horse and buggy were waiting.

"Now, I'm in for it," said Larry, as I locked the gate. "We've spiked one of his guns, but I've given him a new one to use against myself. But come, and I will show you the Door of Bewilderment before I skip."

CHAPTER XXIV

A PROWLER OF THE NIGHT

Down we plunged into the cellar, through the trap and to the Door of Bewilderment.

"Don't expect too much," admonished Larry; "I can't promise you a single Spanish coin."

"Perish the ambition! We have blocked Pickering's game, and nothing else matters," I said.

We crawled through the hole in the wall and lighted candles. The room was about seven feet square. At the farther end was an oblong wooden door, close to the ceiling, and Larry tugged at the fastening until it came down, bringing with it a mass of snow and leaves.

"Gentlemen," he said, "we are at the edge of the ravine. Do you see the blue sky? And yonder, if you will twist your necks a bit, is the boat-house."

"Well, let the scenic effects go and show us where you found those papers," I urged.

"Speaking of mysteries, that is where I throw up my hands, lads. It's quickly told. Here is a table, and here is a tin despatch box, which lies just where I found it.

304

It was closed and the key was in the lock. I took out
that packet—it wasn't even sealed—saw the character
of the contents, and couldn't resist the temptation to
try the effect of an announcement of its discovery on
your friend Pickering. Now that is nearly all. I found
this piece of paper under the tape with which the envelope was tied, and I don't hesitate to say that when
I read it I laughed until I thought I should shake
down the cellar. Read it, John Glenarm!"

He handed me a sheet of legal-cap paper on which
was written these words:

HE LAUGHS BEST WHO LAUGHS LAST

"What do you think is so funny in this?" I demanded.

"Who wrote it, do you think?" asked Stoddard.

"Who wrote it, do you ask? Why, your grandfather
wrote it! John Marshall Glenarm, the cleverest, grand-
est old man that ever lived, wrote it!" declaimed Larry,
his voice booming loudly in the room. "It's all a great
big game, fixed up to try you and Pickering,—but prin-
cipally you, you blockhead! Oh, it's grand, perfectly,
deliciously grand,—and to think it should be my good
luck to share in it!"

"Humph! I'm glad you're amused, but it doesn't
strike me as being so awfully funny. Suppose those

papers had fallen into Pickering's hands; then where would the joke have been, I should like to know!"

"On you, my lad, to be sure! The old gentleman wanted you to study architecture; he wanted you to study his house; he even left a little pointer in an old book! Oh, it's too good to be true!"

"That's all clear enough," observed Stoddard, knocking upon the despatch box with his knuckles. "But why do you suppose he dug this hole here with its outlet on the ravine?"

"Oh, it was the way of him!" explained Larry. "He liked the idea of queer corners and underground passages. This is a bully hiding-place for man or treasure, and that outlet into the ravine makes it possible to get out of the house with nobody the wiser. It's in keeping with the rest of his scheme. Be gay, comrades! To-morrow will likely find us with plenty of business on our hands. At present we hold the fort, and let us have a care lest we lose it."

We closed the ravine door, restored the brick as best we could, and returned to the library. We made a list of the Pickering notes and spent an hour discussing this new feature of the situation.

"That's a large amount of money to lend one man," said Stoddard.

"True; and from that we may argue that Mr. Glenarm didn't give Pickering all he had. There's more somewhere. If only I didn't have to run—" and Larry's face fell as he remembered his own plight.

"I'm a selfish pig, old man! I've been thinking only of my own affairs. But I never relied on you as much as now!"

"Those fellows will sound the alarm against Donovan, without a doubt, on general principles and to land a blow on you," remarked Stoddard thoughtfully.

"But you can get away, Larry. We'll help you off to-night. I don't intend to stand between you and liberty. This extradition business is no joke,—if they ever get you back in Ireland it will be no fun getting you off. You'd better run for it before Pickering and his sheriff spring their trap."

"Yes; that's the wise course. Glenarm and I can hold the fort here. His is a moral issue, really, and I'm in for a siege of a thousand years," said the clergyman earnestly, "if it's necessary to beat Pickering. I may go to jail in the end, too, I suppose."

"I want you both to leave. It's unfair to mix you up in this ugly business of mine. Your stake's bigger than mine, Larry. And yours, too, Stoddard; why, your whole future—your professional standing and prospects would be ruined if we got into a fight here with the authorities."

"Thank you for mentioning my prospects! I've never had them referred to before," laughed Stoddard. "No; your grandfather was a friend of the Church and I can't desert his memory. I'm a believer in a vigorous Church militant and I'm enlisted for the whole war. But Donovan ought to go, if he will allow me to advise him."

Larry filled his pipe at the fireplace.

"Lads," he said, his hands behind him, rocking gently as was his way, "let us talk of art and letters,—I'm going to stay. It hasn't often happened in my life that the whole setting of the stage has pleased me as much as this. Lost treasure; secret passages; a gentleman rogue storming the citadel; a private chaplain on the premises; a young squire followed by a limelight; sheriff, school-girls and a Sisterhood distributed through the landscape,—and me, with Scotland Yard looming duskily in the distance. Glenarm, I'm going to stay."

There was no shaking him, and the spirits of all of us rose after this new pledge of loyalty. Stoddard stayed for dinner, and afterward we began again our eternal quest for the treasure, our hopes high from Larry's lucky strike of the afternoon, and with a new eagerness born of the knowledge that the morrow would certainly bring us face to face with the real crisis. We

ranged the house from tower to cellar; we overhauled
the tunnel, for, it seemed to me, the hundredth time.

It was my watch, and at midnight, after Stoddard and
Larry had reconnoitered the grounds and Bates and I
had made sure of all the interior fastenings, I sent
them off to bed and made myself comfortable with a
pipe in the library.

I was glad of the respite, glad to be alone,—to consider my talk with Marian Devereux at St. Agatha's,
and her return with Pickering. Why could she not always have been Olivia, roaming the woodland, or the
girl in gray, or that woman, so sweet in her dignity,
who came down the stairs at the Armstrongs'? Her
own attitude toward me was so full of contradictions;
she had appeared to me in so many moods and guises,
that my spirit ranged the whole gamut of feeling as I
thought of her. But it was the recollection of Pickering's infamous conduct that colored all my doubts of
her. Pickering had always been in my way, and here,
but for the chance by which Larry had found the notes,
I should have had no weapon to use against him.

The wind rose and drove shrilly around the house.
A bit of scaffolding on the outer walls rattled loose
somewhere and crashed down on the terrace. I grew
restless, my mind intent upon the many chances of the

morrow, and running forward to the future. Even if I won in my strife with Pickering I had yet my way to make in the world. His notes were probably worthless,—I did not doubt that. I might use them to procure his removal as executor, but I did not look forward with any pleasure to a legal fight over a property that had brought me only trouble.

Something impelled me to go below, and, taking a lantern, I tramped somberly through the cellar, glanced at the heating apparatus, and, remembering that the chapel entrance to the tunnel was unguarded, followed the corridor to the trap, and opened it. The cold air blew up sharply and I thrust my head down to listen.

A sound at once arrested me. I thought at first it must be the suction of the air, but Glenarm House was no place for conjectures, and I put the lantern aside and jumped down into the tunnel. A gleam of light showed for an instant, then the darkness and silence were complete.

I ran rapidly over the smooth floor, which I had traversed so often that I knew its every line. My only weapon was one of Stoddard's clubs. Near the Door of Bewilderment I paused and listened. The tunnel was perfectly quiet. I took a step forward and stumbled over a brick, fumbled on the wall for the opening which we had closed carefully that afternoon, and at

the instant I found it a lantern flashed blindingly in
my face and I drew back, crouching involuntarily, and
clenching the club ready to strike.

"Good evening, Mr. Glenarm!"

Marian Devereux's voice broke the silence, and Marian Devereux's face, with the full light of the lantern
upon it, was bent gravely upon me. Her voice, as I
heard it there,—her face, as I saw it there,—are the
things that I shall remember last when my hour comes
to go hence from this world. The slim fingers, as they
clasped the wire screen of the lantern, held my gaze for
a second. The red tam-o'-shanter that I had associated
with her youth and beauty was tilted rakishly on one
side of her pretty head. To find her here, seeking, like
a thief in the night, for some means of helping Arthur
Pickering, was the bitterest drop in the cup. I felt as
though I had been struck with a bludgeon.

"I beg your pardon!" she said, and laughed. "There
doesn't seem to be anything to say, does there? Well,
we do certainly meet under the most unusual, not to say
unconventional, circumstances, Squire Glenarm. Please
go away or turn your back. I want to get out of this
donjon keep."

She took my hand coolly enough and stepped down
into the passage. Then I broke upon her stormily.

"You don't seem to understand the gravity of what

you are doing! Don't you know that you are risking your life in crawling through this house at midnight? —that even to serve Arthur Pickering, a life is a pretty big thing to throw away? Your infatuation for that blackguard seems to carry you far, Miss Devereux."

She swung the lantern at arm's length back and forth so that its rays at every forward motion struck my face like a blow.

"It isn't exactly pleasant in this cavern. Unless you wish to turn me over to the lord high executioner, I will bid you good night."

"But the infamy of this—of coming in here to spy upon me—to help my enemy—the man who is seeking plunder—doesn't seem to trouble you."

"No, not a particle!" she replied quietly, and then, with an impudent fling, "Oh, no!" She held up the lantern to look at the wick. "I'm really disappointed to find that you were a little ahead of me, Squire Glenarm. I didn't give you credit for so much—perseverance. But if you have the notes—"

"The notes! He told you there were notes, did he? The coward sent you here to find them, after his other tools failed him?"

She laughed that low laugh of hers that was like the bubble of a spring.

"I beg your pardon!" she said, and laughed. *Page 311*

"Of course no one would dare deny what the great Squire Glenarm says," she said witheringly.

"You can't know what your perfidy means to me," I said. "That night, at the Armstrongs', I thrilled at the sight of you. As you came down the stairway I thought of you as my good angel, and I belonged to you, —all my life, the better future that I wished to make for your sake."

"Please don't!" And I felt that my words had touched her; that there were regret and repentance in her tone and in the gesture with which she turned from me.

She hurried down the passage swinging the lantern at her side, and I followed, so mystified, so angered by her composure, that I scarcely knew what I did. She even turned, with pretty courtesy, to hold the light for me at the crypt steps,—a service that I accepted perforce and with joyless acquiescence in the irony of it. I knew that I did not believe in her; her conduct as to Pickering was utterly indefensible,—I could not forget that; but the light of her eyes, her tranquil brow, the sensitive lips, whose mockery stung and pleased in a breath,—by such testimony my doubts were alternately reinforced and disarmed. Swept by these changing moods I followed her out into the crypt.

"You seem to know a good deal about this place, and I suppose I can't object to your familiarizing yourself with your own property. And the notes—I'll give myself the pleasure of handing them to you to-morrow. You can cancel them and give them to Mr. Pickering,— a pretty pledge between you!"

I thrust my hands into my pockets to give an impression of ease I did not feel.

"Yes," she remarked in a practical tone, "three hundred and twenty thousand dollars is no mean sum of money. Mr. Pickering will undoubtedly be delighted to have his debts canceled—"

"In exchange for a life of devotion," I sneered. "So you knew the sum—the exact amount of these notes. He hasn't served you well; he should have told you that we found them to-day."

"You are not nice, are you, Squire Glenarm, when you are cross?"

She was like Olivia now. I felt the utter futility of attempting to reason with a woman who could become a child at will. She walked up the steps and out into the church vestibule. Then before the outer door she spoke with decision.

"We part here, if you please! And—I have not the slightest intention of trying to explain my errand into that passage. You have jumped to your own conclusion, which will have to serve you. I advise you not to think very much about it,—to the exclusion of more important business,—Squire Glenarm!"

She lifted the lantern to turn out its light, and it made a glory of her face, but she paused and held it toward me.

"Pardon me! You will need this to light you home."

"But you must not cross the park alone!"

"Good night! Please be sure to close the door to the passage when you go down. You are a dreadfully heedless person, Squire Glenarm."

She flung open the outer chapel-door, and ran along the path toward St. Agatha's. I watched her in the starlight until a bend in the path hid her swift-moving figure.

Down through the passage I hastened, her lantern lighting my way. At the Door of Bewilderment I closed the opening, setting up the line of wall as we had left it in the afternoon, and then I went back to the library, freshened the fire and brooded before it until Bates came to relieve me at dawn.

CHAPTER XXV

BESIEGED

It was nine o'clock. A thermometer on the terrace showed the mercury clinging stubbornly to a point above zero; but the still air was keen and stimulating, and the sun argued for good cheer in a cloudless sky. We had swallowed some breakfast, though I believe no one had manifested an appetite, and we were cheering ourselves with the idlest talk possible. Stoddard, who had been to the chapel for his usual seven o'clock service, was deep in the pocket Greek testament he always carried.

Bates ran in to report a summons at the outer wall, and Larry and I went together to answer it, sending Bates to keep watch toward the lake.

Our friend the sheriff, with a deputy, was outside in a buggy. He stood up and talked to us over the wall.

"You gents understand that I'm only doing my duty. It's an unpleasant business, but the court orders me to eject all trespassers on the premises, and I've got to do it."

"The law is being used by an infamous scoundrel to

316

protect himself. I don't intend to give in. We can hold out here for three months, if necessary, and I advise you to keep away and not be made a tool for a man like Pickering."

The sheriff listened respectfully, resting his arms on top of the wall.

"You ought to understand, Mr. Glenarm, that I ain't the court; I'm the sheriff, and it's not for me to pass on these questions. I've got my orders and I've got to enforce 'em, and I hope you will not make it necessary for me to use violence. The judge said to me, 'We deplore violence in such cases.' Those were his Honor's very words."

"You may give his Honor my compliments and tell him that we are sorry not to see things his way, but there are points involved in this business that he doesn't know anything about, and we, unfortunately, have no time to lay them before him."

The sheriff's seeming satisfaction with his position on the wall and his disposition to parley had begun to arouse my suspicions, and Larry several times exclaimed impatiently at the absurdity of discussing my affairs with a person whom he insisted on calling a constable, to the sheriff's evident annoyance. The officer now turned upon him.

"You, sir,—we've got our eye on you, and you'd better come along peaceable. Laurance Donovan—the description fits you to a 't'."

"You could buy a nice farm with that reward, couldn't you—" began Larry, but at that moment Bates ran toward us calling loudly.

"They're coming across the lake, sir," he reported, and instantly the sheriff's head disappeared, and as we ran toward the house we heard his horse pounding down the road toward St. Agatha's.

"The law be damned. They don't intend to come in here by the front door as a matter of law," said Larry. "Pickering's merely using the sheriff to give respectability to his manœuvers for those notes and the rest of it."

It was no time for a discussion of motives. We ran across the meadow past the water tower and through the wood down to the boat-house. Far out on the lake we saw half a dozen men approaching the Glenarm grounds. They advanced steadily over the light snow that lay upon the ice, one man slightly in advance and evidently the leader.

"It's Morgan!" exclaimed Bates. "And there's Ferguson."

Larry chuckled and slapped his thigh.

"Observe that stocky little devil just behind the leader? He's my friend from Scotland Yard. Lads! this is really an international affair."

"Bates, go back to the house and call at any sign of attack," I ordered. "The sheriff's loose somewhere."

"And Pickering is directing his forces from afar," remarked Stoddard.

"I count ten men in Morgan's line," said Larry, "and the sheriff and his deputy make two more. That's twelve, not counting Pickering, that we know of on the other side."

"Warn them away before they get much nearer," suggested Stoddard. "We don't want to hurt people if we can help it,"—and at this I went to the end of the pier. Morgan and his men were now quite near, and there was no mistaking their intentions. Most of them carried guns, the others revolvers and long ice-hooks.

"Morgan," I called, holding up my hands for a truce, "we wish you no harm, but if you enter these grounds you do so at your peril."

"We're all sworn deputy sheriffs," called the care-taker smoothly. "We've got the law behind us."

"That must be why you're coming in the back way," I replied.

The thick-set man whom Larry had identified as the English detective now came closer and addressed me in a high key.

"You're harboring a bad man, Mr. Glenarm. You'd better give him up. The American law supports me, and you'll get yourself in trouble if you protect that man. You may not understand, sir, that he's a very dangerous character."

"Thanks, Davidson!" called Larry. "You'd better keep out of this. You know I'm a bad man with the shillalah!"

"That you are, you blackguard!" yelled the officer, so spitefully that we all laughed.

I drew back to the boat-house.

"They are not going to kill anybody if they can help it," remarked Stoddard, "any more than we are. Even deputy sheriffs are not turned loose to do murder, and the Wabana County Court wouldn't, if it hadn't been imposed on by Pickering, lend itself to a game like this."

"Now we're in for it," yelled Larry, and the twelve men, in close order, came running across the ice toward the shore.

"Open order, and fall back slowly toward the house," I commanded. And we deployed from the boat-house, while the attacking party still clung together,—a strategic error, as Larry assured us.

"Stay together, lads. Don't separate; you'll get lost if you do," he yelled.

Stoddard bade him keep still, and we soon had our hands full with a preliminary skirmish. Morgan's line advanced warily. Davidson, the detective, seemed disgusted at Morgan's tactics, openly abused the caretaker, and ran ahead of his column, revolver in hand, bearing down upon Larry, who held our center.

The Englishman's haste was his undoing. The light fall of snow a few days before had gathered in the little hollows of the wood deceptively. The detective plunged into one of these and fell sprawling on all fours,—a calamity that caused his comrades to pause uneasily. Larry was upon his enemy in a flash, wrenched his pistol away and pulled the man to his feet.

"Ah, Davidson! There's many a slip! Move, if you dare and I'll plug you with your own gun." And he stood behind the man, using him as a shield while Morgan and the rest of the army hung near the boat-house uncertainly.

"It's the strategic intellect we've captured, General," observed Larry to me. "You see the American invaders were depending on British brains."

Morgan now acted on the hint we had furnished him and sent his men out as skirmishers. The loss of the detective had undoubtedly staggered the caretaker, and we were slowly retreating toward the house, Larry with one hand on the collar of his prisoner and the other grasping the revolver with which he poked the man frequently in the ribs. We slowly continued our retreat, fearing a rush, which would have disposed of us easily enough if Morgan's company had shown more of a fighting spirit. Stoddard's presence rather amazed them, I think, and I saw that the invaders kept away from his end of the line. We were far apart, stumbling over the snow-covered earth and calling to one another now and then that we might not become too widely separated. Davidson did not relish his capture by the man he had followed across the ocean, and he attempted once to roar a command to Morgan.

"Try it again," I heard Larry admonish him, "try that once more, and The Sod, God bless it! will never feel the delicate imprint of your web-feet again."

He turned the man about and rushed him toward the house, the revolver still serving as a prod. His speed gave heart to the wary invaders immediately behind him and two fellows urged and led by Morgan charged our line at a smart pace.

"Bolt for the front door," I called to Larry, and Stoddard and I closed in after him to guard his retreat.

"They're not shooting," called Stoddard. "You may be sure they've had their orders to capture the house with as little row as possible."

We were now nearing the edge of the wood, with the

open meadow and water-tower at our backs, while Larry was making good time toward the house.

"Let's meet them here," shouted Stoddard.

Morgan was coming up with a club in his hand, making directly for me, two men at his heels, and the rest veering off toward the wall of St. Agatha's.

"Watch the house," I yelled to the chaplain; and then, on the edge of the wood Morgan came at me furiously, swinging his club over his head, and in a moment we were fencing away at a merry rate. We both had revolvers strapped to our waists, but I had no intention of drawing mine unless in extremity. At my right Stoddard was busy keeping off Morgan's personal guard, who seemed reluctant to close with the clergyman.

I have been, in my day, something of a fencer, and my knowledge of the foils stood me in good stead now. With a tremendous thwack I knocked Morgan's club flying over the snow, and, as we grappled, Bates yelled from the house. I quickly found that Morgan's wounded arm was still tender. He flinched at the first grapple, and his anger got the better of his judgment. We kicked up the snow at a great rate as we feinted and dragged each other about. He caught hold of my belt with one hand and with a great wrench nearly dragged me from my feet, but I pinioned his arms and bent him backward, then, by a trick Larry had taught me, flung him upon his side. It is not, I confess, a pretty business, matching your brute strength against that of a fellow man, and as I cast myself upon him and felt his hard-blown breath on my face, I hated myself more than I hated him for engaging in so ignoble a contest.

Bates continued to call from the house.

"Come on at any cost," shouted Stoddard, putting himself between me and the men who were flying to Morgan's aid.

I sprang away from my adversary, snatching his revolver, and ran toward the house, Stoddard close behind, but keeping himself well between me and the men who were now after us in full cry.

"Shoot, you fools, shoot!" howled Morgan, and as we reached the open meadow and ran for the house a shotgun roared back of us and buckshot snapped and rattled on the stone of the water tower.

"There's the sheriff," called Stoddard behind me.

The officer of the law and his deputy ran into the park from the gate of St. Agatha's, while the rest of Morgan's party were skirting the wall to join them.

"Stop or I'll shoot," yelled Morgan, and I felt Stoddard pause in his gigantic stride to throw himself between me and the pursuers.

"Sprint for it hot," he called very coolly, as though

he were coaching me in a contest of the most amiable sort imaginable.

"Get away from those guns," I panted, angered by the very generosity of his defense.

"Feint for the front entrance and then run for the terrace and the library-door," he commanded, as we crossed the little ravine bridge. "They've got us headed off."

Twice the guns boomed behind us, and twice I saw shot cut into the snow about me.

"I'm all right," called Stoddard reassuringly, still at my back. "They're not a bit anxious to kill me."

I was at the top of my speed now, but the clergyman kept close at my heels. I was blowing hard, but he made equal time with perfect ease.

The sheriff was bawling orders to his forces, who awaited us before the front door. Bates and Larry were not visible, but I had every confidence that the Irishman would reappear in the fight at the earliest moment possible. Bates, too, was to be reckoned with, and the final struggle, if it came in the house itself, might not be so unequal, providing we knew the full strength of the enemy.

"Now for the sheriff—here we go!" cried Stoddard— beside me—and we were close to the fringe of trees that shielded the entrance. Then off we veered suddenly to the left, close upon the terrace, where one of the French windows was thrown open and Larry and Bates stepped out, urging us on with lusty cries.

They caught us by the arms and dragged us over where the balustrade was lowest, and we crowded through the door and slammed it. As Bates snapped the bolts Morgan's party discharged its combined artillery and the sheriff began a great clatter at the front door.

"Gentlemen, we're in a state of siege," observed Larry, filling his pipe.

Shot pattered on the walls and several panes of glass cracked in the French windows.

"All's tight below, sir," reported Bates. "I thought it best to leave the tunnel trap open for our own use. Those fellows won't come in that way,—it's too much like a blind alley."

"Where's your prisoner, Larry?"

"Potato cellar, quite comfortable, thanks!"

It was ten o'clock and the besiegers suddenly withdrew a short distance for parley among themselves. Outside the sun shone brightly; and the sky was never bluer. In this moment of respite, while we made ready for what further the day might bring forth, I climbed up to the finished tower to make sure we knew the enemy's full strength. I could see over the tree-tops, beyond the chapel tower, the roofs of St. Agatha's. There, at least, was peace. And in that moment, looking over the black wood, with the snow lying upon the ice of the lake white and gleaming under the sun, I felt unutterably lonely and heart-sick, and tired of strife. It seemed a thousand years ago that I had walked and talked with the child Olivia; and ten thousand years more since the girl in gray at the Annandale station had wakened in me a higher aim, and quickened a better impulse than I had ever known.

Larry roared my name through the lower floors. I went down with no wish in my heart but to even matters with Pickering and be done with my grandfather's legacy for ever.

"The sheriff and Morgan have gone back toward the lake," reported Larry.

"They've gone to consult their chief," I said. "I wish Pickering would lead his own battalions. It would give social prestige to the fight."

"Bah, these women!" And Larry tore the corner from a cartridge box.

Stoddard, with a pile of clubs within reach, lay on his back on the long leather couch, placidly reading his Greek testament. Bates, for the first time since my arrival, seemed really nervous and anxious. He pulled a silver watch from his pocket several times, something I had never seen him do before. He leaned against the table, looking strangely tired and worn, and I saw him start nervously as he felt Larry's eyes on him.

"I think, sir, I'd better take another look at the outer gates," he remarked to me quite respectfully.

His disturbed air aroused my old antagonism. Was he playing double in the matter? Did he seek now an excuse for conveying some message to the enemy?

"You'll stay where you are," I said sharply, and I found myself restlessly fingering my revolver.

"Very good, sir,"—and the hurt look in his eyes touched me.

"Bates is all right," Larry declared, with an emphasis that was meant to rebuke me.

CHAPTER XXVI

THE FIGHT IN THE LIBRARY

"They're coming faster this time," remarked Stoddard.

"Certainly. Their general has been cursing them right heartily for retreating without the loot. He wants his three-hundred-thousand-dollar autograph collection," observed Larry.

"Why doesn't he come for it himself, like a man?" I demanded.

"Like a man, do you say!" ejaculated Larry. "Faith and you flatter that fat-head!"

It was nearly eleven o'clock when the attacking party returned after a parley on the ice beyond the boat-house. The four of us were on the terrace ready for them. They came smartly through the wood, the sheriff and Morgan slightly in advance of the others. I expected them to slacken their pace when they came to the open meadow, but they broke into a quick trot at the water-tower and came toward the house as steady as veteran campaigners.

"Shall we try gunpowder?" asked Larry.

"We'll let them fire the first volley," I said.

329

"They've already tried to murder you and Stoddard, —I'm in for letting loose with the elephant guns," protested the Irishman.

"Stand to your clubs," admonished Stoddard, whose own weapon was comparable to the Scriptural weaver's beam. "Possession is nine points of the fight, and we've got the house."

"Also a prisoner of war," said Larry, grinning.

The English detective had smashed the glass in the barred window of the potato cellar and we could hear him howling and cursing below.

"Looks like business this time!" exclaimed Larry. "Spread out now and the first head that sticks over the balustrade gets a dose of hickory."

When twenty-five yards from the terrace the advancing party divided, half halting between us and the water-tower and the remainder swinging around the house toward the front entrance.

"Ah, look at that!" yelled Larry. "It's a battering-ram they have. O man of peace! have I your Majesty's consent to try the elephant guns now?"

Morgan and the sheriff carried between them a stick of timber from which the branches had been cut, and, with a third man to help, they ran it up the steps and against the door with a crash that came booming back through the house.

Bates was already bounding up the front stairway, a revolver in his hand and a look of supreme rage on his face. Leaving Stoddard and Larry to watch the library windows, I was after him, and we clattered over the loose boards in the upper hall and into a great unfinished chamber immediately over the entrance. Bates had the window up when I reached him and was well out upon the coping, yelling a warning to the men below.

He had his revolver up to shoot, and when I caught his arm he turned to me with a look of anger and indignation I had never expected to see on his colorless, mask-like face.

"My God, sir! That door was his pride, sir,—it came from a famous house in England, and they're wrecking it, sir, as though it were common pine."

He tore himself free of my grasp as the besiegers again launched their battering-ram against the door with a frightful crash, and his revolver cracked smartly thrice, as he bent far out with one hand clinging to the window frame.

His shots were a signal for a sharp reply from one of the men below, and I felt Bates start, and pulled him in, the blood streaming from his face.

"It's all right, sir,—all right,—only a cut across my cheek, sir,"—and another bullet smashed through the glass, spurting plaster dust from the wall. A fierce onslaught below caused a tremendous crash to echo through the house, and I heard firing on the opposite side, where the enemy's reserve was waiting.

Bates, with a handkerchief to his face, protested that he was unhurt.

"Come below; there's nothing to be gained here,"— and I ran down to the hall, where Stoddard stood, leaning upon his club like a Hercules and coolly watching the door as it leaped and shook under the repeated blows of the besiegers.

A gun roared again at the side of the house, and I ran to the library, where Larry had pushed furniture against all the long windows save one, which he held open. He stepped out upon the terrace and emptied a revolver at the men who were now creeping along the edge of the ravine beneath us. One of them stopped and discharged a rifle at us with deliberate aim. The ball snapped snow from the balustrade and screamed away harmlessly.

"Bah, such monkeys!" he muttered. "I believe I've hit that chap!" One man had fallen and lay howling in the ravine, his hand to his thigh, while his comrades paused, demoralized.

"Serves you right, you blackguard!" Larry muttered.

I pulled him in and we jammed a cabinet against the door.

Meanwhile the blows at the front continued with in-

creasing violence. Stoddard still stood where I had left
him. Bates was not in sight, but the barking of a revolver above showed that he had returned to the window
to take vengeance on his enemies.

Stoddard shook his head in deprecation.

"They fired first,—we can't do less than get back at
them," I said, between the blows of the battering-ram.

A panel of the great oak door now splintered in, but
in their fear that we might use the opening as a
loophole, they scampered out into range of Bates' revolver. In return we heard a rain of small shot on the
upper windows, and a few seconds later Larry shouted
that the flanking party was again at the terrace.

This movement evidently heartened the sheriff, for,
under a fire from Bates, his men rushed up and the log
crashed again into the door, shaking it free of the upper
hinges. The lower fastenings were wrenched loose an
instant later, and the men came tumbling into the hall,
—the sheriff, Morgan and four others I had never seen
before. Simultaneously the flanking party reached the
terrace and were smashing the small panes of the French
windows. We could hear the glass crack and tinkle
above the confusion at the door.

In the hall he was certainly a lucky man who held to
his weapon a moment after the door tumbled in. I
blazed at the sheriff with my revolver as he stumbled

and half-fell at the threshold, so that the ball passed over him, but he gripped me by the legs and had me prone and half-dazed by the rap of my head on the floor.

I suppose I was two or three minutes, at least, getting my wits. I was first conscious of Bates grappling the sheriff, who sat upon me, and as they struggled with each other I got the full benefit of their combined, swerving, tossing weight. Morgan and Larry were trying for a chance at each other with revolvers, while Morgan backed the Irishman slowly toward the library. Stoddard had seized one of the unknown deputies with both hands by the collar and gave his captive a tremendous swing, jerking him high in the air and driving him against another invader with a blow that knocked both fellows spinning into a corner.

"Come on to the library!" shouted Larry, and Bates, who had got me to my feet, dragged me down the hall toward the open library-door.

Bates presented at this moment an extraordinary appearance, with the blood from the scratch on his face coursing down his cheek and upon his shoulder. His coat and shirt had been torn away and the blood was smeared over his breast. The fury and indignation in his face was something I hope not to see again in a human countenance.

"My God, this room—this beautiful room!" I heard

him cry, as he pushed me before him into the library. "It was Mr. Glenarm's pride," he muttered, and sprang upon a burly fellow who had come in through one of the library doors and was climbing over the long table we had set up as a barricade.

We were now between two fires. The sheriff's party had fought valiantly to keep us out of the library, and now that we were within, Stoddard's big shoulders held the door half-closed against the combined strength of the men in the hall. This pause was fortunate, for it gave us an opportunity to deal singly with the fellows who were climbing in from the terrace. Bates had laid one of them low with a club and Larry disposed of another, who had made a murderous effort to stick a knife into him. I was with Stoddard against the door, where the sheriff's men were slowly gaining upon us.

"Let go on the jump when I say three," said Stoddard, and at his word we sprang away from the door and into the room. Larry yelled with joy as the sheriff and his men pitched forward and sprawled upon the floor, and we were at it again in a hand-to-hand conflict to clear the room.

"Hold that position, sir," yelled Bates.

Morgan had directed the attack against me and I was driven upon the hearth before the great fireplace. The sheriff, Morgan and Ferguson hemmed me in. It was evident that I was the chief culprit, and they wished to eliminate me from the contest. Across the room, Larry, Stoddard and Bates were engaged in a lively rough and tumble with the rest of the besiegers, and Stoddard, seeing my plight, leaped the overturned table, broke past the trio and stood at my side, swinging a chair.

At that moment my eyes, sweeping the outer doors, saw the face of Pickering. He had come to see that his orders were obeyed, and I remember yet my satisfaction, as, hemmed in by the men he had hired to kill me or drive me out, I felt, rather than saw, the cowardly horror depicted upon his face.

Then the trio pressed in upon me. As I threw down my club and drew my revolver, some one across the room fired several shots, whose roar through the room seemed to arrest the fight for an instant, and then, while Stoddard stood at my side swinging his chair defensively, the great chandelier, loosened or broken by the shots, fell with a mighty crash of its crystal pendants. The sheriff, leaping away from Stoddard's club, was struck on the head and borne down by the heavy glass.

Smoke from the firing floated in clouds across the room, and there was a moment's silence save for the sheriff, who was groaning and cursing under the debris of the chandelier. At the door Pickering's face appeared again anxious and frightened. I think the scene in the room and the slow progress his men were making against us had half-paralyzed him.

We were all getting our second wind for a renewal of the fight, with Morgan in command of the enemy. One or two of his men, who had gone down early in the struggle, were now crawling back for revenge. I think I must have raised my hand and pointed at Pickering, for Bates wheeled like a flash and before I realized what happened he had dragged the executor into the room.

"You scoundrel—you ingrate!" howled the servant.

The blood on his face and bare chest and the hatred in his eyes made him a hideous object; but in that lull of the storm while we waited, watching for an advantage, I heard off somewhere, above or below, that same sound of footsteps that I had remarked before. Larry and Stoddard heard it; Bates heard it, and his eyes fixed upon Pickering with a glare of malicious delight.

"There comes our old friend, the ghost," yelled Larry.

"I think you are quite right, sir," said Bates. He threw down the revolver he held in his hand and leaned upon the edge of the long table that lay on its side, his gaze still bent on Pickering, who stood with his overcoat buttoned close, his derby hat on the floor beside him, where it had fallen as Bates hauled him into the room.

The sound of a measured step, of some one walking, of a careful foot on a stairway, was quite distinct. I even remarked the slight stumble that I had noticed before.

We were all so intent on those steps in the wall that we were off guard. I heard Bates yell at me, and Larry and Stoddard rushed for Pickering. He had drawn a revolver from his overcoat pocket and thrown it up to fire at me when Stoddard sent the weapon flying through the air.

"Only a moment now, gentlemen," said Bates, an odd smile on his face. He was looking past me toward the right end of the fireplace. There seemed to be in the air a feeling of something impending. Even Morgan and his men, half-crouching ready for a rush at me, hesitated; and Pickering glanced nervously from one to the other of us. It was the calm before the storm; in a moment we should be at each other's throats for the final struggle, and yet we waited. In the wall I heard still the sound of steps. They were clear to all of us now. We stood there for what seemed an eternity—I suppose the time was really not more than thirty seconds—inert, waiting, while I felt that something must happen; the silence, the waiting, were intolerable. I grasped my pistol and bent low for a spring at Morgan, with the over-turned table and wreckage of the chandelier between me and Pickering; and every man in the room was instantly on the alert.

All but Bates. He remained rigid—that curious smile on his blood-smeared face, his eyes bent toward the end of the great fireplace back of me.

That look on his face held, arrested, numbed me; I followed it. I forgot Morgan; a tacit truce held us all again. I stepped back till my eyes fastened on the broad paneled chimney-breast at the right of the hearth, and it was there now that the sound of footsteps in the wall was heard again; then it ceased utterly, the long panel opened slowly, creaking slightly upon its hinges, then down into the room stepped Marian Devereux. She wore the dark gown in which I had seen her last, and a cloak was drawn over her shoulders.

She laughed as her eyes swept the room.

"Ah, gentlemen," she said, shaking her head, as she viewed our disorder, "what wretched housekeepers you are!"

Steps were again heard in the wall, and she turned to the panel, held it open with one hand and put out the other, waiting for some one who followed her.

Then down into the room stepped my grandfather, John Marshall Glenarm! His staff, his cloak, the silk hat above his shrewd face, and his sharp black eyes were unmistakable. He drew a silk handkerchief from the skirts of his frock coat, with a characteristic flourish that I remembered well, and brushed a bit of dust from his cloak before looking at any of us. Then his eyes fell upon me.

"Good morning, Jack," he said; and his gaze swept the room.

"God help us!"

It was Morgan, I think, who screamed these words as he bolted for the broken door, but Stoddard caught and held him.

"Thank God, you're here, sir!" boomed forth in Bates' sepulchral voice.

It seemed to me that I saw all that happened with a weird, unnatural distinctness, as one sees, before a storm, vivid outlines of far headlands that the usual light of day scarce discloses.

I was myself dazed and spellbound; but I do not like to think, even now, of the effect of my grandfather's appearance on Arthur Pickering; of the shock that seemed verily to break him in two, so that he staggered, then collapsed, his head falling as though to strike his knees. Larry caught him by the collar and dragged him to a seat, where he huddled, his twitching hands at his throat.

"Gentlemen," said my grandfather, "you seem to have been enjoying yourselves. Who is this person?"

He pointed with his stick to the sheriff, who was endeavoring to crawl out from under the mass of broken crystals.

"That, sir, is the sheriff," answered Bates.

"A very disorderly man, I must say. Jack, what have you been doing to cause the sheriff so much inconvenience? Didn't you know that that chandelier was likely to kill him? That thing cost a thousand dollars, gentlemen. You are expensive visitors. Ah, Morgan,—and Ferguson, too! Well, well! I thought better of both of you. Good morning, Stoddard! A little work for the Church militant! And this gentleman?"—he indicated Larry, who was, for once in his life, without anything to say.

"Mr. Donovan,—a friend of the house," explained Bates.

"Pleased, I'm sure," said the old gentleman. "Glad the house had a friend. It seems to have had enemies enough," he added dolefully; and he eyed the wreck of the room ruefully. The good humor in his face reassured me; but still I stood in tongue-tied wonder, staring at him.

"And Pickering!" John Marshall Glenarm's voice

broke with a quiet mirth that I remembered as the preface usually of something unpleasant. "Well, Arthur, I'm glad to find you on guard, defending the interests of my estate. At the risk of your life, too! Bates!"

"Yes, Mr. Glenarm."

"You ought to have called me earlier. I really prized that chandelier immensely. And this furniture wasn't so bad!"

His tone changed abruptly. He pointed to the sheriff's deputies one after the other with his stick. There was, I remembered, always something insinuating, disagreeable and final about my grandfather's staff.

"Clear out!" he commanded. "Bates, see these fellows through the wall. Mr. Sheriff, if I were you I'd be very careful, indeed, what I said of this affair. I'm a dead man come to life again, and I know a great deal that I didn't know before I died. Nothing, gentlemen, fits a man for life like a temporary absence from this cheerful and pleasant world. I recommend you to try it."

He walked about the room with the quick eager step that was peculiarly his own, while Stoddard, Larry and I stared at him. Bates was helping the dazed sheriff to his feet. Morgan and the rest of the foe were crawling and staggering away, muttering, as though imploring the air of heaven against an evil spirit.

Pickering sat silent, not sure whether he saw a ghost or real flesh and blood, and Larry kept close to him, cutting off his retreat. I think we all experienced that bewildered feeling of children who are caught in mischief by a sudden parental visitation. My grandfather went about peering at the books, with a tranquil air that was disquieting.

He paused suddenly before the design for the memorial tablet, which I had made early in my stay at Glenarm House. I had sketched the lettering with some care, and pinned it against a shelf for my more leisurely study of its phrases. The old gentlemen pulled out his glasses and stood with his hands behind his back, reading. When he finished he walked to where I stood.

"Jack!" he said, "Jack, my boy!" His voice shook and his hands trembled as he laid them on my shoulders. "Marian,"—he turned, seeking her, but the girl had vanished. "Just as well," he said. "This room is hardly an edifying sight for a woman." I heard, for an instant, a light hurried step in the wall.

Pickering, too, heard that faint, fugitive sound, and our eyes met at the instant it ceased. The thought of her tore my heart, and I felt that Pickering saw and knew and was glad.

"They have all gone, sir," reported Bates, returning to the room.

"Now, gentlemen," began my grandfather, seating himself, "I owe you an apology; this little secret of mine was shared by only two persons. One of these was Bates," —he paused as an exclamation broke from all of us; and he went on, enjoying our amazement,—"and the other was Marian Devereux. I had often observed that at a man's death his property gets into the wrong hands, or becomes a bone of contention among lawyers. Sometimes," and the old gentleman laughed, "an executor proves incompetent or dishonest. I was thoroughly fooled in you, Pickering. The money you owe me is a large sum; and you were so delighted to hear of my death that you didn't even make sure I was really out of the way. You were perfectly willing to accept Bates' word for it; and I must say that Bates carried it off splendidly."

Pickering rose, the blood surging again in his face, and screamed at Bates, pointing a shaking finger at the man.

"You impostor,—you perjurer! The law will deal with your case."

"To be sure," resumed my grandfather calmly: "Bates did make false affidavits about my death; but possibly—"

"It was in a Pickwickian sense, sir," said Bates gravely.

"And in a righteous cause," declared my grandfather. "I assure you, Pickering, that I have every intention of taking care of Bates. His weekly letters giving an account of the curious manifestations of your devotion to Jack's security and peace were alone worth a goodly sum. But, Bates—"

The old gentleman was enjoying himself hugely. He chuckled now, and placed his hand on my shoulder.

"Bates, it was too bad I got those missives of yours all in a bunch. I was in a *dahabiyeh* on the Nile and they don't have rural free delivery in Egypt. Your cablegram called me home before I got the letters. But thank God, Jack, you're alive!"

There was real feeling in these last words, and I think we were all touched by them.

"Amen to that!" cried Bates.

"And now, Pickering, before you go I want to show you something. It's about this mysterious treasure, that has given you—and I hear, the whole countryside—so much concern. I'm disappointed in you, Jack, that you couldn't find the hiding-place. I designed that as a part of your architectural education. Bates, give me a chair."

The man gravely drew a chair out of the wreckage and placed it upon the hearth. My grandfather stepped upon it, seized one of the bronze sconces above the mantel and gave it a sharp turn. At the same moment, Bates, upon another chair, grasped the companion bronze and wrenched it sharply. Instantly some mechanism creaked in the great oak chimney-breast and the long oak panels swung open, disclosing a steel door with a combination knob.

"Gentlemen,"—and my grandfather turned with a quaint touch of humor, and a merry twinkle in his bright old eyes—"gentlemen, behold the treasury! It has proved a better hiding-place than I ever imagined it would. There's not much here, Jack, but enough to keep you going for a while."

We were all staring, and the old gentleman was unfeignedly enjoying our mystification. It was an hour on which he had evidently counted much; it was the triumph of his resurrection and home-coming, and he chuckled as he twirled the knob in the steel door. Then Bates stepped forward and helped him pull the door open, disclosing a narrow steel chest, upright and held in place by heavy bolts clamped in the stone of the chimney. It was filled with packets of papers placed on shelves, and tied neatly with tape.

"Jack," said my grandfather, shaking his head, "you wouldn't be an architect, and you're not much of an engineer either, or you'd have seen that that paneling was heavier than was necessary. There's two hundred thousand dollars in first-rate securities—I vouch for them! Bates and I put them there just before I went to Vermont to die."

"I've sounded those panels a dozen times," I protested.

"Of course you have," said my grandfather, "but solid steel behind wood is safe. I tested it carefully before I left."

He laughed and clapped his knees, and I laughed with him.

"But you found the Door of Bewilderment and Pickering's notes, and that's something."

"No; I didn't even find that. Donovan deserves the credit. But how did you ever come to build that tunnel, if you don't mind telling me?"

He laughed gleefully.

"That was originally a trench for natural-gas pipes. There was once a large pumping-station on the site of this house, with a big trunk main running off across country to supply the towns west of here. The gas was exhausted, and the pipes were taken up before I began to build. I should never have thought of that tunnel in the world if the trench hadn't suggested it. I merely deepened and widened it a little and plastered it with cheap cement as far as the chapel, and that little room there where I put Pickering's notes had once been the cellar of a house built for the superintendent of the gas plant. I had never any idea that I should use that passage as a means of getting into my own house, but Marian met me at the station, told me that there was trouble here, and came with me through the chapel into the cellar, and through the hidden stairway that winds around the chimney from that room where we keep the candlesticks."

"But who was the ghost?" I demanded, "if you were really alive and in Egypt?"

Bates laughed now.

"Oh, I was the ghost! I went through there occasionally to stimulate your curiosity about the house. And you nearly caught me once!"

"One thing more, if we're not wearing you out—I'd like to know whether Sister Theresa owes you any money."

My grandfather turned upon Pickering with blazing eyes.

"You scoundrel, you infernal scoundrel, Sister Theresa never borrowed a cent of me in her life! And you have made war on that woman—"

His rage choked him.

He told Bates to close the door of the steel chest, and then turned to me.

"Where are those notes of Pickering's?" he demanded; and I brought the packet.

"Gentlemen, Mr. Pickering has gone to ugly lengths in this affair. How many murders have you gentlemen committed?"

"We were about to begin actual killing when you arrived," replied Larry, grinning.

"The sheriff got all his men off the premises more or less alive, sir," said Bates.

"That is good. It was all a great mistake,—a very great mistake,"—and my grandfather turned to Pickering.

"Pickering, what a contemptible scoundrel you are! I lent you that three hundred thousand dollars to buy securities to give you better standing in your railroad enterprises, and the last time I saw you, you got me to release the collateral so you could raise money to buy more shares. Then, after I died"—he chuckled—"you thought you'd find and destroy the notes and that would end the transaction; and if you had been smart enough to find them you might have had them and welcome. But as it is, they go to Jack. If he shows any mercy on you in collecting them he's not the boy I think he is."

Pickering rose, seized his hat and turned toward the shattered library-door. He paused for one moment, his face livid with rage.

"You old fool!" he screamed at my grandfather. "You old lunatic, I wish to God I had never seen you! No wonder you came back to life! You're a tricky old devil and too mean to die!"

He turned toward me with some similar complaint ready at his tongue's end; but Stoddard caught him by the shoulders and thrust him out upon the terrace.

A moment later we saw him cross the meadow and hurry toward St. Agatha's.

CHAPTER XXVII

CHANGES AND CHANCES

John Marshall Glenarm had probably never been so happy in his life as on that day of his amazing home-coming. He laughed at us and he laughed with us, and as he went about the house explaining his plans for its completion, he chaffed us all with his shrewd humor that had been the terror of my boyhood.

"Ah, if you had had the plans of course you would have been saved a lot of trouble; but that little sketch of the Door of Bewilderment was the only thing I left, —and you found it, Jack,—you really opened these good books of mine."

He sent us all away to remove the marks of battle, and we gave Bates a hand in cleaning up the wreckage,— Bates, the keeper of secrets; Bates, the inscrutable and mysterious; Bates, the real hero of the affair at Glenarm.

He led us through the narrow stairway by which he had entered, which had been built between false walls, and we played ghost for one another, to show just how the tread of a human being around the chimney sounded. There was much to explain, and my grandfather's

351

contrition for having placed me in so hazardous a predicament was so sincere, and his wish to make amends so evident, that my heart warmed to him. He made me describe in detail all the incidents of my stay at the house, listening with boyish delight to my adventures.

"Bless my soul!" he exclaimed over and over again. And as I brought my two friends into the story his delight knew no bounds, and he kept chuckling to himself; and insisted half a dozen times on shaking hands with Larry and Stoddard, who were, he declared, his friends as well as mine.

The prisoner in the potato cellar received our due attention; and my grandfather's joy in the fact that an agent of the British government was held captive in Glenarm House was cheering to see. But the man's detention was a grave matter, as we all realized, and made imperative the immediate consideration of Larry's future.

"I must go—and go at once!" declared Larry.

"Mr. Donovan, I should feel honored to have you remain," said my grandfather. "I hope to hold Jack here, and I wish you would share the house with us."

"The sheriff and those fellows won't squeal very hard about their performances here," said Stoddard. "And they won't try to rescue the prisoner, even for a reward, from a house where the dead come back to life."

"No; but you can't hold a British prisoner in an American private house for ever. Too many people know he has been in this part of the country; and you may be sure that the fight here and the return of Mr. Glenarm will not fail of large advertisement. All I can ask of you, Mr. Glenarm, is that you hold the fellow a few hours after I leave, to give me a start."

"Certainly. But when this trouble of yours blows over, I hope you will come back and help Jack to live a decent and orderly life."

My grandfather spoke of my remaining with a warmth that was grateful to my heart; but the place and its associations had grown unbearable. I had not mentioned Marian Devereux to him, I had not told him of my Christmas flight to Cincinnati; for the fact that I had run away and forfeited my right made no difference now, and I waited for an opportunity when we should be alone to talk of my own affairs.

At luncheon, delayed until mid-afternoon, Bates produced champagne, and the three of us, worn with excitement and stress of battle, drank a toast, standing, to the health of John Marshall Glenarm.

"My friends,"—the old gentleman rose and we all stood, our eyes bent upon him in, I think, real affection, —"I am an old and foolish man. Ever since I was able to do so I have indulged my whims. This house

is one of them. I had wished to make it a thing of
beauty and dignity, and I had hoped that Jack would
care for it and be willing to complete it and settle here.
The means I employed to test him were not, I admit,
worthy of a man who intends well toward his own flesh
and blood. Those African adventures of yours scared
me, Jack; but to think"—and he laughed—"that I
placed you here in this peaceful place amid greater dangers probably than you ever met in tiger-hunting! But
you have put me to shame. Here's health and peace to
you!"

"So say we all!" cried the others.

"One thing more," my grandfather continued, "I don't
want you to think, Jack, that you would really have
been cut off under any circumstances if I had died while
I was hiding in Egypt. What I wanted, boy, was to
get you home! I made another will in England, where
I deposited the bulk of my property before I died, and
did not forget you. That will was to protect you in case
I *really* died!"—and he laughed cheerily.

The others left us—Stoddard to help Larry get his
things together—and my grandfather and I talked for
an hour at the table.

"I have thought that many things might happen
here," I said, watching his fine, slim fingers, as he pol-
ished his eye-glasses, then rested his elbows on the table

and smiled at me. "I thought for a while that I should certainly be shot; then at times I was afraid I might not be; but your return in the flesh was something I never considered among the possibilities. Bates fooled me. That talk I overheard between him and Pickering in the church porch that foggy night was the thing that seemed to settle his case; then the next thing I knew he was defending the house at the serious risk of his life; and I was more puzzled than ever."

"Yes, a wonderful man, Bates. He always disliked Pickering, and he rejoiced in tricking him."

"Where did you pick Bates up? He told me he was a Yankee, but he doesn't act or talk it."

My grandfather laughed. "Of course not! He's an Irishman and a man of education—but that's all I know about him, except that he is a marvelously efficient servant."

My mind was not on Bates. I was thinking now of Marian Devereux. I could not go on further with my grandfather without telling him how I had run away and broken faith with him, but he gave me no chance.

"You will stay on here,—you will help me to finish the house?" he asked with an unmistakable eagerness of look and tone.

It seemed harsh and ungenerous to tell him that I wished to go; that the great world lay beyond the confines of Glenarm for me to conquer; that I had lost as well as gained by those few months at Glenarm House, and wished to go away. It was not the mystery, now fathomed, nor the struggle, now ended, that was uppermost in my mind and heart, but memories of a girl who had mocked me with delicious girlish laughter,— who had led me away that I might see her transformed into another, more charming, being. It was a comfort to know that Pickering, trapped and defeated, was not to benefit by the bold trick: she had helped him play upon me. His loss was hers as well, and I was glad in my bitterness that I had found her in the passage, seeking for plunder at the behest of the same master whom Morgan, Ferguson and the rest of them served.

The fight was over and there was nothing more for me to do in the house by the lake. After a week or so I should go forth and try to win a place for myself. I had my profession; I was an engineer, and I did not question that I should be able to find employment. As for my grandfather, Bates would care for him, and I should visit him often. I was resolved not to give him any further cause for anxiety on account of my adventurous and roving ways. He knew well enough that his old hope of making an architect of me was lost beyond redemption—I had told him that—and now I wished to depart in peace and go to some new part of the world, where there were lines to run, tracks to lay and bridges to build.

These thoughts so filled my mind that I forgot he was patiently waiting for my answer.

"I should like to do anything you ask; I should like to stay here always, but I can't. Don't misunderstand me. I have no intention of going back to my old ways. I squandered enough money in my wanderings, and I had my joy of that kind of thing. I shall find employment somewhere and go to work."

"But, Jack,"—he bent toward me kindly,—"Jack, you mustn't be led away by any mere quixotism into laying the foundation of your own fortune. What I have is yours, boy. What is in the box in the chimney is yours now—to-day."

"I wish you wouldn't! You were always too kind, and I deserve nothing, absolutely nothing."

"I'm not trying to pay you, Jack. I want to ease my own conscience, that's all."

"But money can do nothing for mine," I replied, trying to smile. "I've been dependent all my days, and now I'm going to work. If you were infirm and needed me, I should not hesitate, but the world will have its eyes on me now."

"Jack, that will of mine did you a great wrong; it put a mark upon you, and that's what hurts me, that's what I want to make amends for! Don't you see? Now don't punish me, boy. Come! Let us be friends!"

He rose and put out his hands.

"I didn't mean that! I don't care about that! It was nothing more than I deserved. These months here have changed me. Haven't you heard me say I was going to work?"

And I tried to laugh away further discussion of my future.

"It will be more cheerful here in the spring," he said, as though seeking an inducement for me to remain. "When the resort colony down here comes to life the lake is really gay."

I shook my head. The lake, that pretty cupful of water, the dip and glide of a certain canoe, the remembrance of a red tam-o'-shanter merging afar off in an October sunset—my purpose to leave the place strengthened as I thought of these things. My nerves were keyed to a breaking pitch and I turned upon him stormily.

"So Miss Devereux was the other person who shared your confidence! Do you understand,—do you appreciate the fact that she was Pickering's ally?"

"I certainly do not," he replied coldly. "I'm surprised to hear you speak so of a woman whom you can scarcely know—"

"Yes, I know her; my God, I have reason to know her! But even when I found her out I did not dream that the plot was as deep as it is. She knew that it was a scheme to test me, and she played me into Pickering's hands. I saw her only a few nights ago down there in the tunnel acting as his spy, looking for the lost notes that she might gain grace in his eyes by turning them over to him. You know I always hated Pickering,—he was too smooth, too smug, and you and everybody else were for ever praising him to me. He was always held up to me as a model; and the first time I saw Marian Devereux she was with him—it was at Sherry's the night before I came here. I suppose she reached St. Agatha's only a few hours ahead of me."

"Yes. Sister Theresa was her guardian. Her father was a dear friend, and I knew her from her early childhood. You are mistaken, Jack. Her knowing Pickering means nothing,—they both lived in New York and moved in the same circle."

"But it doesn't explain her efforts to help him, does it?" I blazed. "He wished to marry her,—Sister Theresa told me that,—and I failed, I failed miserably to keep my obligation here—I ran away to follow her!"

"Ah, to be sure! You were away Christmas Eve, when those vandals broke in. Bates merely mentioned it in the last report I got as I came through New York.

That was all right. I assumed, of course, that you had gone off somewhere to get a little Christmas cheer; I don't care anything about it."

"But I had followed *her*—I went to Cincinnati to see her. She dared me to come—it was a trick, a part of the conspiracy to steal your property."

The old gentleman smiled. It was a familiar way of his, to grow calm as other people waxed angry.

"She dared you to come, did she! That is quite like Marian; but you didn't have to go, did you, Jack?"

"Of course not; of course I didn't have to go, but—"

I stammered, faltered and ceased. Memory threw open her portals with a challenge. I saw her on the stairway at the Armstrongs'; I heard her low, soft laughter, I felt the mockery of her voice and eyes! I knew again the exquisite delight of being near her. My heart told me well enough why I had followed her.

"Jack, I'm glad I'm not buried up there in that Vermont graveyard with nobody to exercise the right of guardianship over you. I've had my misgivings about you; I used to think you were a born tramp; and you disappointed me in turning your back on architecture,—the noblest of all professions; but this performance of yours really beats them all. Don't you know that a girl like Marian Devereux isn't likely to become the agent of any rascal? Do you really believe for a minute that she tempted you to follow her, so you might forfeit your rights to my property?"

"But why was she trying to find those notes of his? Why did she come back from Cincinnati with his party? If you could answer me those things, maybe I'd admit that I'm a fool. Pickering, I imagine, is a pretty plausible fellow where women are concerned."

"For God's sake, Jack, don't speak of that girl as women! I put her in that will of mine to pique your curiosity, knowing that if there was a penalty on your marrying her you would be wholly likely to do it,—for that's the way human beings are made. But you've mixed it all up now, and insulted her in the grossest way possible for a fellow who is really a gentleman. And I don't want to lose you; I want you here with me, Jack! This is a beautiful country, this Indiana! And what I want to do is to found an estate, to build a house that shall be really beautiful,—something these people hereabouts can be proud of,— and I want you to have it with me, Jack, to link our name to these woods and that pretty lake. I'd rather have that for my neighbor than any lake in Scotland. These rich Americans, who go to England to live, don't appreciate the beauty of their own country. This landscape is worthy of the best that man can do. And I didn't undertake to build a crazy house so much as one that should have some dignity and character. That passage around the chimney is an indulgence, Jack,— I'll admit it's a little bizarre,—you see that chimney isn't so big outside as it is in!"—and he laughed and rubbed his knees with the palms of his hands,—"and my bringing foreign laborers here wasn't really to make it easier to get things done my way. Wait till you have seen the May-apples blossom and heard the robins sing in the summer twilight,—help me to finish the house,— then if you want to leave I'll bid you God-speed."

The feeling in his tone, the display of sentiment so at variance with my old notion of him, touched me in spite of myself. There was a characteristic nobility and dignity in his plan; it was worthy of him. And I had never loved him as now, when he finished this appeal, and turned away to the window, gazing out upon the somber woodland.

"Mr. Donovan is ready to go, sir," announced Bates at the door, and we went into the library, where Larry and Stoddard were waiting.

CHAPTER XXVIII

SHORTER VISTAS

Larry had assembled his effects in the library, and to my surprise, Stoddard appeared with his own hand-bag.

"I'm going to see Donovan well on his way," said the clergyman.

"It's a pity our party must break up," exclaimed my grandfather. "My obligations to Mr. Donovan are very great—and to you, too, Stoddard. Jack's friends are mine hereafter, and when we get new doors for Glenarm House you shall honor me by accepting duplicate keys."

"Where's Bates?" asked Larry, and the man came in, respectfully, inperturbably as always, and began gathering up the bags.

"Stop—one moment! Mr. Glenarm," said Larry. "Before I go I want to congratulate you on the splendid courage of this man who has served you and your house with so much faithfulness and tact. And I want to tell you something else, that you probably would never learn from him—"

363

"Donovan!" There was a sharp cry in Bates' voice, and he sprang forward with his hands outstretched entreatingly. But Larry did not heed him.

"The moment I set eyes on this man I recognized him. It's not fair to you or to him that you should not know him for what he is. Let me introduce an old friend, Walter Creighton; he was a student at Dublin when I was there,—I remember him as one of the best fellows in the world."

"For God's sake—no!" pleaded Bates. He was deeply moved and turned his face away from us.

"But, like me," Larry went on, "he mixed in politics. One night in a riot at Dublin a constable was killed. No one knew who was guilty, but a youngster was suspected,—the son of one of the richest and best-known men in Ireland, who happened to get mixed in the row. To draw attention from the boy, Creighton let suspicion attach to his own name, and, to help the boy's case further, ran away. I had not heard from or of him until the night I came here and found him the defender of this house. By God! that was no servant's trick,—it was the act of a royal gentleman."

They clasped hands; and with a new light in his face, with a new manner, as though he resumed, as a familiar garment, an old disused personality, Bates stood transfigured in the twilight, a man and a gentleman. I think we were all drawn to him; I know that a sob clutched my throat and tears filled my eyes as I grasped his hand.

"But what in the devil did you do it for?" blurted my grandfather, excitedly twirling his glasses.

Bates (I still call him Bates,—he insists on it) laughed. For the first time he thrust his hands into his pockets and stood at his ease, one of us.

"Larry, you remember I showed a fondness for the stage in our university days. When I got to America I had little money and found it necessary to find employment without delay. I saw Mr. Glenarm's advertisement for a valet. Just as a lark I answered it to see what an American gentleman seeking a valet looked like. I fell in love with Mr. Glenarm at sight—"

"It was mutual!" declared my grandfather. "I never believed your story at all,—you were too perfect in the part!"

"Well, I didn't greatly mind the valet business; it helped to hide my identity; and I did like the humor and whims of Mr. Glenarm. The housekeeping, after we came out here, wasn't so pleasant"—he looked at his hands ruefully—"but this joke of Mr. Glenarm's making a will and then going to Egypt to see what would happen,—that was too good to miss. And when the heir arrived I found new opportunities of practising amateur theatricals; and Pickering's efforts to enlist

me in his scheme for finding the money and making me
rich gave me still greater opportunities.   There were
times when I was strongly tempted to blurt the whole
thing; I got tired of being suspected, and of playing
ghost in the wall; and if Mr. Glenarm hadn't got here
just as he did I should have stopped the fight and
proclaimed the truth.   I hope," he said, turning to
me, "you have no hard feelings, sir."   And he threw
into the "sir" just a touch of irony that made us all
roar.

"I'm certainly glad I'm not dead," declared my grandfather, staring at Bates.   "Life is more fun than I ever
thought possible.   Bless my soul!" he said, "if it isn't a
shame that Bates can never cook another omelette for
me!"

We sent Bates back with my grandfather from the
boat-house, and Stoddard, Larry and I started across the
ice; the light coating of snow made walking comparatively easy.   We strode on silently, Stoddard leading.
Their plan was to take an accommodation train at the
first station beyond Annandale, leave it at a town forty
miles away, and then hurry east to an obscure place in
the mountains of Virginia, where a religious order
maintained a house.   There Stoddard promised Larry
asylum and no questions asked.

We left the lake and struck inland over a rough country road to the station, where Stoddard purchased tickets only a few minutes before the train whistled.

We stood on the lonely platform, hands joined to hands, and I know not what thoughts in our minds and hearts.

"We've met and we've said good-by in many odd corners of this strange old world," said Larry, "and God knows when we shall meet again."

"But you must stay in America—there must be no sea between us!" I declared.

"Donovan's sins don't seem heinous to me! It's simply that they've got to find a scapegoat,"—and Stoddard's voice was all sympathy and kindness. "It will blow over in time, and Donovan will become an enlightened and peaceable American citizen."

There was a constraint upon us all at this moment of parting—so many things had happened that day—and when men have shared danger together they are bound by ties that death only can break. Larry's effort at cheer struck a little hollowly upon us.

"Beware, lad, of women!" he importuned me.

"Humph! You still despise the sex on account of that affair with the colleen of the short upper lip."

"Verily. And the eyes of that little lady, who guided your grandfather back from the other world, reminded me strongly of her! Bah, these women!"

"Precious little you know about them!" I retorted.

"The devil I don't!"

"No," said Stoddard, "invoke the angels, not the devil!"

"Hear him! Hear him! A priest with no knowledge of the world."

"Alas, my cloth! And you fling it at me after I have gone through battle, murder and sudden death with you gentlemen!"

"We thank you, sir, for that last word," said Larry mockingly. "I am reminded of the late Lord Alfred:

" 'I waited for the train at Coventry;
   I hung with grooms and porters on the bridge,
   To watch the three tall spires,—' "

he quoted, looking off through the twilight toward St. Agatha's. "I can't see a blooming spire!"

The train was now roaring down upon us and we clung to this light mood for our last words. Between men, gratitude is a thing best understood in silence; and these good friends, I knew, felt what I could not say.

"Before the year is out we shall all meet again," cried Stoddard hopefully, seizing the bags.

"Ah, if we could only be sure of that!" I replied. And in a moment they were both waving their hands to me from the rear platform, and I strode back homeward over the lake.

A mood of depression was upon me; I had lost much that day, and what I had gained—my restoration to the regard of the kindly old man of my own blood, who had appealed for my companionship in terms hard to deny— seemed trifling as I tramped over the ice. Perhaps Pickering, after all, was the real gainer by the day's event. My grandfather had said nothing to allay my doubts as to Marian Devereux's strange conduct, and yet his confidence in her was apparently unshaken.

I tramped on, and leaving the lake, half-unconsciously struck into the wood beyond the dividing wall, where snow-covered leaves and twigs rattled and broke under my tread. I came out into an open space beyond St. Agatha's, found the walk and turned toward home.

As I neared the main entrance to the school the door opened and a woman came out under the overhanging lamp. She carried a lantern, and turned with a hand outstretched to some one who followed her with careful steps.

"Ah, Marian," cried my grandfather, "it's ever the task of youth to light the way of age."

CHAPTER XXIX

AND SO THE LIGHT LED ME

He had been to see Sister Theresa, and Marian was walking with him to the gate. I saw her quite plainly in the light that fell from the lamp overhead. A long cloak covered her, and a fur toque capped her graceful head. My grandfather and his guide were apparently in high spirits. Their laughter smote harshly upon me. It seemed to shut me out,—to lift a barrier against me. The world lay there within the radius of that swaying light, and I hung aloof, hearing her voice and jealous of the very companionship and sympathy between them.

But the light led me. I remembered with bitterness that I had always followed her,—whether as Olivia, trailing in her girlish race across the snow, or as the girl in gray, whom I had followed, wondering, on that night journey at Christmas Eve; and I followed now. The distrust, my shattered faith, my utter loneliness, could not weigh against the joy of hearing that laugh of hers breaking mellowly on the night.

I paused to allow the two figures to widen the distance between us as they traversed the path that curved away toward the chapel. I could still hear their voices, and see the lantern flash and disappear. I felt an impulse to turn back, or plunge into the woodland; but I was carried on uncontrollably. The light glimmered, and her voice still floated back to me. It stole through the keen winter dark like a memory of spring; and so her voice and the light led me.

Then I heard an exclamation of dismay followed by laughter in which my grandfather joined merrily.

"Oh, never mind; we're not afraid," she exclaimed.

I had rounded the curve in the path where I should have seen the light; but the darkness was unbroken. There was silence for a moment, in which I drew quite near to them.

Then my grandfather's voice broke out cheerily.

"Now I must go back with *you!* A fine person you are to guide an old man! A foolish virgin, indeed, with no oil in her lamp!"

"Please do not! Of course I'm going to see you quite to your own door! I don't intend to put my hand to the lantern and then turn back!"

"This walk isn't what it should be," said my grandfather, "we'll have to provide something better in the spring."

They were still silent and I heard him futilely striking a match. Then the lantern fell, its wires rattling

as it struck the ground, and the two exclaimed with renewed merriment upon their misfortune.

"If you will allow me!" I called out, my hand fumbling in my pocket for my own match-box.

I have sometimes thought that there is really some
sort of decent courtesy in me. An old man caught in
a rough path that was none too good at best! And a
girl, even though my enemy! These were, I fancy, the
thoughts that crossed my mind.

"Ah, it's Jack!" exclaimed my grandfather. "Marian
was showing me the way to the gate and our light went
out."

"Miss Devereux," I murmured. I have, I hope, an
icy tone for persons who have incurred my displeasure,
and I employed it then and there, with, no doubt, its
fullest value.

She and my grandfather were groping in the dark for
the lost lantern, and I, putting out my hand, touched
her fingers.

"I beg your pardon," she murmured frostily.

Then I found and grasped the lantern.

"One moment," I said, "and I'll see what's the trouble."

I thought my grandfather took it, but the flame of
my wax match showed her fingers, clasping the wires of
the lantern. The cloak slipped away, showing her arm's

soft curve, the blue and white of her bodice, the purple blur of violets; and for a second I saw her face, with a smile quivering about her lips. My grandfather was beating impatiently with his stick, urging us to leave the lantern and go on.

"Let it alone," he said. "I'll go down through the chapel; there's a lantern in there somewhere."

"I'm awfully sorry," she remarked; "but I recently lost my best lantern!"

To be sure she had! I was angry that she should so brazenly recall the night I found her looking for Pickering's notes in the passage at the Door of Bewilderment!

She had lifted the lantern now, and I was striving to touch the wax taper to the wick, with imminent danger to my bare fingers.

"They don't really light well when the oil's out," she observed, with an exasperating air of wisdom.

I took it from her hand and shook it close to my ear.

"Yes; of course, it's empty," I muttered disdainfully.

"Oh, Mr. Glenarm!" she cried, turning away toward my grandfather.

I heard his stick beating the rough path several yards away. He was hastening toward Glenarm House.

"I think Mr. Glenarm has gone home."

"Oh, that is too bad!" she exclaimed.

"Thank you! He's probably at the chapel by this time. If you will permit me—"

"Not at all!"

A man well advanced in the sixties should not tax his arteries too severely. I was quite sure that my grandfather ran up the chapel steps; I could hear his stick beating hurriedly on the stone.

"If you wish to go farther"—I began.

I was indignant at my grandfather's conduct; he had deliberately run off, leaving me alone with a young woman whom I particularly wished to avoid.

"Thank you; I shall go back now. I was merely walking to the gate with Mr. Glenarm. It is so fine to have him back again, so unbelievable!"

It was just such a polite murmur as one might employ in speaking to an old foe at a friend's table.

She listened a moment for his step; then, apparently satisfied, turned back toward St. Agatha's. I followed, uncertain, hesitating, marking her definite onward flight. From the folds of the cloak stole the faint perfume of violets. The sight of her, the sound of her voice, combined to create—and to destroy!—a mood with every step.

I was seeking some colorless thing to say when she spoke over her shoulder:

"You are very kind, but I am not in the least afraid, Mr. Glenarm."

"But there is something I wish to say to you. I should like—"

She slackened her step.

"Yes."

"I am going away."

"Yes; of course; you are going away."

Her tone implied that this was something that had been ordained from the beginning of time, and did not matter.

"And I wish to say a word about Mr. Pickering."

She paused and faced me abruptly. We were at the edge of the wood, and the school lay quite near. She caught the cloak closer about her and gave her head a little toss I remembered well, as a trick compelled by the vagaries of woman's head-dress.

"I can't talk to you here, Mr. Glenarm; I had no intention of ever seeing you again; but I must say this—"

"Those notes of Pickering's—I shall ask Mr. Glenarm to give them to you—as a mark of esteem from me."

She stepped backward as though I had struck her.

"You risked much for them—for him"—I went on.

"Mr. Glenarm, I have no intention of discussing that, or any other matter with you—"

"It is better so—"

"But your accusations, the things you imply, are unjust, infamous!"

The quaver in her voice shook my resolution to deal harshly with her.

"If I had not myself been a witness—" I began.

"Yes; you have the conceit of your own wisdom, I dare say."

"But that challenge to follow you, to break my pledge; my running away, only to find that Pickering was close at my heels; your visit to the tunnel in search of those notes,—don't you know that those things were a blow that hurt? You had been the spirit of this woodland to me. Through all these months, from the hour I watched you paddle off into the sunset in your canoe, the thought of you made the days brighter, steadied and cheered me, and wakened ambitions that I had forgotten—abandoned —long ago. And this hideous struggle here,—it seems so idle, so worse than useless now! But I'm glad I followed you,—I'm glad that neither fortune nor duty kept me back. And now I want you to know that Arthur Pickering shall not suffer for anything that has happened. I shall make no effort to punish him; for your sake he shall go free."

A sigh so deep that it was like a sob broke from her. She thrust forth her hand entreatingly.

"Why don't you go to him with your generosity? You are so ready to believe ill of me! And I shall not defend myself; but I will say these things to you, Mr. Glenarm: I had no idea, no thought of seeing him at the Armstrongs' that night. It was a surprise to me, and to them, when he telegraphed he was coming. And when I went into the tunnel there under the wall that night, I had a purpose—a purpose—"

"Yes?" she paused and I bent forward, earnestly waiting for her words, knowing that here lay her great offending.

"I was afraid,—I was afraid that Mr. Glenarm might not come in time; that you might be dispossessed,—lose the fight, and I came back with Mr. Pickering because I thought some dreadful thing might happen here—to you—"

She turned and ran from me with the speed of the wind, the cloak fluttering out darkly about her. At the door, under the light of the lamp, I was close upon her. Her hand was on the vestibule latch.

"But how should I have known?" I cried. "And you had taunted me with my imprisonment at Glenarm; you had dared me to follow you, when you knew that my grandfather was living and watching to see whether I kept faith with him. If you can tell me,—if there is an answer to that—"

"I shall never tell you anything—more! You were so eager to think ill of me—to accuse me!"

"It was because I love you; it was my jealousy of that man, my boyhood enemy, that made me catch at any doubt. You are so beautiful,—you are so much a part of the peace, the charm of all this! I had hoped for spring—for you and the spring together!"

"Oh, please—!"

Her flight had shaken the toque to an unwonted angle; her breath came quick and hard as she tugged at the latch eagerly. The light from overhead was full upon us, but I could not go with hope and belief struggling unsatisfied in my heart. I seized her hands and sought to look into her eyes.

"But you challenged me,—to follow you! I want to know why you did that!"

She drew away, struggling to free herself.

"Why was it, Marian?"

"Because I wanted—"

"Yes."

"I wanted you to come, Squire Glenarm!"

Thrice spring has wakened the sap in the Glenarm wood since that night. Yesterday I tore March from the calendar. April in Indiana! She is an impudent tomboy who whistles at the window, points to the sunshine and, when you go hopefully forth, summons the clouds and pelts you with snow. The austere old woodland, wise from long acquaintance, finds no joy in her. The walnut and the hickory have a higher respect for the stormier qualities of December. April in Indiana! She was just there by the wall, where now the bluebird pauses dismayed, and waits again the flash of her golden sandals. She bent there at the lakeside the splash of a raindrop ago and tentatively poked the thin, brittle ice with the pink tips of her little fingers. April in the heart! It brings back the sweet wonder and awe of those days, three years ago, when Marian and I, waiting for June to come, knew a joy that thrilled our hearts like the tumult of the first robin's song. The marvel of it all steals over me again as I hear the riot of melody in meadow and wood, and catch through the window the flash of eager wings.

My history of the affair at Glenarm has overrun the bounds I had set for it, and these, I submit, are not days for the desk and pen. Marian is turning over the sheets of manuscript that lie at my left elbow, and demanding that I drop work for a walk abroad. My grandfather is pacing the terrace outside, planning, no doubt, those changes in the grounds that are his constant delight.

Of some of the persons concerned in this winter's

tale let me say a word more. The prisoner whom Larry left behind we discharged, after several days, with all the honors of war, and (I may add without breach of confidence) a comfortable indemnity. Larry has made a reputation by his book on Russia—a searching study into the conditions of the Czar's empire, and, having squeezed that lemon, he is now in Tibet. His father has secured from the British government a promise of immunity for Larry, so long as that amiable adventurer keeps away from Ireland. My friend's latest letters to me contain, I note, no reference to The Sod.

Bates is in California conducting a fruit ranch, and when he visited us last Christmas he bore all the marks of a gentleman whom the world uses well. Stoddard's life has known many changes in these years, but they must wait for another day, and, perhaps, another historian. Suffice it to say that it was he who married us —Marian and me—in the little chapel by the wall, and that when he comes now and then to visit us, we renew our impression of him as a man large of body and of soul. Sister Theresa continues at the head of St. Agatha's, and she and the other Sisters of her brown-clad company are delightful neighbors. Pickering's failure and subsequent disappearance were described sufficiently in the newspapers and his name is never mentioned at Glenarm.

As for myself—Marian is tapping the floor restlessly with her boot and I must hasten—I may say that I am no idler. It was I who carried on the work of finishing Glenarm House, and I manage the farms which my grandfather has lately acquired in this neighborhood. But better still, from my own point of view, I maintain in Chicago an office as consulting engineer and I have already had several important commissions.

Glenarm House is now what my grandfather had wished to make it, a beautiful and dignified mansion. He insisted on filling up the tunnel, so that the Door of Bewilderment is no more. The passage in the wall and the strong box in the paneling of the chimney-breast remain, though the latter we use now as a hiding-place for certain prized bottles of rare whisky which John Marshall Glenarm ordains shall be taken down only on Christmas Eves, to drink the health of Olivia Gladys Armstrong. That young woman, I may add, is now a belle in her own city, and of the scores of youngsters all the way from Pittsburg to New Orleans who lay siege to her heart, my word is, may the best man win!

And now, at the end, it may seem idle vanity for a man still young to write at so great length of his own affairs; but it must have been clear that mine is the humblest figure in this narrative. I wished to set forth an honest account of my grandfather's experiment in

looking into this world from another, and he has himself urged me to write down these various incidents
while they are still fresh in my memory.

Marian—the most patient of women—is walking toward the door, eager for the sunshine, the free airs of
spring, the blue vistas lakeward, and at last I am ready
to go.